About the Author

Liz Cansdale was born near Brighton in Sussex. She has always loved all things creative and as well as writing has an online shop selling handmade bags and crafts. After bringing up her son in Cornwall, where she had an art gallery, when he was offered a place at Oxford, she returned to Sussex. One day she decided she wanted to try something completely new and different , and so she took the bold step of moving to Italy where she spent a number of years living in Ferrara, teaching English, a job she absolutely loved. She has always loved writing and *May the Fourth* is the result of an idea she had after a conversation about politics during which someone suggested the way to world peace was to eliminate all geographical borders. She now lives in Eastbourne.

May the Fourth

Liz Cansdale

May the Fourth

Vanguard Press

VANGUARD PAPERBACK

© Copyright 2024
Liz Cansdale

The right of Liz Cansdale to be identified as author of
this work has been asserted by her in accordance with the
Copyright, Designs and Patents Act 1988.

All Rights Reserved

No reproduction, copy or transmission of this publication
may be made without written permission.
No paragraph of this publication may be reproduced,
copied or transmitted save with the written permission of the
publisher, or in accordance with the provisions
of the Copyright Act 1956 (as amended).

Any person who commits any unauthorised act in relation to
this publication may be liable to criminal
prosecution and civil claims for damages.

A CIP catalogue record for this title is
available from the British Library.

ISBN 978 1 80016 858 9

This is a work of fiction. Names, characters, businesses, places,
events and incidents are either the product of the author's imagination or
used in a fictitious manner. Any resemblance to actual persons, living or
dead, or actual events is purely coincidental.

Vanguard Press is an imprint of
Pegasus Elliot Mackenzie Publishers Ltd.
www.pegasuspublishers.com

First Published in 2024

Vanguard Press
Sheraton House Castle Park
Cambridge England

Printed & Bound in Great Britain

Dedication

For my wonderful dad, who's always been my strength and rock.

Chapter One

4th May 2222

Were it not for the fact that it would have been a highly unprofessional thing to do, and not to mention that it would have looked ridiculous, Lee would have danced down the corridor in juvenile delight and with an all-consuming excitement. They were almost there!

It wasn't that there weren't still obstacles stacked up one atop another to overcome, because there were. And not only were these obstacles too many to count, but for the most part they were also extremely complicated and would be very dangerous to negotiate. But the thrill and expectation of having got to this point was immense. Everything was finally ready.

Thirty years of a life dedicated to the arrival of this day had been tough to say the least, and at times the question of whether it would ever be possible, although Lee would never have admitted aloud to ever having had such a thought, had inevitably been at the forefront of many a colleague's mind. On occasion even the most dedicated and loyal of them had doubted, and more frequently the less dedicated and loyal had ridiculed and tried to discourage and undermine, before giving it up as a bad job and walking away.

That was fine. Lee had understood their nerves, or lack of staying power, or whatever it was, and sympathised. Who could blame them? Times were hard, and in their delicate position, well, who knew what could happen to them if things went wrong?

And yet, despite everything, here they were. It *had* been possible, and now Lee and a meticulously chosen and vetted team were preparing to begin the biggest and most important political revolution for two hundred years.

Listening to the last-minute briefing of the chief aide as the little group strode towards the private departure gate, Lee grunted approval. This repetition wasn't strictly necessary. It had all been heard a hundred times before and committed to memory long ago. However, protocol dictated this final clarification so once again Lee listened, nodding approval. The aide handed over a sheaf of papers and looked sideways at his boss, biting his lip.

'I really think I should come with you.'

'Honestly, Howard, you do keep on.' Lee sighed deeply so that the shoulders, in their neat black suit, rose and fell with a thumping motion. 'Are you sure you don't just want a free trip to Nevada?'

Howard Dyer's mouth twisted. 'Why would I?'

Lee laughed. It was a light, easy sound that belied its owner's fifty-six years, but their pace slowed slightly as Howard's superior turned to look at him, quickly serious again. 'Is it bad?'

'They're following you, if that's what you mean.'

'They're always following me.'

'I know that,' Howard snapped. 'But don't you wonder what they'll make of this sudden unscheduled departure?'

'It'll put them on higher alert than usual, yes. We know that. It's unavoidable.'

'Well, then...'

It was true, of course. The plane would be tracked, as always, movements would be followed, as always, but there would be a team over there in Nevada, the second the plane took off, wondering what was afoot and planning pre-emptive action against every possible scenario they could think of. Every scenario, that was, except the real one. Lee hoped and prayed they would have no idea about that.

'Oh, for goodness' sake. Do what you like. Come, then, if you think it'll help, though I don't know how you imagine your presence will change anything.' The consent was given in a manner that Lee hoped conveyed reluctance only at having the ever-fussing Howard Dyer as a devil's advocate travelling companion, nagging away in the background like a stuck record, rather than letting it be known that, actually, he was quite right, and some company would be rather useful. The truth was, this mission was likely to turn into a deathly scuffle at best, and the inevitable threat of that would otherwise be not only an ever-present, but a lonely companion. 'Happy now?'

'More so than I was.'

'Well, don't come crying to me if you end up dead in a ditch. I'm only trying to protect you.'

'I give you my word that you shall receive no remonstrances from beyond the grave if that unfortunate end awaits me,' he said with mock seriousness.

Lee's eyes rolled towards the ceiling. 'Let's get on with it, then.'

Howard grinned and they continued on down the corridor.

On arrival at the departure gate, a light and airy room in the westerly annex of the immense complex of buildings in west London in which Lee's headquarters were situated, they were approached by an employee, a young girl in a smart navy-blue uniform and nondescript light brown hair tied back uncompromisingly tightly from her face into a severe ponytail, all the better to work without distraction, no doubt. She was wheeling a small black case at her side.

'Thank you,' said Lee. 'Would you please also arrange for some things to be brought for Mr Dyer? He will be travelling with me. As quickly as you can.'

The girl nodded assent and hurried away to a desk, where she picked up a handset and relayed the message. Lee led the jittery entourage across the room to sit and wait for the plane and the case to be declared ready for them, sighing with mild impatience. The other members of the group who had accompanied them to the departure lounge now took their turns, amid much nervous hand shaking and well-wishing, to hand over various papers and files, before trickling away to return, terrified, to their offices, grateful to be out of it and staying where they were.

Strangely, hard copies of documents were still far safer than digital ones which, of course, over the years had become easier, rather than harder, for prying eyes to find, doctor, or destroy. Therefore, this entire mission had been prepared using only pen and paper, and no document had been drafted with less than three people present, all of whom had sworn and signed papers in front of lawyers to conform with what would in the past have been called the Official Secrets Act. Lee could not have been more careful.

After a couple of minutes, the two who were to travel were alone, but for the staff milling around at the gate.

'Are you sure you need to be in Nevada?' asked Howard. 'I mean, if things are going to get nasty, that's where it's going to kick off.'

'Which is precisely why I do need to be there. You already know my reasons. You've been by my side as I've made every decision on this, and I've made my reasons for each one perfectly clear. Please don't make me go through it all again.'

Howard gave a reluctant nod. 'You know best.'

'I do. And Howard, you do not have to come. You can change your mind. But if you decide to accompany me, I want no more of this negativity. I haven't got time for it. I've got to do the most important job of my life out there, and I haven't got time to be concerning myself with tripping over your sensibilities at every turn. You're either fully with me, without this constant questioning, or you stay here and quake at home in the Shires where I don't have to be bothered by it. You decide. Either way, this goes ahead today.'

'I'm sorry,' the chief aide answered. 'I'll come with you, and you'll hear no more about it.'

'Good. OK then. In that case I shall be glad of your company. Thank you.'

Lee had given up everything to this cause. A family, most importantly, but other things, too. And who knew, if this all went belly up today, then no doubt liberty would be added to the list of deprivations. But that was a risk which had needed and still needed to be taken. Timing was imperative, and the time to act was upon them. It was the reason for the current haste and the reason there was no room to pander to the frights of the staff.

It wasn't that Lee hadn't wanted a family; for a long time, it had been most decidedly tempting. But there had always been a bigger desire burning within; a desire to change the world for the better. And it had been clear on that fateful day, as the subject of marriage had been discussed, dissected, and then ultimately and sadly rejected, that there would not have been room or time in such a life as this to undertake the commitment of matrimony in the way it should be undertaken. It wouldn't have been fair to inflict this life on another person. And so, the two had parted, and Lee had known as it had all been unfolding and hurting, and as accusations were fired, that that was it. The chance was gone. For the same reason that relationship had failed, no other could work, and no other relationship would ever be acceptable anyway because no one could ever replace what was being lost, thrown away and sacrificed. No, not thrown away. Sacrificed, yes, but never thrown away, which made it sound easy. It hadn't been easy.

Loneliness had spread out into the void of Lee's future, but the cause shouted loudly enough if not to fill it completely, then at least to drown out the noise of persistent regret. With a heart shattered into a thousand shards, the die had been cast.

From that moment on, every moment of Lee's days had been dedicated to building the Democratic Party into a viable opposition to the World Administration.

Now, the team and the plan that had been meticulously put together over decades, was ready and they were hurrying down the path signposted freedom. Lee and Howard would catch this flight in order to slot the final piece of the jigsaw into place. If they succeeded, a whole new chapter would begin. A whole new chapter of work. And a whole new chapter for the world. Yes, delight and excitement were two very welcome and well-deserved feelings to be in the presence of right now, even with whatever was awaiting them on the other side of the Atlantic taken into consideration.

There wasn't anything particularly different about the process of flying these days from anything in the past. Progress in aviation had been rather neglected for the last hundred years or so. It was a ridiculous state of affairs, especially when you considered the advances in technology which could have been used to improve the speed of it, if nothing else. The only difference now was that, in theory, you simply got onto a plane and went where you wanted with no questions asked – although things being what they were nowadays, hardly anyone ever did. The idea of going on holiday had become something forgotten, a relic of the past.

For a start, the cost was prohibitive for most people, as the price of the old-fashioned and scarce fuel that was needed was extortionate. The advances made in nuclear fusion provided modern transport only for those few lucky enough to be in a position to afford a personal, short-distance pod. So, either way, travelling had become impossible for most people. Added to that, the twenty-page-long "Reason for Travel" document that had to be filled in before any flight was interrogative, completely contradicted the right to freedom of travel which was supposed to be available to all by law, and sucked the last drops of fun or enjoyment out of any trip.

So, for the most part, aeroplanes had disappeared from the skies, to be replaced only by the handful of pods flown by the police, government officials, and anyone else in authority, most of whom used them simply to flit about between meetings when a land vehicle would have done just as well, in order to flaunt their status, show off, and stamp their authority. Everyone else stayed at home.

Good for the environment, though, you might be thinking? But no. Unfortunately, not. This reduction in air travel was too little, too late, for the temperature continued to rise and the globe was drying unheeded to a crisp.

There was still security control at airports, of course, ironically more rigorous than ever, but no passport checks. Because of course there were no passports.

Naturally, Lee had a private plane, which made life a lot easier. So, there was no problem to be overcome other than time. Lee's urgency was time. They needed to get from London to Nevada as soon as possible, relying on old-fashioned timings and fuel.

However, the second suitcase arrived promptly enough and the two stood and followed a flight attendant through a short tunnel and onto the plane.

Jesus Christ, thought Lee, fighting the rebellious knot of anxiety that had started to bubble up. Calm, calm, calm... just put one foot in front of the other.

But if this goes wrong, we're screwed. The whole world is screwed.

On board, the World Leader sat down in the familiar chair. The plane was comfortable, with its plush carpet, wooden panelling with shiny brass fixtures which Lee hated and had always thought made it seem like an inside-out flying coffin, the personal fridges containing an assortment of Lee's favourite tipples beside each armchair-like upholstered seat, which were widely spaced around a sturdily secured table. But today none of these little luxuries were given as much as a thought of appreciation, if indeed they ever were, and certainly not the brassware. A luxurious aeroplane seemed an absurdity and, anyway, there were far more important things to think about.

The plane taxied to the runway, a journey of no more than a minute or so. For the sake of security, there were three pilots on board the plane today, in case anyone got any funny ideas, not that they knew what was happening of course, and the door to the cabin was left open. No chances were to be taken. Being mid-air while everything kicked off could be argued to be mad enough in itself, but the truth was, it was as safe, or otherwise, as anywhere else.

Lee and Howard buckled themselves in, and Howard handed his boss an electronic device which he removed from his bag with a shaking hand.

'Tell me, Howard, is it excitement or fear which governs your nerves at present?'

'Both. But you have my silence on the matter.'

Lee nodded. 'Yes, quite right. Nevertheless, a healthy mixture, under the circumstances.'

Without another word, the Leader waited until the plane had reached altitude, then accepted a cup of tea with a nod of thanks from what could have been a clone of the girl in the departure lounge, placed it on the table to cool and began a last thorough check-through on the device that had been handed over.

Hours later, as the plane was about to land, after sending up a silent prayer to anyone who was willing to listen and taking a moment or two to double-check and reread the security information on the little screen, the World Leader, savouring the moment, very determinedly pressed a button.

'That's it. It's done. Now let's see what fate has in store for us.'

Chapter Two

The way in which Anthony Hurst was behaving was suspicious. His colleague, Charley Greenway, watched with interest from across the boardroom table as Hurst sat opposite him at their morning briefing, alternately shuffling and reshuffling the papers on the table in front of him and fiddling with something in his lap that appeared to be a small red child's building brick. How very odd.

Hurst's eyes, his colleague noticed, darted about between the faces of the other people present and blinked too much. Added to this, there was a certain tension in his movements that indicated an effort was being made to appear at ease. He calmed down when called upon to speak, Greenway noted, but as soon as his, as always, extremely competent contribution to the morning's proceedings was over, the little irregularities began to snap back into view. Perhaps something was troubling him, but there was clearly something other than work on his mind.

It was interesting. He hadn't observed Hurst to be the sort of man to bring his private problems to work, which strongly indicated that his jitters were likely to be down to something else. Something which, if he was reading the signs correctly, could prove to be very problematic indeed.

The meeting droned on. People spoke, people listened, people gave small presentations. The usual mind-numbing nonsense. And all the while, Hurst was on edge. Perhaps he was on drugs? Agent Greenway looked intently into the blue eyes of the man who sat twitching opposite him, but they looked normal. The pupils were normal. OK, so not that, then.

Hurst was rolling the little red brick between his fingers again now. His hand kept darting under the table, as if he was afraid of being questioned about it.

Yes, there were only two possible explanations left, as far as the other man could see. Either Hurst was suffering some sort of personal problem and was using the brick as a channel for his agitation and anxiety, which would have been rather strange because why a child's brick? It was a strange thing to bring to work. Why not sit and fiddle with the cuff of his shirt or the cap of a pen, which would have been more normal and would probably have gone unnoticed? Or it was something else entirely, something far more sinister, and Agent Hurst had become sloppy. He hoped for Hurst's sake it was the former, but as he watched the man twitching and blinking and then seemingly coming to his senses and putting the brick into his pocket, experience told him it was not.

Oh dear. What a pity.

He would investigate. He would check it out today, and if his checks came to nothing, he would review the footage from the cameras in Hurst's house and, see whether there was anything going on at home that might explain his strange behaviour. He would watch Hurst more closely at work, and even befriend him for a while if needs be, if he couldn't get to the bottom of it the usual way. Instinct told him he *would* get to the bottom of it the usual way.

Yes, it was a pity.

Bored with the meeting, which was drawing to a conclusion anyway, and impatient to get on with things, Greenway coughed, stood up, and excused himself from the room. Nobody took much notice of him. Hurst didn't even raise his head or seem to register his departure.

Once outside in the spacious anteroom, he walked across to the desk and gave orders to the girl who managed the comings and goings in the boardroom and conference rooms to lock the door after everyone had left the meeting, and not to allow anyone else into the room until he had finished some business he had in there. She was to call him when the room was empty and not speak of his request to anyone, and especially not to those currently sitting in the meeting.

Having given his instructions, he returned to his office to wait and gather a few things together that he felt sure he was going to need. This part of his job was exciting, but he had to admit to feeling a bit of regret this time. He sat and tapped his fingers impatiently on his desk. If his hunch was right, then it was most unfortunate. He'd always considered Agent Hurst to be one of the good guys. But the excitement of the situation and love of his job pushed aside and overrode any other emotion as he waited impatiently, keen to get on with it.

He didn't have to wait long. Within fifteen minutes the call came from the girl downstairs, and he returned speedily to the boardroom. He locked the door behind him, drew the blinds all around the glass walls to give himself privacy from the prying eyes of anyone who might happen to pass by in the room outside, then rounded the table and sat in the chair which Hurst had previously occupied. He put his hand under the table in the place he'd seen Hurst's hand disappear and moved his fingers gently and slowly around its underside, a few millimetres at a time, backwards and forwards, side to side, until… yes, there was something.

Keeping his finger firmly in place under the table's edge, he pushed the chair aside and dropped onto the floor, adrenaline pumping. This was what his job was all about, and he loved it. He removed a torch from his pocket and moved his finger to one side, still pointing at the right place. There!

Hardly visible, transparent save for its miniscule dark centre, lay the bug. My, my, who would have thought? 'Who's been a naughty boy, then?' he said aloud. 'Deary me, Mr Hurst.' The man smiled malevolently to himself as he took a pen and drew a circle around the bug before removing his finger from its position. It's always the ones you least expect. Always watch the quiet ones.

With both hands now free, Agent Greenway dug in his pocket for one of the tools he'd brought with him. Using the thin blade of a pocket-knife, he then set about prizing the device gently from its moorings, taking care not to break it, and placed it carefully into a little glass jar, before creeping out from under the table with a satisfied look on his face. He pocketed the evidence of his colleague's deception, drew the blinds to return the room to its usual state and returned once more to his office to orchestrate his next move, humming to himself as he went. There was no room for sentimentality in this job. And besides, he was beginning to imagine his own reward when he presented the device to his boss.

The girl at the desk watched him go with interest, then picked up her bag and fished inside it for a moment before taking out a tissue and blowing her nose without really needing to before getting back to work.

Chapter Three

Lucas Blackmore cursed, which was most unlike him. His assistant nodded his head in doleful agreement. 'I know, sir.'

'Are you certain?'

'Absolutely. It's the most recent one, in fact. It's been moved. There's no other explanation for that other than its having been discovered.'

'This is a disaster. Have you activated the plan?' Lucas paced urgently about the room, his fingers twisting together in agitation. 'This really is awful timing. Why now, for God's sake? After all this time, and as everything's about to get difficult enough.'

'I know,' his assistant repeated. 'But yes, the plan is being put into action as we speak. I can't imagine he'll have much time, so I took the liberty of acting immediately and signalling Janine, without consulting you first. I hope I did the right thing? It's a good job everything was already in place and set up ready to go.'

Lucas nodded. He could trust Paolo. 'Yes, of course. I trust your judgement. There was no alternative but for you to act immediately.' He and his assistant looked at each other anxiously. 'Oh, God, Paolo, why today? It's happening any second, and now we've got this to worry about as well.'

'Yes.'

'I suppose all we can do now is sit and wait.'

'Yes, sir. Indeed. Nothing more than that.'

Chapter Four

'Citizens,

'I am aware that this unscheduled broadcast will be a surprise and a shock to you, and that it will be interfering with your work and your lives and, for many of you, your sleep, and for this I beg your forgiveness. However, I am making this unprecedented address and asking you to listen to me today for a very important reason. As you watch your screens and listen to this announcement, each and every one of you finds yourself becoming an important part of history. A crucial part of history.

'As you know, the World Leader does not often call their citizens to attention in this way, and I am no different. In fact, I have never done it before. It is my role to lead, to oversee, and to rule, if you will, from a position of some distance, and I have always adhered to this. However, in recent years I have become increasingly alarmed at the direction the form of so-called democracy on our planet is taking and about how you, its citizens, are suffering for it, and I know that my alarm mirrors your own.

'As a result, I find myself unable to continue as I have been doing for so long. I am unable to go on holding my silence. And so, whether it is unorthodox or not, I must now speak out and openly oppose the system that I am supposed to be seen to condone, for I do not. My allegiance is with the Democratic Party whose leader I was, as you know, before I was elected to my current position and, whatever your feelings on this, I implore you to pay close attention to what I have got to say, and to heed my warning.

'On this planet, we call ourselves democratic, but the truth is we are not living in a democracy, and we all know it, whether we agree with the regime imposed upon us or not. I believe that on a personal as well as a global level, things are changing for the worse for every one of us in a way that we hope could not have been foreseen by our ancestors two hundred years ago. I say we "hope" it could not have been foreseen, in order to give the benefit of the doubt, because the alternative is a sinister one indeed, full of malevolent intent and a power-hungry thirst for the total control of humankind, the like of which we thought to be confined to history or even to science fiction.

'However, perhaps it was foreseen because that is what we are now living with. Perhaps my faith in the goodness of humanity is misplaced and I should not give the benefit of the doubt, because if you read the old history texts you will see that mistrust and fear were in fact already prevalent at that time, just as has always

been the case but, in my opinion, in the last couple of centuries it has only got worse, and all under the name of the so-called "Free World".

'You do not need me to tell you that ruling by fear is in no way democratic. It is the very opposite definition of democracy, and it is becoming the very thing that, when the system we live by was conceived two centuries ago, the people were told was trying to be avoided, if not eradicated. I believe that even then it was already too late. We had already gone too far.

'It is natural that the people of that time, hopeful of a better future, would have wanted to believe what they were being told. Or perhaps they didn't realise the extent to which they would end up being controlled, as we now, with the truth all around us and the benefit of hindsight, do. Perhaps they were just beginning to see it, but they were lied to, manipulated, and bribed into accepting the new ways. People have paid the price for that misplaced trust ever since. And today, we are paying the price more than ever.

'Desperate contradictions and paradoxes are all around us. The very freedoms, by the promises of which we were lured in, have enslaved us, being cleverly written up in the name of fairness and equality into international laws that in fact put ever-increasing limitations on all that we do, and have become the self-crafted rope with which, if we are not careful, we will hang ourselves. It is a cliché, but humanity is standing poised on the precipice, on the knife-edge summit of a

high mountain, while a terrible storm rages around us. And we are losing our footing.

'We have already lost our freedom of speech, while existing in a world run by computers, where we were told anything would be possible and where we were promised our voices would be heard and that our freedom of speech would be paramount. The reality though is that people today are afraid to express any opinions that stray even slightly off the path of the ever changing and decreasing list of acceptable words, for fear of being cancelled from the very networks of platforms that earn them their living, meaning that innovative thought is closely monitored and regulated. In short, it is disallowed. It is for this reason I am having to speak to you in this way today.

'I am currently surrounded and protected by a heavily armed security team, while opposing teams working for the World Administration toil away in their secret facilities around the globe to shut me down, simply for not towing their party line. But it is not my party line to tow. The World Administration, as you are aware and as I have just said, is not my party.

'Freedom of speech is a basic human right, with which they disagree, but for which I will fight.

'Fear of causing offence means we no longer even allow something as basic as comedy in our society. People have forgotten how to laugh, even at themselves. Our planet has become a serious place, in every way.

We can no longer publicly express any views which could be misinterpreted.

'But it is in our nature to differ, to question, and to challenge. It is how we grow and learn. Our brains and our imaginations should be our best asset – indeed these are the fundamental means by which we evolve – and they are suffering from a collective arrested development. Everything, but everything, is open to misinterpretation if you scrutinise it and pull it apart and, doing this in a calculated enough way that it serves your own selfish purposes seems to be the only talent left, permitted, or indeed encouraged. We have turned upon each other in a most alarming way, no more evolved it would seem than rats in a laboratory.

'There is no spontaneity left in our world. We must think before we speak more than ever before, and while thought before action is often a good thing, we now find ourselves silenced through a genuine fear of the grave consequences of falling foul of the, if you will permit me to be candid, not-so-bright, vindictive, victim-culture-promoting element of society so often intentionally misunderstanding everything we say. We must be seen to be dumbed down to the lowest common denominator, just in order to protect ourselves, in order to survive.

'Where are the freedoms that we were promised? Our lives are interfered with on every conceivable level by the World Administration, who do the very thing they were not supposed to do when we started out on this mission, and that is to control. This is done under the

guise of the WA being helpful, transparent, and inclusive, all for your benefit, but this is no longer working in your favour, if indeed it ever truly did.

'Our children are not being nurtured; they are being turned into automatons. At school, they are not allowed to fail, or to be seen to be achieving beyond the level of their peers. The less capable are nursemaided through school with certificates of participation and rewards for behaving themselves respectably, as if that were a notable achievement, while the ever-more dumbed-down university courses feed an ever-worsening culture of entitlement.

'The intelligent children are not encouraged to shine – rather, they are being taught that if they do, if they try to excel academically, they are somehow implying that they are better than everyone else and are reprimanded for being snobs. I ask, if we do not encourage our bright youngsters to shine and help to propel them forwards, how can we as humans ever hope to evolve further? What will their futures be like? What will any of our futures be like?

'Anyone rejected for a job nowadays can and does find a reason to accuse the interviewer of discrimination. Are we heading for a world where computers are given even more jobs than they have already taken from us, and we become completely redundant, simply because we are not robots?

'We are all different. As humans, we are all different. But that diversity is being used as a weapon

against us. And we are the ones holding the weapon and training it on our own children. We are failing them. We are failing ourselves. We are threatening ourselves. The very future of humanity is at stake, nothing less than that, and I implore you to listen to me, and act, before it is too late.

'If we do not act, we will find ourselves enslaved beyond hope by our own system. We are, I fear, moments away from that fate. Another war is not beyond the realms of possibility, and if that happens, it will probably signal the end of us and this planet we call home. Once again, unrest is building on our planet. It is building fast, and I am here today to ask you all to help me, to help yourselves, avoid it. We must work together to save ourselves from that terrible fate. If you work with me, we can achieve the proper peace and democracy that we, most of us, want, without resorting to the destruction of ourselves and our planet that an unofficial uprising, which I assure you is imminent, would bring.

'It is no secret that I believe we should return to the old order and the System of Nations, taking with us of course all the progressions and benefits that have helped so many of you, and the planet itself. Some of our laws and policies do work, and they work well.

'I still believe in world peace, of course I do, just as the instigator of our system did two hundred years ago, but I believe that changing the way we do things is the only way to achieve it, not this relentless and

desperate ironing-out of our innate differences, which was not part of the original plan.

'This is a pivotal point in the history of humanity. Do we continue as we are, on our rapid path towards self-destruction, or do we acknowledge that we are all supposed to be different and individual, and learn to embrace that once more, returning to a world of excitement, possibility, freedom, and happiness?

'When I have finished speaking, you will get your chance to be a part of history. We will be holding a vote. But first, let me explain to you in as clear a way as possible in the short space of time I've got available to me, exactly how we have come to find ourselves in the position we are now in, and exactly what you will be asked to do.'

Chapter Five

'How did this happen? WHO LET THIS HAPPEN?'

The full force of Agent Ward's wrath burst from his wide cavern of a mouth with the force of a half starving wild bear pursuing difficult prey on his first hunt after hibernation as he faced his employees and yelled at them. The dozen colleagues who had been summoned to his office and who were sitting nervously around the table, fidgeting in their chairs, glanced at each other in alarm and shrank down in their seats, like children who hope the angry teacher's words won't be directed at them. He was always an unsmiling angry man, but they'd never before seen him behave quite like this.

With his fists clenched like a couple of uncooked hams on the end of his arms and his malevolent, almost colourless, grey eyes swivelling wildly in their sockets, Ward screamed at them with a fury that caused the fleshy, reddening skin around his double chin to wobble over the top of his crisp white shirt collar, and the sight of it and of him made each one of them flinch, simultaneously in fear and disgust.

A huge bright screen on the wall beside them showed the unfolding of the World Leader's speech in all its hideous glory. Although the sheer audacity of it was to be admired, the nervous tension in the room was such that it could have been harvested for power. The sparks of it were almost visible. The screen was the only light in the room, and that fact contributed to the sinister edge that sat heavily over the scene as the Leader's face was projected out at them, larger than life and unstoppable.

The gathered group of men and women had been going about their work as usual before this catastrophe had struck. It had been a regular Monday morning, just like any other. At ten o'clock, as they were being brought drinks and snacks by the reassuringly old-fashioned looking tea lady wheeling her trolley in her neat little flowered apron and wrinkled brown tights, and as most of the people who had offices on that floor were sticking their heads out of their doors to greet her and say hello to their colleagues in the corridor, chatting amiably to her and each other about the day's offerings of cakes and biscuits, their workstations had simultaneously gone blank and emitted a high-pitched whistle in the rooms behind them.

Turning as one to face back into their offices, they had stood and stared in shock. This had never happened before. Could there be a problem with the power supply? But surely not. They had ample backups of power and, anyway, none of the lights had gone out. Tea and coffee and cake forgotten, they had raced back to their stations to try to see what the problem was, only to find that they were, each and every one of them, frozen out of whatever they had happened to be working on. And then, as they scrambled frantically to try to get back into their work, with a sudden flash the World Leader's face had appeared before them. From the rooms along the corridor, there were gasps of shock, shouts, and even one or two screams of horror. The tea lady scuttled away with her trolley, her grey curls bobbing around her little round face as she went.

The screens were frozen onto the channel the Leader was using – a new channel that these agents had not even been aware existed – and they found themselves unable to change the image on the screens, mute or reduce the volume, or even switch them off, not that any of them had thought to try to do so, such was their morbid fascination at this unprecedented intrusion. Besides, everyone knew that if they started switching off parts of the network, it was enough to get them fired at best, sent to prison or, at worst, dispensed with at the hands of their boss' unspoken-of and denied, though indisputably real, assassins.

One by one, they had returned to the corridor to talk to their colleagues. Everyone was in the same situation and none of them had any idea what was happening, how it had happened, or indeed what to do about it. A stirring of fear had immediately started to circulate among them, as they debated what their boss was going to do and how he was going to react. This speech was set to ruin him. And they knew that unless they did something about it, it was set to ruin them all.

Predictably enough, within seconds of this nervous conversation, every agent on their floor had been summoned by a terrified-looking intern, who'd come running breathlessly along the corridor towards them, to come here to Ward's office, where they now were, and where they had unceremoniously been plunged into a sinister half-darkness as he had turned off the room's lights with a vicious punch, so they could better feel the impact of what was unfolding around them, much like turning off the lights to watch a horror film.

The room at large had stared unblinkingly at the Leader as the words boomed out all around them, trying not to look interested or indeed show any other emotion on their faces than the outrage that was expected of them, lest they be accused of sympathising, and braced themselves for what was about to follow.

What was about to follow, it very soon became clear, was carnage. From the messages from their sister facilities across the world that they could hear being replied to across the corridor by the secretaries, through the open door of Ward's office, this message was not just being streamed into this headquarters facility, or even into the sister World Administration facilities, but it was in fact a worldwide broadcast. Of course it was. The Leader was addressing the "citizens". This wasn't a threat or a preview of something to come, it was happening now. And with no warning. At this moment in time, every screen in every home all across the globe, had been hacked, switched on, and was showing the same thing: this broadcast.

Everyone was watching. Everyone was waiting. The agents, nervously shuffling from foot to foot in Ward's office, were waiting. Their boss, turning purple with fury, his chest heaving with indignation, had slammed the door shut on the noise of the secretaries and ordered his agents to sit.

He had paced the room for a few long seconds, apparently without words, before he'd bawled the question at them as to how this had happened. He gasped now in outrage and clutched his throat, making the assembled staff momentarily stiffen in their chairs and wonder whether they were about to have two catastrophes on their hands, before yanking his collar open so that a small metal button popped off and skittered away across the polished floor to sit glinting in the half light in the corner of the room.

'You people are to blame for this,' Agent Ward continued in a menacingly low voice. 'All of you.' His gimlet-like beady little eyes, that were slightly too close together, especially for such a large round face, scanned the table, meeting every set of their own eyes in turn. 'And for your own sakes you'd better hope that one of you can sort it out and sort it out within the next few minutes. You realise what's happening here? You realise what that maniac is going to do?' He took another huge, heaving breath and clutched this time at his head, a quizzical look flitting momentarily across his face that suggested he was wondering why his hair was not long enough to get hold of and pull out. 'You're responsible for tracking, monitoring, and watching the Leader's every movement,' he continued, 'For looking at every tiny piece of online activity, every private activity, listening to every word, and predicting EVERY THOUGHT, damn it to hell!' He banged his fists hard on the table, and again the agents around it flinched as one as computers, pens and mugs rattled. 'Damn *you* all to hell,' he spat. 'You should not have allowed this to happen.'

Taking yet another rasping breath as the speech continued on the vast screen to his left, he turned abruptly to one agent in particular and, leaning towards him with his hands now flat on the table, bawled over the Leader's voice, 'You! Hurst!' A small globule of spit flew from his mouth and landed on the table in front of Agent Hurst. Everyone looked at it. It was hard not to. 'You're supposed to be in charge of this lot.' Ward pushed himself upright and waved his hands around the table at Hurst's colleagues. 'You're useless. Get to your station, you blithering idiot. I want you personally to find a way to break through the security they've put around this broadcast, and I want you to do it IMMEDIATELY! Get it off air before anymore damage is done.'

Agent Hurst got unsteadily to his feet, the Leader's speech still bursting forth and gathering momentum from the screen on the wall, and gathered up with shaking hands the paper and pen he'd brought with him. Beads of sweat had sprung up on his forehead, not quite hidden by the fringe of slightly greying sandy blond hair that fell forwards over it.

'Yes, sir,' he whispered, not daring to meet Agent Ward's eyes.

'How long will it take?' barked his boss, with the first hint of what could either have been worry, or a grudging admission that Hurst knew more than he did about these things, now breaking through his rage. 'You haven't forgotten that if a vote of no confidence in us is taken and we lose it, we are bound by the laws of this planet to honour the result? If that's what's happening here, we would lose everything we've worked for, for years, in an instant. A goddamn instant. All of it. Our entire way of life wiped out by nothing more than an ill-informed idiot. So? How long?' His face was by now the colour of a quivering over ripe plum, and his teeth were gritted and bared at his quarry as he waited for a response.

'I don't know, sir,' Hurst replied cautiously, thinking that the biggest ill-informed idiot was standing right in front of him. 'The security is bound to be extremely complex. They kept it well hidden, of course.' He needed to prepare Ward to understand, in order to save his own skin, that it might not be possible to hack it at all, the way you'd try and talk calmly to a kidnapper so that they didn't kill you. 'Nobody had any inkling that this was going to happen,' he ventured, slightly worried about what would become of his colleagues once he was out of the room. Not that his presence had any bearing on that, of course.

'Well, that's what you're paid for, you damn fool. You and your team...' Ward waved his clenched fist around the room once more, 'are supposed to be the best there is at HAVING INKLINGS.' Hurst thought for a moment that Ward was about to stamp his foot, making the over ripe plum of his head fall gracelessly from the tree of his thick sweaty neck, and the thought almost made him laugh. How had this uneducated fool risen to his current position of total power over the world? How had it been possible?

'Have you got any idea of the consequences of what that lunatic is doing?' Ward continued, apparently oblivious to the moment of mirth that had arisen in his best agent. Hurst opened his mouth to reply that yes, he did, but Ward snapped, 'That was rhetorical, man.' Hurst closed his mouth. Ward's insults were hardly conducive to his getting what he wanted. 'So? What are you waiting for?' Ward howled, as Hurst stood there considering him, nervous on the outside, contemptuous within. 'Go and get it done and get it done now.' Ward's tone became slightly more conversational again for a moment as if he'd just remembered the fact that, for the time being at least, he needed Hurst. 'We need to stop this broadcast before it goes any further,' he said in a pause for breath in the Leader's address. 'If we can cut it off mid-stream, we can pass it off as the Leader having gone insane, don't you see? Middle-aged madness, or some such.' His eyes bulged crazily, desperately. 'And then... well, then we deal with our oh so popular one-of-the-bloody-people Leader. Get to it. And pick that button up and give it to me,' he added irritably.

'Yes, sir, of course.' With a small incline of his head, Hurst made his way towards the door, and bent down to retrieve the metal button. He held it out to Ward, who fell silent for a moment and turned to stare at the screen.

'Oh, bugger off!' he yelled.

Assuming Ward was addressing him, Hurst stumbled gratefully from the office, absent-mindedly stuffing the forgotten button into his trouser pocket, and scurried away at a run down the brightly lit corridor, which hurt his eyes after the gloom of Ward's office. Ward screamed after him, with any pretence at humility gone once more, that heads would roll if the broadcast wasn't stopped within the next two minutes. And his head would be the first to find itself on a spike in the town centre.

Easy for you to say go and sort it out, thought Hurst. His heart was pounding, and his palms were now also wet with sweat. Oh God, why did this responsibility have to fall to him, of all people? Hadn't he done enough for one day? Done his bit? He took a deep breath as he jogged along the corridor, his shoes echoing loudly on the tiles beneath his hurrying feet. However, he acknowledged, perhaps it was better that the responsibility did fall to him. That had been the plan, after all. Some warning might have been nice, though, after all his hard work and risk taking. That was the thanks he got for putting his neck on the line day in day out.

Anyway, at least his being chosen to solve the catastrophe had given him a means of getting out of that awful meeting and away from Ward, whom he loathed. He was also relieved to get away from anyone in that room who might detect anything other than total compliance in his demeanour. It was getting harder and harder these days to keep up the pretence.

He could have put any discernible change in his countenance down to the fact that he didn't appreciate being yelled at and insulted in front of his colleagues, of course, especially as he was the most senior among them in terms of experience, and Ward was so obviously just a thug in a suit, but even so. You never could tell with people. That was one of the problems with working in intelligence; you never really knew who was on your side or who you could trust. Counterintelligence by its very nature doubled those concerns. As a result, Hurst wisely trusted no one.

He hurried along the corridor with a look of urgent concern on his face, unerringly conscious of the cameras blinking away all around him, and got into an open lift, which would take him up the three floors to his office. The nervous tapping of his long slim fingers on the wall of the lift was quite genuine. He had every reason to be nervous. If this didn't work, he was done for. It really was not unknown for people who didn't quite tow the line or measure up to expectation to disappear. It wasn't just rumours or urban myths. People were expendable in this world. Robots, as the Leader had said.

If it did work, he realised, he was probably also done for. But still, needs must when the devil drives. And stopping the devil from driving was the whole point of this terrifying exercise. The Leader was talking about taking part in history. He wondered momentarily how his own story would read. He supposed it all depended on the outcome. After all, the winners write the history books, don't they? He wondered whether he would be on the winning team, fit for a mention.

The lift came to a smooth stop and the doors gave an innocent ping as they opened right outside Hurst's office. He crossed the hall and opened the door with a hand that trembled slightly. This large room was located on the top floor of the building, and Hurst was grateful for that fact. The reason for this gratitude was that he tended to get rather claustrophobic on occasion and what with this facility being located underground, it meant he could always remind himself, if he started to feel panicky, that at least he was nearer to the surface than the poor sods who worked on the lower floors. And if ever there were an emergency, he consoled himself with the cheerful knowledge that he would be able to get out before Ward, and would, with luck on his side, be able to surreptitiously lock the doors before the nasty bastard reached the surface. Ah, happy thoughts indeed…

He pulled himself quickly back from his musings, however, and took a few deep breaths to steady himself as he stepped into his room where, naturally, the Leader's speech was continuing to wreak its mayhem, ringing out into the still and humid air. He tried not to look as if he was listening, but that was almost impossible given the fact that the Leader's face was speaking out through the screen he had to work from. It was better if he went straight to work on checking the procedure with his eyes averted from the screen and his concentration focused on the keyboard below. He moved quickly towards his desk.

There were no windows in the room, of course, but at least it was large, he thought again. It was quite luxurious, really. He flicked on the air conditioning to cool himself while he worked.

He had a lovely big antique wooden desk standing on a plush cream rug, that always made him feel important when he sat at it. Silly. But wood such as this was no longer allowed to be used in the production of furniture, of course. Well, there was scarcely any left, was there, what with the world's forests being so mercilessly decimated over the past centuries, and the few remaining twigs of the world's forests now so fiercely protected. Thin veneers of cheap mass-produced wood were nowadays glued onto even cheaper frames and was all that was available. Furniture of the calibre of this desk was a thing of the past unless one could afford antiques. And hardly anyone could afford antiques. Hardly anyone could afford the cheap stuff either, truth be told. Anyway…

Banks of screens occupied the walls of this room, as they did in every other room in this facility, and the Leader's face was therefore duplicated many times, giving the room the look of an old-world television shop with the images flashing away in unison. A couple of old-fashioned metal storage and filing cabinets sat forlorn and almost forgotten in the corner of the room, housing as they did the very few handwritten documents that were produced nowadays, and there was not much else of note to see. He couldn't even have a couple of plants in here, he thought gloomily, what with there being no natural light. And he'd never seen the point of artificial plants.

Apart from the door out into the corridor which had been the scene of so much debate and confusion a few short minutes ago, there was also a connecting door into his secretary's office which, mercifully, was shut at the moment. He needed to concentrate, not to be quizzed and asked a load of questions that he either couldn't or wasn't allowed to answer. So yes, to all intents and purposes, this was just a regular office. Desk, secretary, workstation. Boring as hell.

Of course, appearances could be deceptive. There was far more to Agent Hurst, and to this office, than met the eye, he thought with a satisfying inner scoff. As long as he was careful...

Well, he *was* careful. He had spent years perfecting the practice of being careful, and this was the most vital, pivotal moment, he thought now, as he sat his tall thin frame down at his desk in front of a huge panel of buttons, keys, and of course the screen he'd be working beside, and dragged a hand through his damp hair.

This morning had been rather nerve-wracking, to be fair, because he'd had his mind on other things, but he'd been careful and now everything hung on what happened next, on what he did next. Despite what Ward said, he, Hurst, was important. Ward was unaware of quite how important Hurst was, he stewed. Quite how intelligent. Quite how influential. Oh, stop it, he thought. You sound like a child.

But this was the moment that would change everything. All he had to do was go through his carefully worked out and planned, approved-by-Ward-himself routine of hacking into the Leader's computer network, and hope that it was all easily visible to the people manning the network of cameras in this place, several of which were located in this office and trained on his every move. He wiped his sweaty palms down his thighs and pulled a sheaf of papers out of the top drawer of the desk. Let's show them I'm double-checking the correct procedure, he thought wryly. Let's give them something to watch – not that any of them will understand it.

As he worked his way through this list of procedures, he found himself scowling darkly with a deep resentment and wondering quite why this morning's plant had been necessary. It was a pointless risk, if the speech was to be broadcast today. They had put him at more risk than was necessary.

He hadn't asked for this job, hadn't wanted it. He'd just been plucked, late one rainy Wednesday afternoon, from his workplace in an ordinary computer firm where he had minded his own business and got on with his ordinary routine job of designing computer software. It had been a place where he had actually been happy, he remembered nostalgically. He'd had some good friends there in London, where he used to live. It had been a good team of people, with a normal, relaxed atmosphere, and it had enabled him to live in a normal way and do his fair share in providing for his normal family. They were used to the cameras in the workplace at that time, of course, and nobody liked it, but there had been nothing like the amount of tension and stress that hovered over his life like a storm cloud here, threatening to burst, and violently, mercilessly dump its contents on him at any moment.

Then one day in London, life had changed. What he had initially feared to be a group of four reprobates about to mug him, but now knew to be far more sinister even than that, had been waiting for him in the shadows of the car park as he left his place of work to go home for the evening. They had surrounded him as he had tried to get into his car, issuing threats against making a sound, and then told him that he and his family, for Hurst had a wife and son, would be relocating, and that he would from then on be working in intelligence for the World Administration. Not only that, but he would be working for the boss, the leader no less, of the World Administration.

Utterly bewildered by what he was hearing, their demand for silence had hardly been necessary. Shock at the use of these words in reference to himself had silenced him as effectively as anything physically damaging that they could have inflicted on him. There must have been a mistake. He had hardly known what it meant, to work in intelligence, never mind known what he could say in response to them in that initial moment of shock, and so he had just stood there, car keys in hand, gawping at the four men in mute disbelief. They told him to relock his car and to go with them quietly and calmly, and that nothing bad would happen. Hardly believing these words, he had done as he was told. After all, what choice did he have? He had been outnumbered. And, he thought, he'd been a wimp.

He could certainly never have dreamt that working in intelligence, as they'd put it, could mean that he would be employed to do the low, despicable things he now did. He didn't want to spy on the World Leader. To be perfectly honest, he couldn't have cared less at the time what the World Leader even did. He hardly cared now. He had just wanted to remain a normal person in his normal job. In London.

But no. That hadn't been possible. Once he had regained command of his speech on that fateful day, incarcerated as he had been inside their car, he had tried to argue, tried to reason with them, tried to say no, but it had been very firmly pointed out to him that refusal was not an option. That in fact he should feel honoured and consider himself extremely lucky that he'd been chosen. He had not felt anything of the kind. He disagreed wholeheartedly with everything the WA stood for.

The memory of that time still caused a simultaneous burning fear and white-hot rage to ignite inside him. The fact that he had been so incapable of coherent or successful argument or of getting himself and his family out of it was partly to blame. He was ashamed of himself and of what he still saw as his inarticulate weakness. The only thing to lessen this self-criticism was the knowledge that they would have taken him regardless. Or so he'd thought.

What might his life and that of his family be like now, though, if he hadn't been singled out for this work, or if he had at least tried to stand up for himself and had not been so easily manipulated? The four men, he remembered, had quickly and easily achieved their aim – they had manhandled him into their own car, squashed him into the middle of the back seat, where, he supposed, they could better control his movements, and driven him home to his house, which was a ground floor flat with a postage stamp of paved garden out the back, dusty and grey and unused except by the rubbish bin and as a convenient route towards the park for the local cats on their night-time prowl.

Of course, the men had not needed directions to Anthony Hurst's abode. They had parked directly outside, which further annoyed him because it was something he himself could rarely manage to do, and accompanied him into his living room where his wife had been sitting on the floor playing with their two-year-old son. Without preamble or any apology for their intrusion, they repeated their narrative to her.

Sally had worked as a hairdresser at that time, in their previous life in London. Well, she still did work as a hairdresser, but she'd been a normal hairdresser back then. Everything had been normal back then, within the context of what they were used to at least. They'd had a regular life where they minded their own business and others minded theirs, where there had only been as much interference from the authorities towards them as there had been towards anyone else, for crying out loud, and she surely hadn't wanted to move anymore than he had. She had protested. In fact, she had protested far more eloquently than he himself had done, albeit in a haltering and nervous manner. But her protestations hadn't been met with anymore sympathy than his own half-hearted attempt. It was scant consolation.

Only afterwards was it, Hurst thought now as these memories came rushing back to him in perfect sequence, that he had found out that, in actual fact, his wife had not been remotely surprised to find a group of darkly clothed men with an attitude to match escorting her husband home from work and announcing this plan to her. She had been expecting it and had merely been acting a part. Her whole speech had been as well thought out and rehearsed as theirs. When she'd told him this, he'd wondered what the hell she'd been talking about.

The only thing to be hoped, Sally had said later, was that their uninvited guests had not picked up on her lack of surprise and gone away to report any suspicion back to their superiors. One had to assume they would have done, she said; it was the only safe way to think, and one had to fine-tune one's behaviour accordingly. She had said this with the only tinge of fear or regret she had ever shown with regards the situation in the six long years between then and now.

Mindful of their every move, husband and wife had, from that moment on, conducted their life as if they were on stage, being watched by a particularly judgemental audience. In that decisive moment in the lounge six long years ago, Sally had even managed to produce a few tears, clutch her child protectively to her shoulder and, sobbing, ask the question that had been on his own lips all the while: why us?

Her question remained unanswered of course. At least, it was not answered in a truthful way, but the men did at least listen to her when she told them how much she loved her job and that she didn't want to leave it. She asked if she could open her own salon. They said they would see what they could do, that they were not monsters coming to drag them away to the gallows, and that the request would be submitted for her to continue in her field. It was a measure of how deep Sally's contacts ran that it was decided, after her protests had been made and heard, that she would be allowed, while many were not, to continue in her trade while her husband would be doing his bit for humanity, and she was even set up with enough money to open her own salon in their new town, so that it didn't cost them anything. She had been expected to be grateful. And thinking about it now, she probably had been. Grateful that her plan had worked.

Chapter Six

As it turned out, the performance she'd given those four men was just the start of Sally's acting abilities. Abilities that Hurst had known absolutely nothing about. He knew that he should have been proud of her for this, because it had undoubtedly gone a long way towards keeping them trusted and, therefore, it had probably saved their bacon on more than one occasion. But he wasn't. He wasn't proud.

She had been much better at pretending, as she had argued for her job and then once she'd been presented with the gift of the new salon, that she was perfectly happy with the ghastly situation that they had found themselves in, than Hurst himself could ever have hoped to have been. Sally was far more controlled and together than he was. She could talk her way out of anything, and she never seemed to be scared, for them or for the world. It unnerved him.

Well of course she hadn't been scared, had she, he thought again. As he had been about to discover, she had already been privy to the fact that this day would come. She had known from the start, been in on all the planning, and she was certain that they would triumph over adversity. Bizarrely, she had almost appeared to be enjoying herself. Her husband was stunned, and not in a good way.

She had thrown herself into the process of planning her new salon, asking the sort of practical questions that anyone starting a new business would ask. And the people they had been put in touch with to talk about the practicalities of their move really seemed to appreciate this and took her under their wing as if it was the first time anyone had shown any enthusiasm for their enforced move. It probably was.

He thought again about the time, the actual moment, when his wife had revealed her involvement in all of this to him. As soon as they had been left alone in their lounge on that fateful day, with orders to be packed and ready to move in one week's time – there was apparently no need for Hurst to go back to his old place of work, or for him to go and collect his car, which would, they said, be delivered back to him – Sally, still carrying their now almost sleeping son, had taken her husband calmly by the elbow and steered him upstairs into the bathroom, closed the door, and turned on the water in the bath, the shower, and the basin, and then explained to him in a very low whisper not only about her concerns that her reaction had been pre-planned, but also, and far more shockingly, that she was working for the World Leader.

He could still remember all this as clearly as if it had only happened an hour ago, how his eyes had widened uncomprehendingly. What the hell was she talking about? How was it possible? It *couldn't* be possible. Who was this woman standing in front of him, calmly supporting their child's sleepy head on her shoulder and talking in this way? Did he not know her at all? Before he had the chance to respond and tell her that the very idea of her working with or for the Leader was more mental than anything he'd ever heard, more insane than any turn the day had already taken, she had put up a silencing hand and continued to whisper.

He was to follow the instructions that she, Sally herself, would give him, as well as the instructions of the people in his new place of work. They were both to act as if they were one hundred per cent trustworthy and loyal to his new employers, and they must never speak candidly about any of this again, unless they were outside and away from any threat of being overheard by a listening device. She said she was certain one had been planted in their living room when the men had been there, so their loyalty and an enthusiasm for the move was to begin being acted out immediately. Hurst could hardly hear what was being whispered over the sound of the water and had to lean close to catch the words. Was she serious?

He turned his head towards the bathroom door, imagining a bug in the lounge. He could hardly believe she was speaking in this way, that she knew what she was saying. What on earth had happened to them today? What did she mean she'd been working with the

Leader? How the hell did she even know the Leader? It was madness.

Sally then went on to explain that she had a supply of a special washing detergent. When he raised his eyebrows in further questioning bewilderment, Sally quickly explained that their son did not in fact really have an allergy to the regular kind of washing liquids, but the story had been made up so as she could be given access to a type of detergent that had to be ordered and sent to her from a specialist. Her orders of this special liquid came from a company where one of the Leader's agents was working, and Sally's orders always came shipped out containing a chemical that destroyed any tiny listening devices that might be placed on their clothes by the spies who would now inevitably be around them and who had no doubt already been following them and evaluating them closely while deciding on whether or not to take them for relocation.

Hurst was furious. He opened his mouth to speak, to ask her what the hell she thought she was thinking, doing, playing at, getting involved in, letting him believe their son had this allergy, exposing not only him but all three of them to chemicals which no doubt *could* give them skin conditions.

Sally shook her head urgently. They didn't have time for this now. She told him that they would go for lots of walks when they arrived in their new town, and she would explain further. At first, however, they would be just that – walks. It was essential that they prove themselves compliant, and she would explain everything to him as and when she could. Right now, they needed to go back downstairs and act as if nothing out of the ordinary was happening, and vocalise something positive about the move.

With that, she had told him that as the water was on and no doubt being detected, that he should have a shower before joining her downstairs. Then she walked out of the bathroom and along to the nursery to put the small boy down for a nap, before calmly going back down the stairs.

Hurst had watched her go, dumbstruck. Then he'd done as she'd suggested and got into the shower, as much to gather his thoughts together as anything else, but his head was swirling and misting more than the steam on the glass. This was madness. Did she really think those men had planted a bug? He hadn't noticed anything. And device-destroying detergent, for crying out loud? What was this?

But he decided to comply for now, give himself a chance to process it all and think things through. After all, there didn't seem to be much of an alternative. If what Sally was saying were true, and she'd seemed pretty serious, then they were already in too deep to walk away. And so, he had done exactly as his wife had suggested. After all, she had said she would explain when she could, so he could do nothing but trust her, and trusting her was better and easier than trusting anyone else. However, he had to admit that the situation was making him angrier by the minute. He felt sick to his stomach.

After letting the hot water pound down on his head for another ten minutes or so, he turned off the tap and, with a heavy breath, got out of the shower and dried himself. He wrapped the towel around his waist and trod carefully along the hall, mindful of his sleeping son who, he noticed with a pull of affection as he looked in on him, was sucking his thumb in his sleep, all innocence. Hurst entered his own bedroom, that of himself and his wife, his scheming, plotting bloody wife, and the anger continued to brew. Just how closely would their lives be monitored, he wondered, as he threw the towel on the floor and got dressed. Jesus, was nothing sacred anymore?

Had Sally closed the bathroom door and turned on the water merely – merely! – to close off the sound of them speaking, or had she imagined the device she was so sure had been dropped could fly? Yes, Hurst felt sick. And that feeling was intensified by the knowledge that he couldn't talk about any of this with her. It wasn't safe, she had said, and she was quite right. If there was a bug, their house was no longer safe. Their lives were no longer safe.

It was true. His whole life had been turned on its head in the space of a couple of hours, and more by her than by the men who had accosted him in the car park. Somehow, he had managed to go back downstairs and eat his dinner, but to his mind he was hardly behaving naturally.

This, he guessed, was all right for now. He couldn't have cared less, anyway. He had had a terrible shock. His mood was bound to be a bit off. A bit off? He'd had a bellyful before the real nightmare had even started.

Clearly following his thoughts and thinking that avoiding the subject entirely was even more damaging, not to say unnatural, Sally had begun to talk about moving. She had put a few questions to him: did he think their son would take to the move all right; what did he think their new house would be like; where did he think they were going?

He had shot furious daggers of scowling resentment at her across the table and answered her in the same tone as he had used when their earlier uninvited guests had announced this preposterous plan. Yes, he thought their son would be fine. He didn't really care for someone else to be choosing where he lived. He didn't have a clue where they would be going, and he doubted they were even supposed to know themselves. He'd thrown his spoon down into his dessert bowl with a sharp clatter and sat back in his chair with his arms folded defensively across his chest.

This last could have been construed as dissent, he knew, so, already scared, he justified his answer by saying that the work he would be doing was supposed to be top secret, remember, so they probably weren't allowed to know for security reasons. Then he'd sat forward and gone back to glowering into his apple pie and custard.

Things had been decidedly frosty between husband and wife for a number of weeks following that horrible day that had changed their lives forever. Hurst had felt iced-up from the inside out. Partly because of Sally's furtiveness and the fact that she had kept all this from him, kept him in complete ignorance as to what she had been doing and the fact that what she had dragged him into as a result could and probably would put them all in unimaginable danger. He preferred to keep his mouth shut and concentrate on the practicalities of packing their stuff for the move, rather than challenge her about it. Well, he couldn't challenge her, could he? She'd condemned him to this and there wasn't a damn thing he could do about it.

What he really wanted to do was to simply pack a suitcase and leave her. But of course, he couldn't. Had she possibly invented the story of the bug just in case, just so he wouldn't do exactly that? Was it simply an extra layer of security, put in place by her to guard against his leaving, like a bitter icing on top of the poisoned cake of his hopeless incarceration by her, by the World Leader, and by his new employers, the World Administration? He felt emasculated, deceived, used. He was not at all happy.

However, an ability to keep up indefinitely the defensive shield of embittered martyr that he'd cloaked himself with, proved impossible, and his mood began very slowly to thaw. He focused a lot of attention onto his son, reminding himself constantly how much he loved him and how important it was to ensure his happiness.

As the days passed and the move became imminent and the prospect of finding themselves God alone knew where drew ever closer, he found himself in need of his wife's support. She and their son were all he had, and even more so now. Besides, what was the point of staying angry? It wouldn't change anything; it wouldn't make him miraculously wake up from the nightmare Sally had put them into the middle of. So, bit by bit his mood had returned, if not exactly to the normality of before, then to a sort of grudging outward acceptance of the situation, as he did his best to arrange his thoughts so as they wouldn't destroy him. He loved her, after all, he must remember that, and would need to support her, too. You stupid cow, he thought to himself with a sigh.

If she had only told him. If she had only explained what she was involved with before things got out of hand. Maybe he could have talked her out of it. Maybe he himself would be a bit more sympathetic towards her. Maybe he wouldn't now be putting his life in danger because of her. He was under no illusions; the work he would be doing would be dangerous. Why else was it secret? Intelligence work didn't involve breeding Easter bunnies, did it?

One day following their move, as they were taking a stroll around the town to get their bearings, Sally had finally begun to talk to him in more detail. She had taken hold of his hand and, when he'd looked round at her in response to this unexpected show of affection that had been distinctly lacking of late, she smiled kindly, like the Sally he loved and who he used to think he knew and, with his attention on her, she had finally begun to speak about it.

Through a mouth that didn't move, and after telling him not to react, she explained that she had been communicating with the Leader all along, for months even before his encounter with that group of men in the car park, that yes, their arrival had been engineered, yes, she had been waiting for it, and that, by the way, there was a device on the inside wall of the microwave oven that he must make sure he never touched. Quite how he hadn't laughed out loud at that particular piece of information, he didn't know. It took every ounce of self-control he possessed to arrange his face into a mask of ordinariness, even though he was pretty sure there were no cameras where they were, walking along a quiet road behind their house on the outskirts of town. The device was to be used only by her. He listened to her murmured words and responded normally when she interjected a piece of normal speech, utterly bewildered by her and by the situation he found himself in.

How on earth had his wife been doing this? His sweet, kind wife, the mother of their child, the softly spoken woman who got on well with everyone and who worked in a normal little hairdresser's. For crying out loud, he had thought they told each other everything. Why hadn't she told him what was going on from the start? Because she knew damn well that he would never have agreed to have any part in it, in this insane scheme, that's why. But that was the point – insane scheme to do what, exactly? He supposed he would have to wait to hear the answers to that particular question, along with the hundreds of others he had for her, until she deemed it safe or necessary to enlighten him.

The first time she had spoken to him without moving her mouth, as they had first walked up the path to their new home, having just endured a trip that felt to all intents and purposes like a kidnapping, he'd thought there was something wrong with her. If it hadn't been for the fact that the first words she'd spoken in this way had been a harshly worded order not to react, and that in actual fact he was by then, from the stress of the trip, almost returned to the point of being beyond as much as even turning his head in her direction, such was his renewed flare-up of anger, he would have raced to call her a doctor.

As it was, in a few precious seconds, grabbed while their escort had been occupied with finding keys and depositing their bags on the pavement, as she had clutched their son's little hand and led him to the door, she had hissed at him, Hurst, not to say a word because their house would surely be bugged. Here we go again, he'd thought.

And so, it had not been a difficult instruction to follow. By now he was getting used to the absurd which, in itself, made him even more angry and resentful. So, he had simply walked back down the path and begun to help their driver with the bags, wondering on top of everything else how long his damned wife had been skilled in the art of ventriloquism. He certainly felt like her dummy, with her hand up his arse controlling everything he did. Bitch. How could she do this to him? To them? He'd picked up a couple of bags and stomped up the path after his ruined family.

Their new house wasn't at all bad. In fact, it was a lot better than Hurst himself had been expecting and, in terms of real estate, was actually quite a considerable step up from the flat they used to live in. For one thing, it was a house rather than a flat. It was detached and stood on a rather large plot of land that included a garage and a lawned garden. A gated driveway separated it from the street, and a cute little path led up to the white-painted front door, which had a large potted bush each side of it. Inside, they had three good sized bedrooms, already furnished, and a state-of-the-art kitchen, that Sally was delighted about. Her enthusiasm over this particular room was quite genuine, of that Hurst had no doubt. He had glared at her. All this is OK then, as long as you've got a decent bloody kitchen, he'd thought. The lounge was cosy, with an open fireplace and a window overlooking the back garden. Two large cream sofas sat snugly against the walls, with a glass-topped coffee table on a small cream rug in front of them. He wondered briefly whether, if they decided they wanted to rearrange the furniture, they would be accused of searching for bugs – of the surveillance variety, he'd thought bitterly. They had a spacious bathroom, there was a utility room off the kitchen, and there was even a separate dining room – a sure sign of affluence, he'd growled to himself. It was all so obviously too good to be true, and Hurst wondered whether the people who had provided all this for them were so stupid as to think the Hursts wouldn't find it all a bit suspicious if they, the WA, really believed them to be under their sole employ. Did everyone get a house like this? Perhaps so. These ponderings, as with so many others by this point, he had naturally kept to himself. However, as if reading his mind, the men who had driven them to the new house, upon seeing him staring at the arrangement of furniture, told him that they were of course free to make whatever changes they liked to the décor. He'd just grunted a non-committal response. The whole thing was too unnerving for words.

However bitter he was, no one could deny that the house was beautiful, and for that at least Hurst tried not to be too resentful. It would be good for their son to have all this space and a garden to play in, and there was even enough room to accommodate a second child, should they wish to have one.

Hurst did not wish to have one. Apart from the fact that, at the moment, he could barely even bring himself to look at his wife, other than to keep up the pretence of marital bliss for the sake of their unseen audience, it was bad enough that the child they already had had been uprooted from all that he had known in his young life and forced to come to this foreign backwater hell full of sand and dust. He wasn't about to inflict that on anyone else. But yes, the house was nice. Quite the softener in fact, if you were materially minded, he had thought to himself resentfully. His skills must really be respected and needed. But needed to do what, exactly?

A tiny stirring of curiosity had raised its head within him, and at last he began to be genuinely interested in what his wife had to say.

Gradually, Sally had revealed all the information that had been coming her way. She apologised, admitting that his misery had all been her fault, but, despite his slight softening towards her, Hurst was still angry.

Yes, he thought again now, he'd been angry with her for a long time afterwards, in fact, despite his newfound curiosity. But he'd been in a position where he could not even express that anger, and she knew it. He still felt used, and he still felt trapped. And there was nothing he could do about it.

Every chance she got Sally reiterated how sorry she was for all the secrecy she had been forced to put between them. But the secrecy, she told him, was just because she had been following orders. And quite apart from that, she had known that he wouldn't have wanted her to get involved, but that it was something she herself felt so strongly about that she felt the risks were worth it. If she succeeded in her mission, if she succeeded in her mission with his help, then they could change the world. They could really make a difference and help the Leader to achieve the aim of bringing down the current regime of fear, control, and dictatorial brainwashing.

Was she insane? How did she think she was going to bring down the regime?

She was excited, she told him. It could work. Think of the benefits for their son of growing up in a world where he was allowed to think for himself, be free of observation, and properly settled in his old homeland. He could live in a proper country which would have a name, and which would give him a nationality he'd never otherwise know.

She had a point, of course. Hurst's fear and reluctance was due entirely to the effects of the regime under which they currently lived. This was in fact *not* Sally's fault. If he could be a part of the downfall of the current regime, crazy though that sounded, if he could help his son to have a better future, one where he could be happy and free, if they could all go home to England and be allowed to call it such, well then of course, he would do whatever he had to.

And so it began. Hurst fully on board, with the thoughts of a world two centuries before, where people had lived within the borders of their own countries and by a set of fairer rules than they had today planted firmly in his head, he finally began to pay attention.

Chapter Seven

'Permit me to give you all a brief, summarised reminder of how our present situation came about. In the year 2022, the area of the world that was once called Italy had at its helm the now infamous prime minister, Vincenzo Codardo. His core political belief was, as you all know, for we are all taught to revere him, that all people, wherever they happened to live in the world, should have an equal right to relocate to whatever part of the globe they desired. He was sure that this no-borders freedom would bring lasting peace to the world.

'In principle, it seemed to be a noble desire, with a genuine belief that the idea could work. In fact, I believe the man really did envisage that gaining world peace in this way was possible. But his ideal was the ill-thought-out plan of a man who could not see that if you give leaders enough rope, they will not hang themselves, but they will hang their citizens, and that ultimately his New World would become a prison. He could not have imagined that his ideas would have no collocation with what we have actually ended up with as a result of the actions of his successors. And I also believe that, were he alive today to witness the ultimate outcome of his

naivety, of his determination to believe that all of humanity was able, wanted, or could be gently persuaded to see the world as he did, he would be horrified.

'Perhaps I am wrong. We know he was never a man to admit to his mistakes, or to take responsibility. He would no doubt say that the mess we are now in is as a direct result of the misinterpretation of his ideal by others. Probably his biggest mistake was to imagine that in using nothing but his manifesto of fairness, he could open the eyes, as he saw it, of the ignorant people of the world to his truth, and that people everywhere would bow down to what he thought to be his superior knowledge and follow his ideal without challenge. In other words, his arrogance was the world's downfall.

'At the time, two centuries ago, the twenty-eight member states, or countries, within a smaller, more basic, model of this freedom of movement ideal, within the continent of Europe, had just become twenty-seven, when the people of what was then known as the United Kingdom of Great Britain and Northern Ireland voted by a miniscule margin to leave this union, and once again become a fully independent union of their own four countries.

'Codardo didn't seem to draw any lessons from the fiasco that followed this move, this proof that you can't please everyone all the time. He didn't understand that a lot of the British people who wanted to remain in the union, and who were committed to it, nevertheless

agreed with the pro-leavers in that they felt the controls over them were becoming too tight. He was convinced that not just a unified Europe, but a unified world, could be made to work better for everyone by abandoning all sovereignty and coming together as one, even though he could see the unified continent of Europe completely falling apart before his eyes following the departure of the United Kingdom, and the remaining member states being then also spurred into taking action against the tight controls themselves. And this coming only fifty years or so from the date of the union's creation.

'The union was seen by many in the less wealthy member states as forcing tighter controls upon them for the benefit of the handful of countries that were most powerful, while at the same time, conversely, the people of the wealthier nations objected to what they saw as the forcing of an equality of economies and an even spreading out of wealth, which made the more affluent nations responsible for holding up the rest, while more and more, smaller and poorer European countries applied for membership so as they also could take advantage of the system. The people of the wealthier nations in particular were not happy, and after the departure of the United Kingdom, the people of these nations were the first to start speaking up in their millions and calling for the dissolution of the whole union. They may have had freedom of movement, the right to come and go as they pleased within the member states, to live and work where they wanted within the

union, but beyond that, the controls and regulations being imposed upon them were, many believed, too high a price to pay just to satisfy those who wished to work abroad.

'Of course, a friendly union between neighbouring, and indeed world, nations, is ideal. It's what any right-minded person wants, and that union within Europe was created to ensure that after the Second World War the nations of Europe remained friendly and never went down that terrible, destructive path again. But the centralisation of laws and various financial matters was always going to cause a problem, especially when there began to be talk of a centralised European army. People were afraid. They wanted the security of being back within the safety of their own nations, and answerable to no one else, like going home to the safety of your own house after spending time away travelling in places whose cultures are alien to you.

'However, the Italian prime minister remained resolute, if not obstinate. If anything, this questioning of the system made him more determined than ever to prove that his vision could work, could be fairer for all, and could indeed provide all the freedoms that the union between those member states had failed to do in the eyes of the protesting citizens – but on a global scale.

'To begin with, he wanted a global currency for those who wished to enter his New World, English to be taught as a mandatory second language for those with a different mother tongue, a cap on property ownership,

with compulsory requisitioning of any property which was deemed surplus to your needs, enforced charity donations for the super-rich to rid them of their wealth, a channelling back down of money to those who in his opinion needed it more, as well as the freedom for all people to come and go as they pleased and to live and work wherever the fancy took them, with no barriers for doing so within participating countries.

'Unfortunately, people tend to love nothing more than a bandwagon to jump on, and the moment Codardo started saying he would take away the money from the super-rich, people were rushing forwards, ready with their support. The super-rich have always been in the minority and have always been hated and resented by many of the less well off who tend to assume they are out to do nothing but exploit them, and so of course this minority couldn't get enough backing to oppose him.

'And so, the changes began.

'Once he had the backing of the people for his scheme, he saw to it that a law was quickly passed within Italy which meant the borders of his country were effectively erased. The country no longer used its name, the citizens could no longer refer to themselves as Italian, and the country became nothing more than an area of land containing cities and towns that anyone from any country who chose to join Codardo's vision could go to with no questions asked and, armed only with a set of civil laws to keep the peace, he invited all other countries to follow his lead and do the same.

'When described in this way, it sounds naïve at best, insane at worst, and who knows, perhaps it was, but it came at a time when the world was recovering from a global virus that completely changed the way people lived and that for a long time took away their freedom – to the extent that they were forbidden for weeks at a time to leave their houses. While the authorities struggled with the logistics of getting an effective vaccine produced and rolled out as quickly as possible to combat this virus, to see to it that the world's population then actually went on to get themselves vaccinated, and struggled to make people believe that being locked into their homes for weeks on end was for the benefit of all, most countries saw an inevitable response of protests, riots and general civil unrest. Stoking the fires even further were all the conspiracy theories that were naturally prevalent. In some places, people even had their front doors welded shut to stop them going out. It is easy to understand their anger.

'After this restrictive situation had been going on for more than two years, even the general, law-abiding populace started to get more than a bit restless. Unsurprising then that they should begin in greater numbers to listen to the proclamations of the man who was promising them not only the return of their freedom, but freedom on a level that had never been seen before. People's reaction to the global closures – for people lost their businesses, jobs, and livelihoods, as well – was to embrace wholeheartedly any chance they were given

to move around again, to live again, and this ideal of a better and freer world that was being offered to them by Codardo was intoxicating. People didn't stop to think about the fact that in order to keep the peace on a global scale you have to increase controls, laws and restrictions, not loosen them. And neither did Codardo.

'Pressure mounted on the authorities everywhere around the world and, one by one, other countries joined the "Free World". Its idea was to offer the same opportunities to every person in every country by way of losing every country's name and borders and, generations later, to sum it up in a couple of sentences, it encompassed the whole world, with an overseeing body, the World Administration who, thus far, have had total dominance, imposing the laws, and generation after generation of children being taught that this system of unification was the best and indeed the only way. Very soon, it was forbidden to speak the names of the old countries. Countries as the world once knew them, no longer existed. We all became simply "Citizens of the World".'

Chapter Eight

Every so often, Sally would receive parcels through the post of what looked like innocent items bought online. Some of them were. Others were less so, and these could contain anything from children's toys to pens and came with coded instructions on the delivery notes. Essentially, the items were fitted with miniscule, almost invisible, bugging devices. The instructions explained where these bugs were on the item and Hurst's job was to "accidentally" take them to work with him and transfer the sticky devices to the offices in his building, as indicated on the coded instructions.

For Hurst's part, it had been yet another absurdity. It had felt as surreal and the method as rudimentary as if they had been back in the nineteen eighties and living in the middle of a cheap spy novel. However, hating his situation as he did, and desperate to get out and return to the relative normality of his old life, Hurst had, albeit with an ever-present terror rolling around inside him, undertaken this mission. It scared the hell out of him. Every time he took one of the little devices to work, every time he held the item it was attached to in his hand and surreptitiously rolled it where he wanted it to stick, before seemingly absent-mindedly replacing the now genuinely innocent item into his pocket, he felt convinced that this would be the day he was caught. And if he was caught... well, it didn't bear thinking about.

Another thing that was extraordinary was not just the old-fashioned means of getting the bugs placed, but the paradox that such technology could be concealed in something so small. The little sticky bugs were no bigger than a grain of sand. Nowadays, of course, there was much better technology available than ever before: listening devices concealed in what looked like crumbled leaves in plant pots, and in tiny drones that appeared to be flies. However, Hurst supposed that this old method was favoured because it was generally assumed by the Leader and the Leader's operatives that nobody would be looking for them.

Added to that, as old-fashioned as they appeared to be, Sally explained that the little sticky bugs were unique in that they were undetectable by the bug sweeping methods employed at the facility at which Hurst worked. Something to do with the glue, apparently, kept them hidden. The only risk to this ingenious plan was to Hurst himself and, only if they could prove it, for all the delivery notes to Sally were burnt, should he be caught. He was the one in the firing line. Not she. He. And yes, he thought now, that's the correct grammar – which was something else that bugged him, pardon the pun, about being here in what was essentially America. No one could speak properly.

He wondered, if this scheme of the Leader's was successful, how long it would be until they were able to return home. Would their old home still be there? Would it have been sold off to someone else by the time they returned? Would he even survive to see that glorious day of going home? Would Sally survive to see that day? What would happen to their son if the two of them were killed? He couldn't think about it. Thinking that way would drive him crazy. He had to stay focused and keep telling himself that one day very soon all this would be over, and they would indeed be able to go home and get on with their lives as a normal family in a genuinely free and democratic world. In their own country.

They could no longer see or communicate with their old friends, of course, but had at least been able to say goodbye. They had been given a cover story to tell people about how Hurst had been offered the opportunity to work in a top facility that was serving the greater good of the people of the world, and naturally everyone had said they were proud of him. Well, they had to say that, didn't they? Who knew what people had really thought? People had been fed just enough information to keep them quiet, and everyone knew better than to ask too many questions. The family was given a good send-off and that was that. Goodbye old life.

Hurst wondered whether the reason it had been easy for Sally and her contacts in the Leader's office (how did she know these people?) to arrange for the so-called World Administration to target him was because neither he nor his wife had any other family. There was nobody for their now eight-year-old son to ask questions about or be sad at not seeing. It was all very convenient. It was all very creepy. Surveillance was part of life, everyone knew that, but in his opinion, it was one thing if it was used to keep people safe on the streets but quite another if it was abused in the way it had started to be over the last fifty years or so. What it was, was sinister. The speed with which technology moved on made increased surveillance inevitable in a world such as theirs, he supposed, but nevertheless he didn't like it and he knew that he was far from the only one to feel that way. Cameras in the workplace could be argued to be useful, but the trouble was, you had no way of knowing, if you worked in his sort of field, even though everyone's houses were watched, whether your house had also been fitted with extra surveillance devices, as his wife had suspected from the outset. She was right – one had to assume they were. Therefore, it would be most unwise for anyone at all to voice their thoughts on anything other than family matters or trivial topics, even in their own home, and it was wrong.

Anyway, they hadn't had any choice. He hadn't been told where they were relocating to when he had had his men in black experience and, truth be told, he wasn't supposed to know even now. He did, of course. For anyone with an averagely functioning brain, he fumed, the matter had been simple. Frankly, it was insulting. Plus, Sally had been helped on her way in working out this glaringly obvious answer by the Leader's people, by being told their destination would be towards the western side of what used to be America and so it hadn't been difficult to work out that they were in the middle of the Nevada desert.

Put on a plane and sedated though he and his family had been, like a cargo of endangered animals being sent to a zoo where they could be monitored, he and his wife had been able to work this information out from the fact that they had woken up after a ten-hour flight and that in their new town there was dry earth as far as the eye could see and the horizon encircled them with dusty looking red mountains. No, it didn't take a genius to work it out.

Nobody in their right mind would choose to live in the middle of this harsh landscape. They were nowhere near any other towns or cities and there was no public transport to speak of. Buses were laid on for people without cars to get to their places of work, or to the shops, but they did not run services outside the town. Cars were fitted with trackers. To all intents and purposes, they were prisoners. Invisible to the outside world, and practically invisible within the confines of the town. No one to notice or care if they disappeared.

And so of course, aware of the dangers, they hadn't spoken about any of these kinds of things while inside their house because, apart from the fact that it was bugged, it was also likely to be riddled with cameras, and they both knew it. They understood that they had virtually no privacy whatsoever. Consequently, they went for a lot of walks and runs, pretending to be fans of keep fit, and spoke in low voices through gritted teeth; now two whispering ventriloquists rather than one.

Their subterfuge must have worked well, because one day, after about eighteen months, Hurst was suddenly summoned before Agent Ward and told that he had proven himself to be trustworthy and that he was being promoted to the position he now held, overseeing the work of the team of special agents on his floor. He'd gone home that evening and spoken about it with Sally. They'd put on quite a show of enthusiasm about it over dinner that night for the benefit of whoever was tasked with listening to that evening's conversation.

Oh, he thought now, as he consulted the bank of screens and buttons in front of him, if they only knew. He was glad he had an excuse for his face being screwed up in anger.

Before he got to work on Ward's orders, he sent a quick message to his wife.

I might be a bit late home for dinner. Perhaps you should put something in the microwave.

Chapter Nine

Sally Hurst dragged her eyes away from the Leader's speech that was playing out on the screen on the living room wall and picked up her communication device, or CD as they were known. She read her husband's message with no outward sign of interest. Avoiding making any kind of reaction, she simply replied, *OK*, placed the device back onto the sofa where it had been lying, stood up, slid her feet into her fluffy pink slippers and headed for the kitchen, which was located just off the back of the living room.

On her way, and for the sake of normality, she made a point of calling loudly up the stairs to her son to ask if he wanted a drink. The children had been given the first part of the morning off to study for a test that afternoon and that's what Toby was currently doing in his bedroom. Sally's salon was closed on Mondays and so she'd been able to spend the morning at home with him. He was due back at school at eleven thirty.

Now eight years old, he was a very placid boy. He never asked questions, always did as he was told, and respected authority with the unquestioning passive acceptance of all children nowadays. It broke Sally's heart. She longed for him to have the freedom to think out and plan his own future for himself and to show some signs of curiosity about the world. She longed to be able to go into his room and tell him off for listening to music rather than doing his homework but knew that that situation would never arise for him. Unless things changed.

He and all other children were the reason the Democratic Party were doing this. He was certainly the reason *she* was doing it. Once in the kitchen she opened the freezer, a careful look of serenity painted on her face, and tucked her long dark hair casually behind her ear as she bent to rummage through its contents, listening all the while to the speech that she could still easily hear filtering through from the lounge. What exciting times these were, and how thrilling that she should be so closely involved.

Sally loved to cook, and always made sure she froze plenty of spare portions of whatever she made, for occasions such as this; occasions when her husband would be home late. Being seen to be the embodiment of a normal wife and mother was of the utmost importance, and she genuinely loved her kitchen. Smiling happily to herself now, she took some pastry she'd made out of the freezer, muttering audibly that she'd make an apple pie later, to validate what she was about to do. She took the lid off the container and opened the door of the microwave oven. No camera could have detected the tiny switch that she brushed her hand over as she placed the frozen ball of pastry in its container inside. This signal to the Leader would let it be known that her husband was doing his job. Things were going to plan.

What a good actor she was, she thought with satisfaction. Yes, this was all rather thrilling, she had to admit. Fancy, being alive at such a momentous time in history, and actually doing something to help write the next chapter. Yes, it was quite, quite thrilling, and none but a small select group of trusted individuals had the slightest idea of what was going on, making it, quite honestly, even more thrilling. What an honour it was to be involved.

Closing the microwave door and setting the timer, she took a tub containing already cooked apple out of the freezer and put it on a plate on the draining board to thaw, before wandering sedately back through to the lounge to continue watching the Leader, her excitement growing stronger by the minute. She coughed and bit back her smile as she rearranged her face back into its serene blank mask. She must not become complacent.

Sally settled herself back contentedly against a softly plump purple cushion to watch the rest of the Leader's speech, kicking off her slippers, thoroughly satisfied and pleased with herself.

Chapter Ten

Hurst got to work. With an expression of the utmost concentration on his face, his pale blue eyes scanned the screen in front of him, which was filled with nothing but the Leader's face, and, looking for clues, he pressed a couple of buttons. There weren't any clues of how to do this, of course, but it was vital that he went through the process of trying everything he could to stop the broadcast in a textbook and very visible way. For once he was glad of the cameras blinking away around him. They would be his proof that he had done what he could. He consulted the notes that he'd just scrambled to retrieve from his desk drawer and typed in a code.

The computer beeped and a message appeared on the screen, as he had known it would, telling him that the function he'd just performed had, rather than getting him closer to hacking into the Leader's computer network, created yet another wall of security around it. With the warning flashing and beeping in front of him, he bit the inside of his mouth to stop himself smiling in satisfaction. The Leader really did have the most intelligent minds working in that office. He mustn't smile. Instead, he voiced the word, 'Damn', sat back in his chair and made as if to study the screen, wondering if, one day, he would be able to join them, or even work in the government of his old country, the United Kingdom. What a wonderful thought that was.

He punched in another combination of keys, numbers and functions. Nothing. Good, that was how it should be. All he had to do was keep up this pretence for long enough that the Leader's full message could be delivered. That was his mission. He turned back to his notes, not knowing for sure how long that would take, for the speech to reach its conclusion, and ran his finger down the long list of handwritten instructions, wishing he was granted access to more detailed information from the Leader's people, rather than the few select things he needed to know coming to him via Sally in order for him to carry out his duties for this mission. Mind you, if the point of his not being told when this'd been going to happen was to make him look as bewildered as everyone else, then it had succeeded. He tried again, using another pathway. Another message popped up, warning him of the dangers of trying to infiltrate the system. Christ, dangers everywhere. Not that he was worried about this particular threat; it had been planned for, after all. The threat from his boss was the thing most playing on his mind at the moment. What was Ward going to do if he, Hurst, couldn't at least make it look as if he'd made some progress? Perhaps it was time to make this thing look more successful. Also planned for, naturally. He sat there for a moment, scratched his chin in thought and then feigned a theatrical lightbulb moment before trying a different combination. There! One wall of security was broken. He needed a password to get any further.

What could he do? He wished he'd been given a few false ones to try. He also wished he had some coffee. Suddenly, he felt parched, and wondered vaguely how long it had been since he'd had anything to drink. This fiasco meant he'd missed his morning cup of tea, he recalled.

Of course, the password was programmed to change every ten seconds, so the likelihood of his stumbling across the correct one was a few million to one, but even so. His fingers trembled as they hovered over the keyboard while he thought about it. He tried a few basic ones and after the third attempt the message on the screen informed him that he had only one attempt remaining. Oh God, Ward would go insane. When he entered the fourth wrong combination, he'd be back to square one and have to go through the whole procedure again. Not a problem as far as his orders from the Leader were concerned, of course, but the delay would not go down well with his boss here. Still, it couldn't be helped. There was nothing he could do about it. If Ward thought he could do better, let him try.

Chapter Eleven

'Let us answer a few questions in this short time we have available to us.

'Ask yourselves: are we capable – could the human race ever be capable – of genuine peaceful freedom in any way on a global scale? Can you teach peace to those who have never had it, understood it, or indeed wanted it? Possibly. But could it be done in the way outlined by Codardo? If I had been around then, I would have said it was unlikely. Looking at the world from the viewpoint of today, I would have to say I'd have been right to doubt.

'For example, when this new way of doing things was in its infancy, every "old" country that wanted to remain autonomous, and every new, open, non-country, retained its arms. Why, you may well ask? If we were all supposed to be becoming one united world, what was the point? Well, in the beginning, it was decided that the best course of action to protect against distrust and any potential threat from the countries who were yet to join, or who perhaps at that point were never expected to, was to retain existing arms which, the people of the world were told, would gradually be phased out and

destroyed, once the world reached a sufficiently secure point. By this, what was meant was this: arms would be destroyed only once every resisting country had been convinced, either by talks or by more forceful measures, and therefore by the use of those arms, to comply with the new world order.

'Naturally, and as we now know to our detriment, no point of utopia ever came, and so to this day, weapons are still produced. Their existence is hidden from and denied to the general public, but they are still there, and are easily available to the World Administration in whichever part of the globe they decide they may need to use them. Because they are the ones who make them.

'Of course, as I say, this production is kept out of public sight, in that it is forbidden ever to be reported on and is conducted in ever more secretive and illegal ways, but we all know. We are not stupid. Even if we are forbidden to speak of these things, we all know that it is happening, that new, increasingly lethal weapons are still and always will be in production. They are all over the world, trained by the World Administration on the people and areas of the planet deemed to be occupied by the most dangerous rebels who still try to cling to the past.

'This undercover, top secret, arms work, is only a small part of the work being done by people specially chosen by the authorities; people who are watched either throughout their time at university, where they

are finally allowed to achieve, or whose talents are watched and monitored while they work. These unfortunate people are then quietly approached if they are deemed suitably useful and are "persuaded" to leave behind all that they know, to work in the field deemed suitable for them and useful for the WA. They are not allowed to speak about their work to anyone and to safeguard against this, whole families are relocated to facilities in secret locations, often miles away from their homes, or across oceans, where entire new towns and communities have been built to accommodate them. You know this happens. You see it every day. Some of you watching are the victims of it. People disappear from their neighbourhoods, sometimes without even the time to say their goodbyes. And even when they do, families move suddenly, out of the blue, and with no prior warning, and to add insult to injury, they have to lie about it to their friends. It is a fact of life as we know it. So why do we do nothing about it? Because up until now we have been too scared. People feel alone in this supposedly united world. You have been afraid to speak the words that you are thinking for far too long.

'But now is the time to take action. Now is the time to do something about it. Now is the time to stop being scared. We must all act, and we must do so immediately. Today.

'And as I said, it is not simply about arms and military force and dominance. If our world is as safe and secure as we are led to believe, and this system we

live by is so successful, then why is it necessary for all the cloak and dagger underground surveillance and criminal behaviour against you, the people, by the very ones, the overseers, who are supposed to be working for all our good? And when I say "criminal behaviour" I am putting it mildly. It should not be necessary to spy upon your citizens, and the fact that it is deemed necessary for the world to be living such a double life shows just one of the many glaring flaws in this system that, rather than working for the benefit of all, is set on a path to destroy us.'

Chapter Twelve

'I will bloody well destroy *you*,' muttered Ward, alone again now in his darkened bunker of an office. 'I'll see to it that this is the last speech you ever give, you self-righteous, pompous fool. Sitting there spouting a load of bollocks that you've taken and twisted from long ago abandoned history books as if they are the holy bloody grail, when they've got no more relevance today than some stupid child's story book. Global control is the only way. *My* way is the only way. You should be irrelevant now, and I shall see to it that you are.'

He turned away from the screen and looked down at his hand, where sat on his open palm a miniscule bugging device, and wondered how manymore there were, how long this had been going on, and just how much intelligence had been given away to the Democratic Party and the so-called World Leader by the treacherous Agent Hurst, who had been trying for who knew how long to undermine not only his, Ward's, authority, but everything he and his party stood for and believed in. Agent Greenway had told him there could be any number of the things all over the facility. And the most worrying thing of all was that Greenway had tested this one against the bug-sweeper, he'd reported, his face grim, and it hadn't registered. Not a flicker. It had passed completely unnoticed under the powerful devices they used to safeguard against exactly this.

Ward felt stupid. How could it be that unbeknownst to him those people had developed the technology to fool his state-of-the-art anti-bug scanners? As far as he knew, the Leader and certainly the Democratic Party hadn't even been aware of the scanners' technology. There must be someone reporting from that department, too, because to his knowledge, Hurst never had reason to go there.

It seemed Ward had let standards slide. Clearly, his intelligence team was lacking credibility in a big way. When all this was over, he needed to have a proper shake-up of his staff so no situation such as this could ever be allowed to happen again. But for now, he'd sent Greenway off to the laboratory to try and come up with an interim method of detection so that they could rid the facility of this plague that'd been unleashed upon them by Hurst. He knew it was an impossible task. That type of work took months, and to develop ideas into a useable system could only be achieved by using the brains and knowhow of whole teams of highly trained experts, not just one man chancing his luck on the off chance of a breakthrough, just because it suited his boss to have one.

Ward's hand quivered with rage at finding himself in such a predicament, and his fist closed tightly around the little sticky bug that sat clinging to his flesh like the leech that it was. He'd had to think of a way to keep Hurst out of the way until he could decide what to do with him. His first instinct had been to have him shot, but he'd decided regretfully that that might not be such a great idea if they needed to use him to locate the rest of the bugs. For now, he'd put him to work in isolation on the task of hacking into the Leader's speech. He looked at the screen where, unsurprisingly, the speech was continuing unabated. Just how deeply was Hurst involved with these people?

The Free World might have been Codardo's dream, Ward conceded, but the World Administration, of whom he, Ward, was now the leader, had taken that bud of an idea and turned it into the only workable system. All the mamby-pamby stuff of Codardo's time and thinking, that the old countries could join the system as and when and if they wanted to, and everyone would live together, all dancing around in fields of flowers like a load of hippies, living and letting live and being allowed to run around loose all over the world as and when the fancy took them, at the same time as outlawing wealth, was a total nonsense. It had been asking for trouble, about that the Leader was right. But he, Ward, was in charge now. He had been democratically elected to be just that – in charge – and the way he saw it was that the only way to keep tabs on the population and hold onto peace and stability in an open world was by ensuring he knew everything that was going on and ruling with an iron fist.

It wasn't as if the current system had been recently or radically changed overnight by him and his party. It hadn't. The way the people lived now had been a gradual process, as Codardo's vision had been changed and adapted to fit the progressing times by each new generation that had followed him. Quite how this current World Leader had ever come to power he would never understand. Quite why the people had voted in this person whose ideas so radically opposed the WA, was a mystery to him. The people should be happy with their lot. Did they not realise that the way they lived ensured their continuing safety and security? People behaved as if they were being monitored every minute of every day, but of course they weren't. How could they be? It was done randomly, for the most part, with the focus on the people high up or in positions of potential sensitivity. No, the people had it good under the control of the WA, and they should appreciate that.

Ward looked again at the small device in his hand and ground his teeth. He knew he had a battle ahead of him if he wanted to remain in power, and he knew that battle would be a difficult one. He should have moved sooner – as soon, in fact, as the World Leader had been elected – to ensure a change in the law in order to safeguard his own position in the event of a disaster such as this. He should have foreseen it. As it was, if this crazy person got their way, he would be redundant, in every sense of the word. And he was not about to let that happen. He scowled darkly to himself, peeling the little device off his hand and replacing it in the small glass bottle he'd taken it out of. He screwed the lid tightly shut on it, then pocketed the bottle and stalked out of his office to find out how Greenway was getting on. The Leader's voice continued to ring out behind him.

Hurst. Bloody Hurst. He'd thought the man to be a loyal agent, working for the WA in a willing and constructive manner. You couldn't trust anyone and that was the truth. There he was, sitting in his office, being paid good money to do an important job which he should have been proud of and grateful for and all the while he was colluding with the enemy. Faking it. Laughing at his employers.

Ward wondered whether, if he were in the World Leader's position, he'd have trusted Hurst enough to give him the means to get into the computers. Of course not. But trust didn't have anything to do with it. That speech was as protected as it was possible for it to be, and Hurst knew nothing of the security, he was sure. His job was to stall the WA, not help them, even under threat. The Leader's people would have been careful about that and he, Ward, was sure Hurst didn't have the means to hack the system. Well, he'd put an end to it. Agent Greenway would be put on a mission to dispose of him, just as soon as he could be spared, and if he did not succeed in it there would be dire consequences for him as well. Ward was not about to tolerate anymore dissent and Hurst would be used as an example to hold up to all the rest of the miserable bastards.

Chapter Thirteen

'Will our survival of the fittest instinct always prevail?

'Of course it will. Strength overpowers weakness. And by this I do not mean the brute force and violent threats as dished out by the World Administration. We are animals, with the instinct to care for and protect our own, of course we are. Our own can be our fellow humans, yes. But our own starts with the people around us, those we are close to. Our families. For the vast majority of people who have children, at the moment of becoming a parent we put our children's needs above our own. We are social, pack animals, not the cold empty robots that our enemy (for that is what the WA are) would like us to be, and it has been shown time and again over the course of our history that people will defend themselves and their rights no matter what the cost. Nothing has changed in this regard.

'We need to defend ourselves now. We need to survive. We need to be the fittest. Looking out for ourselves and our interests in relation to the rest of the world is the only way we can, as humans, take care of each other. Having properly regulated governments overseeing the best interests of every individual country

in a peaceful way and in relation to and respect of the rest of the world is what we need. We need to show our strength now and speak up for ourselves and our children. We need to teach our children that living with tolerance and not oppression is the correct way to exist. Controlling is not caring.

'Greed, of course, is ever-present. We can't change it. Since the days of living in caves, of first keeping animals, building shelters, fashioning tools et cetera, since prehistory, it has been in our collective nature to want more or better than our neighbours, to protect our own property and keep it out of the hands of others. But the proper regulation of properly defined countries is the way to keep this in check, not the fear-inducing dictatorial control to which we are currently subjected, which is due, in part, to the fact that it is impossible for one regulatory body and keeper of the peace to oversee billions of people, even with the help of strategically-placed councils and committees around the world, whose job it is to snitch on people like the immoral spies they are.

'Status is important to humans. It is the way we outwardly proclaim our strength. Pushing ourselves higher than those around us and wanting control over them has always been the human way. But if we have our old ways made available to us once more, then innovation will be allowed to shine in a healthy way. People will be allowed to shine in a positive way. Economies will grow. Personal wealth will grow. We

will grow as a species – spiritually, and in every other way. How can you help the poor if you are one of them – if you are all poor? You can't. Inevitably, the forbidding of any great personal wealth leads to rulers with obscenely huge wealth presiding over an increasingly impoverished general populace. The peasants grubbing about in the dirt outside the castle walls to gather a few grains of fallen rice to feed their starving families, while those inside, the privileged few, adorn themselves with gold and jewels and grow fat from the abundance of food. This is what we have gone back to under the WA.

'There has always been a faction of society, of course, who take what they can't make. This has never been able to be controlled by law, and the underground, the black market, and gang corruption has always been present. However, under a System of Nations, these groups are far easier to monitor and control (in a lawful way). As a result, the people are safer. As a result, the world would not be ruled by the biggest underground circle of corruption and unlawful control ever known to man, as it is now. These criminals currently treat every one of you as potential criminals yourselves and don't trust the people to do the right thing. Hypocrisy is what it is. A double standard of the most despicable kind.'

Chapter Fourteen

'What happened when the countries who resolved to stay autonomous finally succumbed to the pressures being put on them and had to unwillingly join the new "free" world?

'It wasn't enough to simply offer them the opportunity. How could that ever be enough? The opportunity to do what? Lose their identity? Lose their nationality? These nations had quite obviously been watching the results thus far and had decided quite rightly that the system was playing out to be a disaster. Inviting this chaos through the doors of their own countries was never going to be an option for any but the most naïve and desperate! Who in their right mind, wanting to live in a civilised and peaceful society, would welcome such a thing? Quite understandably, the problems were all they could see. There were many countries that simply didn't share Codardo's vision, let alone the ever more radical views of his successors.

'You were bound to have a situation where a substantial proportion of the countries of the world felt this way, and these countries who didn't want to join – as should have been their right, by the way – found

themselves as a result of their perceived dissent, in the middle of a long protracted and bloody war against those who were trying to force them to join against their will. This had not been Codardo's aim. His vision, as was clear to a large number of the general public from the start, was being increasingly radicalised, which he should have known from the start that it would be.

'In addition to this, there were those countries who further retreated into themselves, and firmed up their borders against the outside world even more tightly than they had been to start with. It was an obvious and predictable reaction, and one that, under those conditions, is to be sympathised with. And so then, as all this war and destruction ravaged the Earth, Codardo, unbeknownst to him, had succeeded only in creating in his wake, utter global havoc. More closed societies and dictatorships whose movements couldn't be seen, the unpredictability of which was naturally causing concern for the world at large, a huge new dictatorship desperately grappling with and creating a new power for itself in the form of the World Administration, and yet another World War. The non-compliance, the standing up for their own liberty, a liberty for which Codardo claimed to have been fighting, had ironically become a terrible danger to these non-conforming countries, and to everyone else besides.

'You can't deal with the situation by sending in missionaries or using the media, as Codardo tried to do,

peacefully, in the early days, because both those pathways were, naturally, firmly closed to him. He had doors slammed in his face left, right and centre. So, in order to gain the inclusion of those rogue countries, he would have had to open their borders by force, which went against the ideal he was so intent upon bringing about for the world. He was content to sit back and wait for the non-conformist countries to see for themselves the positive effects of his New World. His successors were not.

'The result of this eventual, in my opinion, illegal, warfare, was an increase in an underground resentment which would never fade, even with the implementation of new education laws. People are not stupid. Families taught their children the history that had been banned at school – the real history. And, little by little, generation after generation, the feelings of resentment grew. We are all aware of it. Across the globe, people are asking why, if our world is supposed to be one of fairness, freedom, and inclusion for all, are we watched? Why were cameras eventually fitted in every home? Why are we controlled in such a disgusting way? Why is everything more regulated now than it has ever been before?

'The whispered questions and bewilderment turned bit by bit into what we see around us now – a worldwide discontent with the system and an increasing insistence that something be done about it and a radical change

effected. And this is precisely what I am offering you today, in a peaceful way.

'Wars cannot be kept secret. Of course the truth was taught to the children of those who had been forcibly required to toe the line. How could it not be? We all understand why those children were angry and why their children's children were angry. Just look around you at the situation we now find ourselves in. We are right to be angry!

'I am making this broadcast from a secure location with a level of security around me which I'm sure most of you would be shocked to see. It is a level of security which the governments of Codardo's time could not have dreamt of in their worst nightmares. I won't lie; I am afraid for my life. One can never be too careful in an unprecedented situation such as this, even with the people one trusts. In part, that is why it has taken so long for me to get this broadcast and voting opportunity out to you.

'However, I have worked hard, and I can trust my aides and the people around me. Know that you are all quite, quite safe. I know for certain that the people around me are committed to helping you, the general public. And I know I can also trust some of the people who are, on the surface of it, against me.'

Chapter Fifteen

Hurst shivered. Why was the Leader saying that? If ever there was an admission that there had been inside help, that was it. If ever there was something that was going to get him shot between the eyes, then that was it.

He froze, as a thought occurred to him. He was already in danger! He was in terrible, terrible danger and he suddenly knew it with a deep certainty, the way you know something with a feeling in your gut that you just can't explain in any way other than instinct. He was sure of it. There was someone in this building, and probably on this floor, he thought, with a sick feeling as the realisation dawned, who knew it too, because that person had snitched on him.

Normally, the kind of sensitive damage control work he was currently occupied with would be done by at least two people, never one person working alone. Why hadn't he realised it sooner? Checking and double-checking each other's work should be a fundamental part of the task. It was a fundamental part of any task undertaken in this facility. So why had Hurst been sent away to tackle this by himself?

Because Ward knew.

Had he, Ward, got other agents from that ghastly meeting ensconced in an office somewhere, watching him even now as he had these thoughts, trying to see what he was up to, trying to find proof of his betrayal? He had no way of knowing for sure but suspected that that would be the case. His insides churned in panic as he held onto the look of concentration on his face for the benefit of the cameras. The effort of it made his eyes smart.

Calm down, Anthony, he told himself. Perhaps Ward *didn't* know for sure, and if indeed he was being checked up on, then maybe it was only to try to get proof that there was a double agent in their midst? Why him, though? Why? He didn't believe in coincidences. Why was he working on this alone?

Because Ward *was* sure. There could be no other reason. Hurst swallowed as if his throat was full of sand, panicking.

OK then, it was now more important than ever that he follow these written instructions to the letter and be clearly seen to be doing so. He tried another password and, as expected, was shut down. He began the process again, following his notes as before, his fingers shaking as he keyed in the codes.

How was it possible that he'd been found out? Had he been careless while planting one of the bugs? Had someone noticed a pattern? He'd tried so hard not to create one. And now, as if to confirm the suspicions of the cold and heartless man who was his boss, the Leader was in the process, with those ill-thought-out words, of practically giving him away with a little gift card of explanation. People who are on the surface of it against me. Shit.

Chapter Sixteen

'How could it be possible to keep a country's identity if the status of country was lost?

'How could it possibly be possible? Of course it wasn't possible. You would have your town or city that would be "formerly part of" a country.

'If you weren't allowed to refer to an area of land as a country, where does that leave you? Where does that area of land look to identify itself? Yes, we are all human and we all inhabit the same planet, but countries make us feel secure.

'Just because Codardo himself claimed to have no sense of national pride or allegiance towards his country, didn't mean anyone else would feel the same. It was arrogance of the highest, most dangerous order. He cleverly waited until he had got the disillusioned among the world's populace firmly behind him with his promises of post-pandemic freedom, and voting in their millions for his reforms, before he passed that particular law of a ban for all participants on using your former country's name. No one had been expecting it. They had been double-crossed. Betrayed.

'It was a cause of major civil unrest, of course. People whose countries had signed up for the New World were suddenly rioting in the streets, storming their old parliaments, who were already in a chaotic transition period of dissolution and takeover and were ill-equipped to deal with it, none the wiser themselves as to what was going on, and resentful enough already. World Administrations were hurriedly set up in each former country's parliamentary offices to calm things down, take charge, and stop the protestors in their tracks. The people's behaviour was used against them as justification of the enforcement of much tighter controls. They were told it was the only way and it was for their own good. And it has got worse and worse as the years have passed. People whose countries had not yet signed up for the New World saw this as reason enough not to. We told you so, they said.'

Chapter Seventeen

'On an individual level, how did the people identify themselves if their nationality was removed?

'Well, how could they? Everyone became a "Citizen of the World". This, naturally enough, after the first waves of euphoria at the promise of a better world had calmed down and the rather different reality was starting to dawn, made people insecure and more likely to seek out small groups of illegal protesters to join in secret. It is human nature to want and need to be part of a territorial group – and that doesn't necessarily mean a combative one. If, suddenly, the protective arm of your former country is no longer around you, even if that country was less than perfect, it is quite natural to feel lost, like a small and helpless leaf being blown by a cruel wind around the vast desert of the unknown. Too dramatic? Too poetic? Hardly. Who are we without a sense of self, of identity, of belonging? We feel as if we are nothing, as if we are insignificant. People need to belong; it is only natural. It is in our nature as a species.

'Let's use again the example of the United Kingdom. They were four nations within a mostly strong and happy union, until Codardo arrived with his *mayhem to tear away the borders. Some people, especially in Scotland, would have liked to be separate from the United Kingdom, yes, but the union had always held firm. This would seem to support Codardo's opinion. However, if you had asked back then, for anyone born in Belfast, Edinburgh or Cardiff to state their nationality, they would, in ninety-nine point nine per cent of cases, have told you they were Irish, Scottish or Welsh. Only the English would have been more likely to describe themselves as British rather than English – although Great Britain was only England, Scotland and Wales, so the Northern Irish would never have referred to themselves as such. But the point is this: people are proud of their own countries, even when those countries form part of a union.*

'*One example of this eradication of a sense of belonging was highlighted by the fact that international sport no longer existed. Without countries, how could it? It might seem like a small thing now, to those of us who cannot remember a world with international competitive sport but try to imagine the thrill of going to watch your country play football, or rugby, or being represented in a tennis tournament. We compete now, of course, but only on a city versus city level. We've retained our sports leagues, yes, but they are within the confines of the old countries! What is that if not an admission that we are still proud of our origins? We are told this retention of old sports leagues is purely because of the logistics of travel and the vast number of teams in every sport. But to the people it means something entirely different. It means holding onto their roots.*

'Yes, OK, teams travel and compete in friendly matches across the world, but always with no competitive element, and there doesn't seem to be a lot of point to that. International competition doesn't have to be all about power and control and who can reign supreme over whom; it can be exciting and fun, and it helps us to grow and evolve. It helps us to push ourselves.

'People could identify themselves in the past with their city or town as an extension of their country, but if then they suddenly couldn't identify that city or town with a country, even though they knew that in the past there had been one, they felt lost, cast adrift from any sense of belonging and all that could give them security.

'Certain freedoms should have increased and improved with the new regime designed by Codardo and, at first, they did, before his ideas were twisted into grotesque mutations by succeeding generations, and we will endeavour to resurrect, put right, and keep as many of these original plans going as possible should we win today's vote. For the most part this will focus on human rights, living and working conditions, a right for all to healthcare and schooling et cetera, but with a new and urgent focus on mental health.

'With the New World came unprecedented levels of mental illness, which we absolutely must address as one

of our main priorities if we are to regain any semblance of peace. Depression skyrocketed after the implementation of this new world order, and we need to begin the process of helping people as soon as we possibly can. In the beginning, this increase of mental illness was blamed on the virus that the world had just endured but, in reality, people were suffering and are still suffering from a mass sense of fear, isolation and loneliness because of the thing Vincenzo Codardo's successors were doing. As time went on, this unhappy state got worse and worse until we reached the point at which we now find ourselves – we have become introverted automatons – and it must stop! We need to nurse the human race back to health. And we will.'

Chapter Eighteen

'Who decides on teaching matter in a world with no borders?

'Who decides on anything, come to that? The World Administration, of course. Let's give the benefit of the doubt for a moment and hope that the intention back in the early 2020s was not to create a "Nineteen-Eighty-Four-style" brainwashing of the population, but that they wanted to teach children the truth. How was that ever going to be possible in a world where the truth was forbidden? History was made a mandatory subject in schools. It was considered essential for children to learn about what happened in the past and how much better things were as a result of changing that past.

'That's OK, we can learn from history, and it was arguably better than banning it from classrooms altogether, but when we are rewriting history, from whose perspective should we write? Historically, as we know, the winners of any conflict write the history books, so the new, by this time democratically elected Codardo as World Leader, would have had to have a whole new syllabus of teaching material produced, written entirely from his naïve and blinkered viewpoint,

which of course is exactly what happened. The problem was that this involved the discrediting and tearing apart on paper of every participating country's history, and a grotesque caricature being drawn up to represent those non-participating countries, to support what was happening in the new reality, and it led to the destruction of the very foundation blocks of each old country, painting them as fascist, extremist, communist, or any other offensive label that came to the writers' minds for the purpose of making Codardo's point seem valid.

'Any other method of doing things would have undermined his authority. He would have denied having any authority, of course, and would have claimed that what he was selling to the world and what he was overseeing in his new role as World Leader, was a vision of a modern and peaceful planet. But in order to achieve that aim, anything that pointed towards success or harmony from the past had to be destabilised in recorded history. His new narrative of history that was to be taught to the world's children was, in its entirety, a figment of his so-called neutral team of writers' imagination; a bland work of fiction that concentrated almost entirely on conflicts and differences.

'Another option open to him would have been to allow the old books to continue being used in schools, of course, but he needed history as the new generation knew it to be changed. And so, the truth was not then, and is certainly not now, taught, and the old history

books only exist today in the context of something to be laughed at and ridiculed and they are used as evidence of former barbaric, uneducated, and primitive times. Of course, for those interested enough to hold on to these old works, they mean something entirely different.'

Chapter Nineteen

'Was religion still possible?

'The new law of two hundred years ago said you were still able to practise any religion you wanted, wherever you wanted. However, in practise, in some parts of the world this caused mayhem. There was hardly a country in the old world where multiple religions sat side by side without issue as it was. How on earth (literally) did Codardo ever imagine that this was going to work on a global scale? It was a fantasy, a folly. And little did he no doubt imagine, only taking from his own loose ties to Catholicism when it suited him to do so, and being unable to understand that not everyone thought the way he did, or that it would be impossible for him to change minds in the way and in the numbers that he thought he could, that for others, religion actually went a long way towards giving people the sense of belonging that his new ideas were starting to eradicate.

'It is surprising that he allowed anyone to practise any religion at all. But there you are. A flaw in his thinking? An indicator that he was as prone to fear of judgement from an unseen deity as many others?

Possibly. But whatever his motives for allowing religions to survive, it gave people strength and a sense of community, even for those without any strong beliefs who, crucially, were welcomed in great numbers to every faith around the world as people saw religion as a means of retaining those communities, and I hope that if you are one of these people, genuinely religious or not, it will be one of the factors that helps you find within yourself the strength to make a change.

'*Religion has throughout history been said in itself to be all about power and control, doctrine and fear but, as I said, the people began to cling to their formerly rejected and sidelined religions that they had in greater and greater numbers been slowly leaving behind, as one of the few means left open to them to feel part of a safe and secure group, where they would be protected from the madness that was going on around them. Perhaps Codardo imagined the religions of the world would fizzle out naturally without his having to do anything? If so, he was wrong.*

'*As I just said, people began to flock back to their places of worship and look to their religious leaders to help them. Unrest between different religions was, for a long time, an inevitable consequence of this, and more religious unrest happened as a result of the "unified" world than had ever occurred before, as people struggled to find and fought for a sense of belonging.*

'*This sudden obsession, for want of a better word, with finding safety within the pages of religious texts very nearly saw a return to the old days of witch hunts, with certain localities trying to forcibly recruit their neighbours into their dominant religions, as their need for validation and identification with like-minded people escalated.*

'Nowadays, of course, things have calmed down somewhat, as people are ever increasingly afraid to voice their opinions. But it eventually became clear to religious leaders back then that if they worked together, they could be the basis for an eventual uprising. That hasn't happened up until now, as you know, but, nevertheless, it is coming, and it shows the extent to which the people have been secretly working together for generations to counteract the system by which we now live.'

Chapter Twenty

'*Why do I want to return us to the old ways?*

'*Let me summarise. Humans, as I have already touched upon, find their security and sense of belonging from living in small, safe groups. A worldwide community erases one's sense of belonging. We gain our identity from the differences between us.*

'*If the so-called unified Free World claims to give us freedom, then it should also give us the freedom to choose and decide about our own future.*

'*I am, I hope you will realise, not saying that everything about our current system is wrong. I repeat, many things about our current way of life can and should be retained and carried on in a fairer way within the context of international law.*

'*For example: women's rights, anti-racism, healthcare, working conditions, tax laws, human rights, environmental issues et cetera, but I want to see these laws implemented and working for everyone within the borders of their own countries. I want to give people back their identities and their freedoms.*'

Chapter Twenty-one

'Not everyone agrees with me, of course. There are as many arguments, counter arguments, and questions as there are inhabitants of this planet, and that is the way it should be. However, I would not be doing my duty as leader of a so-called global democracy if I did not try to revive the only system that I believe can bring true democracy to you all, and I now ask for your support in this matter.

'Therefore, I have made the decision that there will be a vote. Now. Today. The question we will ask is this: "Should Planet Earth return to a System of Nations, and re-establish countries with borders?"

'If the result is "No", the idea will be shelved, and I shall tender my resignation forthwith. However, if the answer is "Yes", there will follow an immediate dissolution of the regime under which we now live, and governments will be set up in each old territory. A detailed plan, which I and my team have been working on for a considerable length of time, showing how this transition will take place, what it will mean for each re-established country, and the timescale involved, will be made available to everyone.

'Interim prime ministers chosen from my colleagues, will take the helm in each country until democratically elected leaders – leaders elected by you, the people – can be put into office, and this first and fundamental task of voting in your own governments will take place within six months from now, for all of you – with the dissolution of our current regime being, as I said, immediate.

'I will remain in my job to oversee the transition, and when I am satisfied that I am no longer needed, I will leave my post and there will no longer be a World Leader. You will have your countries and your sovereignty back. You will have your lives and your freedoms back.

'Do not be concerned that the fall of the current administration will lead to violence, or indeed another war. We will do everything we can to avoid that. It is written into the global set of laws that were put in place by Codardo himself two hundred years ago, that in the event that the World Administration is put out of office, the transition to the new government, or in this case governments, must be peaceful and total.

'Make no mistake, the WA will not make it easy, and I am putting myself at great personal risk, even speaking to you in this way. At this moment I am aware that there are teams of secret agents working desperately to find a way into this broadcast to cut me off. They will not succeed, however. I anticipated and pre-empted them, of course, and I have got safeguards

in place. I also know that once they realise that they cannot penetrate the security, their assassins will be on their way to find me.

'Again, they have been anticipated and will not get near to me. At least, not for the time being. I realise that the danger to me is very real, and that we haven't got much time. However, I don't want you to let that influence your choice. A decision needs to be made, and it needs to be made immediately. I believe in your freedom above all else, and I think you do, too. What we have got in our world now is more control than has ever been placed over us before at any time in the history of our planet. We need to regain true democracy.

'Therefore, as I have already said, I have decided that the vote will take place right now, at this moment. I ask you to trust me and not to be afraid.

'On your screens, you will now see two buttons, one labelled YES and the other NO. The question is also on your screens, and, once again, it is this: Should Planet Earth return to a System of Nations, and re-establish countries with borders?

'Understand that if you choose YES, indeed whatever you choose, you will not be in danger. There will be no repercussions for you. The team I have got here working with me has temporarily disabled the tracking on every device on which this transmission is being shown, as well as, for the next ten minutes, all cameras, so your vote will be anonymous. Therefore, even if at this moment you are at work and are

concerned about privacy, you need not worry. If the result of the vote is YES, this disablement will gradually be rolled out over a couple of weeks to include your computers and all other technology. The days of constant surveillance will be over.

'After the vote, my team, should the result be YES, will, once it has been transcribed, make available to you a file which shows exactly the plan for recreating former country territories. This is a very exciting document, and these are very exciting times.

'We need new leaders of the newly established countries, and the people currently in charge will not be permitted to run for these positions. Do not fear them, I beg of you. They may be powerful at the moment, but I am the one who is ultimately in charge. We are aware of the locations of their facilities and of the locations of the world's weapons stores, and my people are already on site to ensure the safety and security of you, the citizens. They will remain there until any threat has passed.

'Lastly, voting is mandatory. It is the only way to remove this screen from your devices. After ten minutes, if you vote, your screens will return to normal. If you do not vote, then when the ten minutes are up, your frozen screen will remain and will once again be trackable. Please do not misinterpret this action as a threat. It is not. What it is, is the last mandatory undertaking you will be asked to submit to under the current regime. It is a key to your happier future. This is the time to change

your future and that of your children, for the better. This is the moment to reclaim your national identities.

'You now have ten minutes to cast your vote.'

Chapter Twenty-two

Sally leapt to her feet. Ten minutes! Dare she believe that it had actually worked? Dare she believe that the cameras were truly deactivated? Was it possible? How could she check? She looked up at the visible camera on the ceiling of the lounge. Its light had gone out. Yes! She went hurrying into the kitchen, as if to make it look as if she had just remembered about the food that was defrosting, and that that was the reason for her sudden leap to her feet… just in case. The camera there was also dead. The cameras, for the first time, were actually deactivated. It was a miracle.

Peering into the microwave, she joyfully noted that the little switch she'd clicked earlier had now turned pink. Her heart skipped a beat. Sally had never seen this before – well, she wouldn't have done – but knew of course what it meant. Message received and understood that Anthony was at least one of the people working on trying to hack in. He was in place to oversee proceedings. Sally now had to wait for the light to turn green to confirm that the deactivation of the cameras had gone ahead. It was only a precaution, this second light, because although she could see quite clearly for herself that the cameras weren't working, it had been considered too high a risk for Sally to vote until the Leader's office had double-checked the deactivation. It was timed to happen one minute after the illumination of the pink. She tapped her fingers on the worktop and waited. At last, there it was. The confirmation. It was safe for her to vote.

Smiling widely, she hurriedly took the pastry out of the microwave and, still keeping up the pretence out of sheer habit, stuck a skewer through it to see if it was thawed, then put it back in for another minute before rushing back into the lounge and pressing the button on the screen: YES.

It felt exhilarating. It had happened. But now what? What about her husband, she wondered with a tug of apprehension, as she watched in nevertheless delighted fascination as the little bar showing the percentage of votes for YES and NO steadily increasing in overwhelming favour of YES. The Leader was going to win.

But what was happening to Anthony? Would he be able to get out of that place and get home safely at the end of the day, without anyone realising he'd had a hand in this? Was one of those votes his, she wondered stupidly? Of course, her husband's safe return home tonight was the most important thing, and his one vote, if it was denied him, would hardly make any difference in the great scheme of things, but she couldn't help wondering at just what an amazing opportunity had been unleashed and given to the world by this spectacular feat of bravery on the part of the Leader and all the people who'd been helping and working undercover for so long and at such risk to themselves to bring this about. Their achievement, including Sally and her husband's, had already gone a long way towards helping to change the world. She was proud of herself.

But there would be time, she hoped, to think about that later, and to bask in their success and in the glory of it. Right now, the important thing was to ensure that her husband would get home safely. He had to. The message he'd sent was not a good sign. Although he was saying he was at work on trying to hack in, he was also saying he was stuck.

Even though the little green light in the microwave indicated that the cameras were deactivated, she couldn't imagine he'd be left alone for a moment, and she couldn't begin to imagine what anyone could do to help him if he was in trouble. *Would* anyone try to help? Or would he be sacrificed to the cause? He hadn't been issued with instructions on how to send a distress signal. It was a terrible oversight. But would it have even been possible for him to send one? Surely not. All he could do was what he'd done, and Sally had a bad feeling about it.

Perhaps she should send a signal to the Leader, ask what they were supposed to do in the event of a problem? But she didn't want to bother the office with such things as her own worries when there was work enough to be done already. She'd have to wait a while, maybe rethink the situation later this afternoon if she didn't hear from Anthony again before then.

She had no idea what she would do in a practical sense if anything happened to him, but at the same time, she had been planning for it in a personal and silent way for a number of months. Her instinct told her that, if discovered, his survival was unlikely unless he found a way of getting out of that place after voting. He would have to vote NO, of course. Sally's worry was that there was no way of telling whether the cameras in the facility could really be disabled, as well as those elsewhere. What if there was some sort of backup that the Leader's people had been unaware of? Ward could be a nasty, vindictive bastard at the best of times, but if he ever found out... well, it didn't bear thinking about. And it was still many hours until the end of the working day. Anything could happen in the meantime.

She watched the timer ticking down on the screen in front of her, and the little vote counter that was steadily rising and giving out its result as the votes were cast. It was looking good for the Leader. At least, it was looking good for a YES result. Who knew what carnage would occur at the end of it? Could things really go as peacefully as the Leader had said?

But Sally trusted the people she'd been working with. She knew that every conceivable possibility would have been thoroughly thought out and investigated before this broadcast went out. Every possibility, that is, except what Sally was supposed to do in the event that her husband was taken into custody, or worse, by the WA. She and her boy would be in terrible danger, and no one had told her what she should do or where she should go. Perhaps a message would come? Perhaps that was another function of the pink light? After turning green, would it change again? Jittery, she darted back into the kitchen to look at it again, for all the good that would do. She was grasping at straws. Of course, it was still green. The light was hardly likely to start flashing at her in code. She wouldn't have known what it meant if it had. Why hadn't anyone told her what to do?

However, as she removed the pastry ball from the microwave, where the light stayed resolutely the same, and put it in the fridge, her attention shifted to a noise on the gravel outside. As she turned her head to look, a chill ran through her. She gripped the fridge door. Oh, no.

Her husband's predicament suddenly became a secondary concern in her mind, and the most pressing question now became this: who was driving that big black car that she could see from the kitchen window and that had turned slowly and menacingly off the street into their driveway?

Chapter Twenty-three

Now? Hurst hadn't expected this. He hadn't known. Of course, he quite understood that he had no right to be told everything, or even anything, beyond the details of the job he was doing. After all, he *was* just doing a job, doing what he was told by the Leader's office, through his wife, and following instructions... but *now*?

Even though he'd already known it since his suspicion at being left to work alone, the full force of the danger he was in now hit him as if it was the first time it had occurred to him. He'd failed to stop the speech and now this... Ward would be finished if the people voted YES. They would vote YES, that much was a certainty. They were doing so now, right in front of his face – and right in front of Ward's face, too. And Ward would assume he'd known this was going to happen. Ward would kill him. That was a certainty, too. He had ten minutes.

A chill ran through his body like a tidal wave, right to his bones; his insides, from head to foot, turned to ice. This was the result of always hiding one's true emotions on the outside; they turned in on you and it was seriously unhealthy.

Hardly believing it was safe to do so, he chanced a look around at his office cameras that usually sat blinking like evil eyes in the corners of the ceiling – well, these were the ones he was aware of, anyway. He had never been able to ascertain whether there were anymore, less obvious surveillance devices trained on him. Those on the ceiling, however, did indeed look dead. For the next ten minutes, they weren't watching him. Ward would be apoplectic.

Sweat began to trickle down Hurst's back, contradicting the chill he felt inside. What was he supposed to do now? Was the Leader expecting him to vote, along with everyone else? Seriously, was that even an option? Did it even matter? Would anyone here see if he did? Would the Leader see if he didn't? Of course. If he didn't vote, the screen would stay locked, remember?

What was everyone else in the building doing right now? Voting NO, even though for the most part they didn't want to? It was madness. This whole situation was madness. And what exactly was Sally's true role in all of it? Support her though he now did, more or less, he'd always had the feeling that the fact he was only ever privy to a percentage of what she knew was her decision alone. His current indecision and uncertainty had the effect of lessening his support for her. He didn't know what to do for the best, and he blamed his lack of knowledge firmly at her door. He heard a noise coming from the adjoining room and remembered his thirst.

As he sat there contemplating his marital doubts, along with his options, he brought his hands to his face and rubbed his eyes. God, he was tired. And not just in the sense of needing sleep. He realised with a jolt that he was probably dead either way regardless of whether he voted or not, regardless of whether that vote if he cast it was for YES or NO, so, standing up on the pretence of going to the door to ask his secretary for some coffee while he still could, and while he waited for the inevitable fallout of his failure to comply with Ward's orders, he casually tapped the YES button on the screen in front of him. It no longer seemed to matter. The YES vote was winning with a current total of eighty-five-odd per cent, anyway.

He realised that he had been naïve to expect any other outcome for himself than that of certain death. His failure in his task of stopping the broadcast had been planned, after all. He was almost certain that Ward couldn't possibly know the full extent of his involvement, even if, as now seemed probable, he'd been alerted to part of it. But, in any case, he, Ward, would not want to sit calmly around a table discussing what had gone wrong. He would be striding the corridors even now, heading to Hurst's office in an ungovernable rage, on a mission to throw him in prison, or worse, for...

For what, exactly? Just because he hadn't got his own way and just because he could? Well yes, exactly that. Ward didn't need a reason, did he? Everything he did was veiled, dark and vile, so he could and would do whatever he wanted to do to Hurst. But Hurst could prove he had tried to help, surely? The camera footage until it had been deactivated would help him, wouldn't it? It would show that he had tried to hack into the Leader's computers, and by using Ward's own methods, at that. His heart sank again as he thought about pressing that YES button. It had been stupid and unnecessary. It had eliminated any bargaining power he might have otherwise had. So stupid.

And yet... Hurst thought of his wife and child at home waiting for him, thought once more of why he was doing this, and a flicker of fresh resolve to safeguard his son's future fluttered to life somewhere in the pit of his stomach, along with the renewed doubts about Sally. It made for an uncomfortable mix, like pouring lemon juice into cream so that it curdled. He'd hardly made a single decision for himself in six years, and that was about to change.

He'd had every right to press that button. He had as much right to his say in the vote as everyone else, and he would do it again. Maybe he could find a way to talk himself out of it. Perhaps he could tell Ward he had just pressed that button to see whether his attempts to block it had worked? But why didn't you press NO, would be Ward's natural and reasonable response. He couldn't answer that. Idiot, he reprimanded himself, even while his jaw tightened in resolve. No, damn it all to hell, he would finally take control of this situation.

His heart was racing as he crossed the room to the secretary's office. He would get her to explain to his furious boss that he had gone home to collect one of his own computers to hook up to the network. He would invent some story that his computer possibly wouldn't be as closely watched as this one, even if that was blatantly untrue, was too late anyway even if it had been true, and was quite possibly the biggest load of rubbish he could have come up with to use to buy himself time. But he couldn't think of anything else as a reason to leave, and he had to try. And then, once he'd told his story to his secretary, he would walk out the door, get in his car, pass legitimately through the security gates, collect his family and drive like the wind to the Democratic Party's offices where they would hopefully all be taken care of until this nightmare was over. It wasn't much of a plan, but he knew he didn't have much time and it was the best he could come up with. Ward would be here any moment; he was sure of it.

Taking a deep breath, he turned the door handle to the secretary's office and pulled it open. As nonchalantly as he could, he put his head around the door and opened his mouth to speak to Linda, his secretary of five years, and spin her his story. But the scene which greeted him turned his blood to ice once more and any hopes he had of an easy passage out of here evaporated in an instant like so much steam. Linda lay sprawled across her desk, the Leader's ten-minute timer ticking loudly from its screen, with a shocked look on her face and a bullet hole in the side of her head.

Hurst's breath wouldn't come. He clutched his chest in terror and forced air into his lungs with a painful rasp. Who had done this? Why? Why the hell had this happened? What possible motive could anyone possibly have had for doing this to Linda, for committing such cold-blooded murder? But instinctively, from the second he'd seen her, and with a sick feeling in his stomach rising up to his throat, he had known why. This had happened to Linda because of him. This was a warning to him that someone was watching his movements. They were telling him that he was right.

They knew. And they were coming for him.

He didn't know what to do. That being the case, and he couldn't think of any other reason for it, so it undoubtedly was, then alerting anyone to it, speaking to anyone, about anything, would have no effect other than to give them what they wanted and speed up the process of his ending up with a matching bullet hole in his own temple.

But if this supposition was correct, and he had no reason to think he was imagining things, well then, frankly, he wondered why he wasn't already dead. Why would they kill Linda? She hadn't done anything against them, as far as he knew. Perhaps there was someone in the building who was simply trying to frighten him, and this awful deed had been carried out to tell him someone was onto him? If so, it was a pretty sick way to go about it. But why else would they have allowed him to hear a noise coming from the room unless they'd intended him to come in here... He swallowed down the chilling fear that was growing stronger by the moment and threatening to overwhelm him and wondered desperately what to do. Whoever had done this, and whatever their motive, he needed to get out of here and he needed to do it fast.

Somewhere he heard a door close, and his heart started racing even faster. It's nothing, just someone working. Murderers don't slam doors.

Oh, for the love of Christ, a voice in his head yelled at him. Yes, they do. This one did. Wake up. They'd already made one deliberate noise to get his attention, why not another? He ran a trembling hand over his chin. For one absurd moment, he wondered whether he was about to cry.

Think, he ordered himself. Think. Pull yourself together.

Right. How had they found out? He had been careless. But how had he been careless, he wondered again? In what way? He was so sure that he'd followed his orders to the letter, and he'd been certain that no one had seen him planting the bugs.

Anthony, stop, he yelled silently at himself. Think about that later. There would be time later to go over the whys and wherefores, assuming he got out of here alive. He had to get out of here alive. Concentrate on getting out of here alive.

He thought about the exit routes from where he stood. There was the main exit, of course, but he was hardly likely to be able to get out that way. There was another exit, leading along to the staff car park, but he was sure that route would be equally perilous. Both routes would take him right through the centre of the building and would also require him to use the lift or the stairs. But perhaps going through the centre of the building wasn't a bad thing, he wondered?

Yes, yes it was, it was a terrible idea. He shook his head. The only other option was to get himself into the cafeteria, at ground level, and the only part of the building that was on the floor above him, where there were not only more exits because of the kitchen safety regulations, but some of those exits would be far less used than the main ones and hidden away from plain sight. Or so he hoped. There was also an exit directly behind the kitchens, he knew; a delivery point that was attached to the preparation area at the rear of the kitchen. But his problem remained the same – getting to one of these exits. Walking around the corridors was not safe, he reminded himself frantically.

Hurst raked his hands desperately through his hair and forced himself to concentrate. What if he could get to the bathroom unseen, then perhaps he could use that age-old method of trying to escape by means of the air conditioning grille. All the building would be connected, surely? It had to be. And that meant there would be some sort of ladder inside to get from one floor to another. It was his only chance if he wanted to avoid detection, but he would have to get in there and out of sight before the ten minutes were up and the cameras sprang back into action, if they were going to. He looked at the screen above Linda's lifeless head. He had already wasted four of the ten minutes. He reached out a trembling hand and closed the girl's eyes, then placed his hand gently onto her hair. 'I'm so sorry, Linda,' he whispered.

It was the final moment of delay he allowed himself. Heart pounding manically against his ribcage, he checked his watch, went back into his own office, closed the door to Linda's, wiped it clean with the sleeve of his jacket, and stepped across to the door to the hallway. His whole body shaking with nerves, he opened it a crack and looked out at the corridor through wild eyes. There didn't appear to be anyone around. It was now or never.

He slipped off his shoes and tucked them under his arm, acutely aware of the noise they would make on the hard tiled floor and, closing the door quietly behind him, walked as confidently as he could out into the hallway and headed briskly for the bathroom, mercifully only a couple of doors down from his office and the scene of brutal murder that lay there.

Darting into the bathroom, Hurst frantically shoved his feet back into his shoes and checked that he was alone. He was.

Relieved, he looked up, scanning the ceiling for the air vent, which he spotted over a cubicle at the end of the row. His heart sank. The metal grille was held in place with the unhelpful use of four screws, one in each corner. His way was barred. How could he get them undone? And even if he somehow managed that task, how would he replace the grille once he'd pulled himself up into the space beyond? This was a bad idea, and he was running out of time. There was no choice. No choice at all, and he must hurry. He must try.

The noxious smell of synthetic orange scented toilet cleaner assaulted his nostrils, threatening to bring on a headache, and a tap dripped rhythmically into one of the sinks as he stood there wondering what to do.

What about his money card? Yes, that was thin. If he could use it to undo the screws… he plunged his hand into his pocket and pulled out the contents. Car keys, his communication device, wallet, and a tissue. Good. Opening his wallet and removing his money card, he stuffed everything else back into his pocket and let himself into the end cubicle. Taking care to leave the door ajar so that hopefully anyone coming into the room after he'd gone would think it empty and not bother to investigate further, he climbed up onto the seat of the toilet. It was a hopeful rather than a realistic assumption because the air vent would of course be the first thing they thought of once they discovered he'd gone. Nevertheless, he didn't see any other path open to him, so he had to die trying. He realised that he probably would.

But still, think of your boy, he reminded himself. Get on with it.

He was just able to pull himself up so as he was sitting on the dividing partition between the end cubicle and the next one along. With one hand on the slippery tiled wall to balance himself, he gripped the card tightly and tried it in the slot of the screw. It didn't fit. Damn it. Panic churning in his stomach, he shoved it back in his pocket and thought about trying his car key. Then he remembered the metal button. Yes! It was small but it could work. It was thin enough. Please let it be thin enough. He fished it carefully out of his other trouser pocket and tried it in the slot. This time, the screw moved.

He chewed on his bottom lip and held his breath as he carefully twisted his improvised screwdriver. He could do it. It was a slow process, but as quickly as he could, he loosened each of the screws and then returned the button to his pocket, before removing his other hand from the wall to steady the grille to prevent it from falling while he removed the screws the rest of the way by hand. He added them to his pocket. Dropping them would be disastrous.

The panel came away easily and Hurst managed, while balancing himself on the thin edge of the toilet partition, to lower it and then tilt it diagonally and slide it up into the space it had revealed above. He looked at his watch. Two of the ten minutes remained before the cameras returned to their normal working state. He raised his hands to find a grip on the edges of the hatch space and took a deep steadying breath.

Never one for the gym or physical activity beyond the walks and runs he went on with his wife, he wondered whether he had the strength to haul himself up. But the truth was he had no choice. The thought of Ward and his security team searching for him and asking why he had failed and why and how his computer system had been rigged to do so, and why he was hanging out of the bathroom roof spurred him on. The thought of Linda lying there with her lifeless eyes and blood puddling across her desk, never to return home to her family, spurred him on.

Adrenaline pumping, and darting a nervous glance at the bathroom door, praying that he wouldn't make any noise loud enough to draw attention to himself, he transferred one foot to the top of the toilet cistern and used it to help project himself upwards. It was a useful aid, and he found it surprisingly straightforward enough thanks also to his tall frame to pull himself up to a point where he could rest his elbows inside the hole. From this point, he had to rather kick and struggle to drag himself completely up through the hole.

But he'd done it. He'd got this far, at least. With sweat now pouring off him, and no longer bothering to look at his watch because it was obvious that the time was now up, he cast around the limited space looking for something onto which to secure the grille. It was too hot up here in this cramped and dirty space with its low ceiling, and the smell had gone from one of putrid orange to dusty, long forgotten attic. It was also dark, and once the grille was back in place – *if* the grille was ever back in place – it would be darker still. He began to feel a different kind of panic attaching itself to the fear that was already threatening to overwhelm him.

Sweat dripping from his chin and stinging his eyes, he fumbled to undo and remove his belt. There was a pipe, insulated with some sort of padded silver coloured foil, just to the side of the space that opened into the toilet. This, presumably, was the air-conditioning, and the pipe he would need to follow to get out. Even if it wasn't the air-conditioning, all the other pipes up here seemed to follow the same route, so it hardly mattered.

Quickly, he threaded his belt down and up through the slats of the grille, posted it back down the hole and pulled it back up. He looped the belt around the pipe, pulling it tightly until the square of metal fitted snugly back into place. He sent up a silent prayer that the action hadn't been caught on camera but was certain it must have been. Which meant there would be someone after him as soon as the camera operators had reported it. Hurst swallowed and forced himself to take a breath.

The next task was to follow the pipes as quickly and as quietly as possible, find a ladder up to the next floor, and hope to God that that the network came out somewhere outside the building. It must do. The canteen was, by his reckoning, about thirty metres ahead of him on the next floor. Sending up another silent prayer, he began to crawl, the space between floor and ceiling being no more than three feet or so, wondering where the ladder would be. There had to be one; it was the only way for the maintenance people to gain access, after all. They'd hardly come in through the bathroom ceiling.

A loud click made him jump. God, what was that? Something in the air conditioning system? Someone coming into the bathroom? Hurry, he told himself. The ceiling space was stuffy and dirty, but it looked as if the dirt on the floor of the space had recently been disturbed, probably by the maintenance people, because the path he was taking around the edge of the room, if you could call it that, next to the pipes, wasn't as grubby as the rest. This was a good sign, as it meant that somewhere he'd find access to the top floor. Nevertheless, before long he was struggling against the urge to sneeze. He pinched his nose. Stay quiet, for God's sake, he willed himself. Perhaps it would be a good idea if maintenance brought a cleaner with them next time. What was the point of servicing the air-conditioning if it was sitting in a swirling mass of filth?

Very quickly, he did spot a ladder. Thank you, thank you, he whispered. It was one of those metal ladders with safety circles around it, and it was just a few more feet in front of him. There still wasn't room for him to stand, though, until he was underneath it, and once he reached the ladder, he had to carefully position himself under it and only assume a standing position while ascending.

Ascending the ladder presented the threat of there being someone up there above him, waiting with total control and advantage over him, he knew, but there wasn't time to dwell on it. He pulled himself into an upright position within the circles of the ladder with his hands, to take the pressure off his joints and therefore hopefully avoiding making any noise from creaking knees. He had no idea how thick the walls were and the shaft he was ascending would be right next to God only knew what; the cafeteria, most likely. And even if he was right about what lay the other side of the wall, and although it should be empty at this time of day, you never knew. He must be extremely quiet.

Chancing his luck, he started to climb, his head tipped up to see anything or anyone that might be waiting for him above. It seemed to be quiet, however. There were about twenty steps up the vertical tunnel, taking him into the ceiling space of the ground-level floor, and therefore, what with it being the only ground-level part of the building, the cafeteria. Yes, he was over the cafeteria, he reassured himself. Now, he needed to find an exit.

After assuming a crawling position again at the top of the ladder, and continuing forwards, a nightmare thought struck him. What if, when he got to the other end of this passageway, the grille that he needed to use as his escape was also screwed shut – from the other side? Worse still, what if Ward and his thugs were waiting for him, having figured out where he would try to emerge and letting him go through this ghastly process just to shoot him dead when he arrived, rather than give chase through the dirty floor space? Would they simply shoot him where he was, and leave him to rot up here, possibly injured, to die a slow and painful death?

He shook his head to rid himself of these thoughts. It occurred to him to wonder, trying to be more optimistic as he crawled quietly along, whether he had in fact replaced the grille in time because so far no one had followed him via the bathroom. Surely, anyone coming up here in pursuit of him would be moving along the route a sight quicker than he was able to. They wouldn't care about noise! So, he thought with a little pop of hope, maybe this could work after all.

But he was sure he'd heard a noise back there. He knew he had. Oh God, where would they be? Would they follow him or wait? He tried to swallow but his throat was dry and full of dust. There was no choice now anyway but to keep going and try, because if whoever had killed Linda returned to the office, they would notice her closed eyes and know that Hurst had found her. Really there had been no point wiping the door handle. In fact, if anything, it pointed the finger of blame in his own direction, even if he himself didn't own a gun and had no reason whatsoever to kill the poor girl.

Chapter Twenty-four

Ward stood in the bathroom and watched, his fat face twisted grotesquely into a malevolent half smile, as one of his men, his agent Charley Greenway, who he'd pulled from the useless task of finding a quick solution to the bug problem, leapt up to sit easily on the dividing wall of the cubicles in a similar position to that which one would adopt to ride side saddle on a horse and calmly sliced through the belt holding the grille in place with a pocket-knife. He watched as the man jumped down and stood the square of metal on the floor before quietly snapping the knife shut, pocketing it, and springing easily back up to disappear stealthily through the gap in the ceiling.

Good. That would be an end to that. He smiled a vindictive smile at his reflection in the dull glass of the bathroom mirror and then, casting a look of utter distaste around the room, he turned to leave. His man could be trusted to finish the job, so there was no more purpose to Ward's hanging around in such a place as a staff bathroom and, anyway, clean enough though it was, it stank of rotten fruit.

It rankled, to put it mildly, that Hurst could have deceived him for so long. And it worried him equally that it had taken so long for one of his other agents, his *loyal* agent Charley Greenway, to rumble the bastard. He was troubled by the knowledge that there could well be at least one other person in the building whose loyalties rested elsewhere. Hurst was highly unlikely to be the only mole. It was also mildly annoying that while he'd been having this very conversation with Greenway, Hurst had been making a run for it. He should have sent Greenway to get rid of him before he'd had the chance to do so. However, it would soon be irrelevant. Greenway was on his tail now, and better late than never.

Was there someone else who had known what Hurst had been up to, he wondered again? Someone who had been helping him? Ward didn't know. What he did know, was that he'd make sure his staff were better watched in future. Greenway would be put straight onto it once Hurst had been dealt with. Such double-crossing disloyalty would not be tolerated, would not happen again, and everyone was going to know it and understand it and understand the consequences of it.

However, for the moment, time was pressing on him, and it was imperative that he get himself out of here and away to his safe house where he could at least evade the humiliation of being publicly turned out of office. The Leader's people had been waiting outside as the end of the vote had happened and the result had been flashed all over the screens, with images of fireworks and party streamers, like some cheap advert for an end of year school dance, and they had already infiltrated the facility, broken in, as he saw it, moments after the result of the vote, and started waving paperwork around and shutting down his surveillance networks, disabling his computers, and dismissing his staff, arresting anyone who protested too violently.

But if anyone thought he, Ward, was going to go quietly, they had another think coming. His loss of power was temporary. He would see to that. It angered him that Hurst had created another thing for him to have to contend with, but his party was still united, even in this so-called defeat, and they would rise again, and soon. And this time with him at the helm in his rightful place. His rightful place as World Leader, where no one would be allowed to get the better of him ever again.

Chapter Twenty-five

Hurst continued to drag himself as quickly and as silently as he could along the tight confinement of the ceiling space, although it was a slow process. Every forward movement of his limbs had to be made gently and slowly so as not to make the slightest sound, which would alert the people in the rooms below. He also had to move extra carefully around the other air vents. Each time he met with one he stopped, listened, and then edged around it after having taken a moment to glance down to get his bearings. It didn't occur to him to wonder whether there might be cameras up here as well. It was a good thing it didn't, because there was enough to think about and drive him crazy already.

As it turned out, the space where he'd first come up above ground had been a storeroom. He'd chanced a quick look down through the slats of the first vent he'd come to and seen nothing but rows of shelves stocked with bathroom supplies. The next had been a cold store containing food. Then an office, the cafeteria itself, mercifully empty, and now he was heading towards what must surely be the kitchen at the end of the building. For once he even forgot his claustrophobia as he tried to work out which direction the facility car park was in from this position. He hoped against hope there would be an easy way out once he got there – there meaning both the end of this network of pipes and out of the facility itself. His arms and legs were beginning to go to sleep and the fabric of his jacket and trousers was beginning to tear on the cuffs and knees as he pulled himself along the rough floor of the roof space.

But suddenly, there it was. The light from the kitchen shone dully ahead of him. He slowed his pace even more and approached with terrified caution. He could hear voices. Slowly, gently, he approached the grille and, heart in his mouth, quickly swept his hand over it. Better they shoot that than his head. Nothing happened. So, very gingerly, he peered down.

The voices he'd heard belonged to a young male chef and an older woman with curls of silver-grey hair escaping from under a hairnet who stood behind him piping cream onto a huge tray of desserts with the air of someone bored to death with the tedium of the job. Hurst wondered what to do. He then noticed another small ladder in a tunnel that veered off to his left at an angle of about forty-five degrees, which consisted of a sort of chute, or slide, with a few steps down its length, culminating in another, larger, grille-like barricade.

With a jolt of delight, he realised that this must indeed be what he'd been looking for – the main outside entry point of the maintenance entrance. All he needed to do was get the attention of one of the people below, perhaps the woman – her age meant she might possibly be keener to help, which sounded all sorts of -ist-types of wrong, but that couldn't be helped. Yes, he needed somehow to get rid of the man, and ask her to go outside and open the door for him. Unless it was possible to open it from inside? Dare he risk going down those steps, those noisy metal steps, and finding out?

As he was contemplating this, luck decided to give him an unexpected helping hand. The woman, he saw, was casting about the room and had spotted a fly. She put down her piping bag and began chasing it towards the door. As she looked around to keep track of it, she turned her head up towards the ceiling and caught a glimpse of Hurst above her, who put his finger to his lips begging for her silence. Curiously, the woman didn't seem remotely surprised to see a man squatting in the ceiling space above her. She didn't scream or make any sort of reaction other than to let out a small tut of annoyance.

'What is it?' asked the chef irritably.

'Nothing, just that there's a blasted fly in here,' she answered easily. 'Would you be a love and go and close the canteen door, so it doesn't get in there, and I'll try to let it out this way. You know how we get it in the neck if any flies get in.'

With a grunt of consent, the chef did her bidding, although not before complaining that he couldn't see any fly.

Hurst knelt in the dust wondering what was going to happen. Was this woman going to help him or call for security? If the latter, then why had she sent the chef away? He held his breath and waited.

As soon as the chef had moved away out sight, the woman grabbed a broom from beside her workstation, opened the door to the delivery area and, without as much as glancing in Hurst's direction, walked outside, flapping her free arm to chivvy the fly out of the room.

If anyone had been observing her, all they would have seen or heard would have been her muttering to herself that the air vents probably needed a clean and their fly nets replaced so they didn't come in, and wielding her broom up to the slats of the maintenance access door to give it a vigorous brush, before accidentally knocking the latch of the door open as she lowered it and went back inside to wash her hands and carry on with preparing the lunchtime desserts.

Hurst hardly dared believe his luck. As quickly as he could, and still making as little noise as possible because, after all, there were people working in the offices on the floor below, the floor where all his own colleagues were, of course, he gently began lowering himself in a sitting position down the thin metal steps. He gave the door a tiny push. As it opened a couple of inches onto the concrete delivery bay, he wondered what to do next. There didn't seem to be anyone around but of course this could be misleading. The surveillance cameras were everywhere and working again by now, he was sure, so crossing this wide-open space to get to the car park was going to be as big a problem as emerging from the trenches of a battlefield into the direct fire of the enemy. As, of course, would be attempting to leave. How could he jump into his car and go charging through the security gate at this time of day? They would be waiting for him. It had been a stupid idea, to imagine he could simply drive away. The very fact that no one seemed to be running around shouting his name and searching for him was suspicious in itself.

He would have to think of an alternative, and fast. Back up in the ceiling space behind him he heard another sound, similar to the first he'd heard, but quieter, and it was followed by another sound, rather like a muffled gunshot. Then came a heavy thud. It was time to take a risk. He didn't have anything with which to defend himself, and they were coming.

But just as he was about to step out into the burning sun and run for his car, for he couldn't think of anything else to do, the door to the kitchen opened once more, delaying his exit. He glanced up the chute towards the space above and wondered why whoever it was up there had not yet caught up with him.

However, his attention was drawn back to what was going on outside. He could easily see the kitchen door from his crouched position, and he waited to see what would happen. Apart from the person in the roof, there was at least one other who knew of his whereabouts, and he didn't know if or for how long she could be trusted to keep his presence to herself, or even whether she was part of Ward's plan to catch him and was working in cahoots with the person who must surely be about to strike. He watched, poised to jump out of the door regardless of the risks if the gunman appeared behind him. Not if. When. A chill ran through him as he watched the goings on outside with urgency.

The same woman who had opened the door for him was back outside. Hurst watched her wheel a cart of what appeared to be tablecloths and towels over to where he sat crouched behind the small metal door.

'That should be all right there until the laundry men come in five minutes,' she said quietly. 'Lucas will know what to do with the extra load. Very helpful is Lucas.' With that, she unhinged the side of the metal cart and dumped a couple of chefs' whites inside on top of the already considerable pile and, leaving the wheeled cart unlocked, walked away.

It was too easy. It had to be a trap, but what choice did he have? As quickly as possible, Hurst glanced once more up at the space in the ceiling above him, removed his jacket to reveal his white shirt, just as an extra precaution, let himself out of the maintenance door into the dry heat of the late morning sun, careful to close it behind him and fix the latch in place, still mightily confused that his pursuer hadn't caught up with him, but grateful for it all the same, and hastily climbed inside the metal cart, pulling the door closed and burying himself underneath the pile of soiled laundry. He wrapped a towel around his hand and held the door closed, praying that no cameras had caught his action and that he was actually, in some as yet unknown way, being helped.

Assuming this was the case, he had timed his move just right. Before long, the rumble of a vehicle's engine could be heard, and what must be the laundry van arrived. Hurst strained his ears to listen as the driver spoke to his liberator and, with mounting hope, he quickly understood what had happened.

'Sorry, luvvie, I'm afraid there are a couple of extra bits in the load today.' Hurst felt the door of the cart click shut and his towel-wrapped hand was stuffed back in through the bars, confirming the intent for him to be there. 'My fault, I caused quite a rumpus when I went to give the security boys their tea and had a coughing fit. Spilt it everywhere, I did. Had them running around after me patting my back and grabbing towels to mop up the mess on the floor. Still, at least no harm done, eh? And they were only away from their work for a minute or so. Daft old bugger, aren't I?'

'Never you mind, angel. No bother for me, but I'll tell Lucas of the extra, just the same. See you tomorrow.'

The cart began to trundle across the tarmac and Hurst felt it being loaded onto a rising tailgate and he and the pile of laundry on top of him disappeared into the back of the van. The door closed and Hurst waited, his heart in his mouth.

Underneath the pile of laundry, he very slowly created an air hole for himself then, inch by slow inch, struggled back into his jacket and wondered what to do. How would he explain his presence once the van was unloaded? What could he give as his reason for escaping from the facility? He fumbled in his pocket for his communication device and switched it off with shaking hands. They could use it to track him. The van began to move.

Also, how would he locate Lucas? He had no idea who Lucas was, what he looked like, or even if he'd understood correctly what that woman, who he now recognised as the tea lady, had meant – that she'd seen him on the camera, bought him some time, and told him Lucas would help.

He was well aware that it could be a trap. Lucas, whoever the hell he was, could very well be waiting for him in a conveniently muffled laundry room with a loaded pistol. Maybe he was about to find out first-hand the procedure for making people disappear.

But no, surely not? They wouldn't go to so much trouble, would they? Surely if the woman was going to turn him in, she would simply have left him in the air vent, or not bothered to make a scene over the spilt tea which, he had to admit with respect, if she was helping him, was quick thinking on her part.

In fact, he wondered, how was it that she'd known he needed help? He could have been anyone, doing anything, when she'd spotted him on that screen and yet she'd helped him. Why? And how come she'd seen him before the people whose job it was to see these things? It was almost as if she'd known what was going to happen before it happened and had set up the whole spilt tea thing in advance. It didn't make any sense. For now, however, he had no way of getting to any answers and no alternative but to wait and see what happened next.

The van stopped. He could hear voices and then the vehicle began to move again. The security gates. They must now be outside the perimeters of the facility and on the road into town. Or out of it. Either way, hurdle number one was cleared. However, he needed to think of a way to explain himself once he was found. Perhaps he could say he'd been about to be accused of something he hadn't done? But in that case, why was he running?

Did he need to be found, he wondered? OK, so this Lucas was someone the tea lady – the tea lady, for God's sake – thought to be trustworthy, but what if she was wrong? Just because she'd helped him, it didn't follow that this Lucas person would. What if he, Lucas, put his own safety first and left Hurst to his fate, as most people would? *Why* had she helped him, he wondered again?

Perhaps the laundry would be wheeled off somewhere and left alone for a time, giving him a chance to escape? All well and good, but there were a couple of problems with that. First of all, he didn't know where the laundry got taken to, and so wouldn't have any idea where he was without turning on his CD. He could hardly climb out of a window and go sneaking around random streets drawing attention to himself. And secondly, how was he supposed to check that the coast was clear without again drawing attention to himself and peeping out of the metal laundry cage? He supposed that would be easy enough to do, as long as he moved extremely slowly, but even so, it was a risk because anyone could be there, standing over him, watching, waiting. They could have padlocked the cart shut, for all he knew, leaving him caged up like an animal. Oh, God.

His only hope was that Lucas was on his side.

Chapter Twenty-six

The black car had now crawled to a stop. Sally couldn't tell whether or not the engine was still running. She stood motionless, rooted to the spot, wondering what to do, her hand gripping the fridge door. Surely, this could not be good, because if it was someone connected with the mission, she didn't know about it, she hadn't been told – it hadn't been part of the plan. But who else could it be? She certainly didn't know anyone who drove a car like that one and, besides, it looked frighteningly official. Her brain grappled for answers. Nothing she could come up with was good. No, this was not good at all. Damn it.

For a few long seconds, nothing happened. The car doors remained closed and she stayed where she was. From her position, Sally was unable to see who was inside the vehicle, but the windows were blacked out anyway, of course. Unlike her own kitchen ones, which meant the occupants of the car would have seen her by now, there was no doubt about it, even though she was at the back of the room. And standing still like this wasn't good for her. It was akin to admitting she had something to hide, that she was frightened of something, and that would never do. So, she had to make a decision, and fast. She had to move.

Sally didn't like improvising; she needed a plan. Plans both excited her and made her feel secure. They meant she could mentally tick off every item towards a goal, and see her objectives being brought slowly to fruition through her own hard work. Life had been full of these plans over the last decade, and it had been so exciting, knowing that she was working undercover for the Leader and the Democratic Party, to make a difference to the world. She hoped against hope that it wasn't all about to come to nothing and end in a shower of bullets.

Ordinarily, these plans that she was used to were slow-moving, but that just made the anticipation all the more thrilling. Usually, if something unforeseen happened, she would have been slightly distanced from it and would have contacted the Leader and asked what she should do, However, with no time available to her for that at this moment, with the unforeseen sitting right there in her driveway, she needed to think on her feet. So, she crossed to the sink, picked up a glass from the draining board and filled it with water, taking a small sip and looking quizzically out of the window as she drank, to give whoever it was the chance to show themselves in a normal friendly way, and also to cover for the fact that with her other hand she had picked up a small vegetable knife and slid it into the belt of her jeans.

Getting no response from her appearance at the window, proved that this meant trouble. Perhaps her husband's cover had been blown and he'd inadvertently given her away? Not that he'd have to, because it would naturally follow that if he was spying for the Leader then so would she be. That type of disaster would indeed be followed up with a visit such as this, and there was now no alternative left to her but to open the door to it and invite it co-operatively into her day.

There was a security chain in place on the door, but what was the point of using that? Men such as the ones she was sure she was about to face would break something as flimsy as a little door chain as easily as snapping a pencil. And then, if they thought she was being deliberately difficult, they would break her neck likewise. She had to look friendly, as if she didn't suspect anything was amiss. So, without further ado, she took a breath and opened the door, hoping her manner didn't give off any hint of anything it shouldn't.

The blade of the knife was poking her lightly in the small of her back, so she simply stood where she was, framed in the doorway with the sun artistically picking out reddish highlights around the edges of her dark hair, still holding the glass of water in her hand just in case she needed to smash it on the wall of the house and ram the shards into someone's face, while hoping she gave off the aura of a regular person. A person without any ideas of anything untoward behind her innocently wide green eyes – or any ideas of the brutal maiming of thugs, anyway. She smiled questioningly towards the big black vehicle and called lightly across to it in her clipped west London accent that she'd so determinedly retained, and that was so strange in these parts.

'Can I help you?'

The driver's door of the car opened, and a man began to emerge. Just one man. This was a surprise to Sally. She had expected there to be two. Didn't hired thugs usually work in pairs? Still, perhaps there was someone else in the car, waiting to help tidy up after she had been disposed of?

Christ, what about Toby? Suddenly, as the thought of her son being hurt or witnessing the murder of his mother played out vividly in her head, her smile disappeared, to be replaced by a cold black terror.

'Who are you?' She moved the glass to her left hand, the easier to reach for the knife with her right.

But as the hulking frame of the black-suited man emerged fully from behind the wheel, the back window of the car was lowered. A familiar voice, but one she hadn't heard for a long time, called to her in an urgent half whisper.

'Sally, go inside, get your boy, and get into the car. Now. Don't ask questions, don't waste time. Just do it. GO.'

Chapter Twenty-seven

For the love of God, what was going on? Something else must have happened. Maybe not Anthony after all. She'd thought things were progressing well, but this impromptu visit was not a good sign. Not a good sign at all. She was dreaming, she had to be. But how foolish to think that the speech had been live. Silly, but she had just assumed. She'd thought...

Idiots assume.

Sally nodded quickly in the direction of the car and turned away into the house, pushing the door closed behind her as she did so. She ran for the stairs and called up to her boy to come downstairs straight away. While she waited for him, she pulled the knife from her belt and put it into her handbag, along with the gun that was kept in the cupboard in the hall, fumbling with the lock in her haste with nervous hands. Quickly, she loaded the weapon. You never knew. The time for worrying about cameras detecting her actions was past. Besides, cameras intruding into people's homes should very soon become a thing of the past themselves. Or so she'd thought. The cameras visible to her in the house all still seemed to be dormant, but who knew? The vote had been won by the Leader. The plan should be progressing well. So, what was going on?

Such had been the urgency in the called instructions from the car that Sally knew there was no time for collecting anything else. But why was she being summoned in this way? And where to? She didn't know what to think. All she knew was, it was imperative that she follow this order.

The young child came obediently down the stairs clutching his favourite toy – a large black and silver robot.

'Yes, Mummy?' he said. 'Is it time to go back to school now?' Holding his robot aloft, he said, 'Look, he's going to kill the emeny.'

Oh Christ, please don't let him be in danger, Sally thought. She sat him down on the bottom stair and helped him on with his shoes. How she wished they could kill the "emeny". She planted a kiss on the top of his sandy little head.

'Not just yet. We have to go for a little ride in a car first, Toby,' she told him, trying to keep her voice from betraying any hint of the fear she was feeling.

Shoving her feet into her own shoes – trainers, because you never knew when you had to run – and grabbing both their coats, because you never knew where they'd end up or for how long, and the evenings could get quite chilly, she hooked her bag over her shoulder, took her son by the hand and led him out to the waiting car, knocking a bag of hairdressing combs and brushes onto the floor from the hall table as she went. A plan was forming in her mind.

The driver, still standing guard beside the car where he'd been just now, watched attentively as Sally and Toby climbed into the big black machine, before himself getting back in behind the wheel. As she sat down, Sally heard the locks click shut. Of course. Normal procedure.

Two rows of three seats faced each other, and a thick black screen divided them from the driver. One side of seats, behind the driver, was empty, and it was onto these that Sally had directed her son and where she herself sat down. On the seat opposite her sat the World Leader, a grim expression on her face. Something was terribly wrong. This was no social call.

'Hello Aunt,' said Sally.

Chapter Twenty-eight

The van stopped after a surprisingly lengthy trip of what was in Hurst's estimation around forty minutes. He hadn't dared to move, even to look at his watch. He waited. Before long, he heard the door of the van open and then close and the soft thud of footsteps on a hard floor as the driver approached the rear of the vehicle. It sounded as if they were inside a building.

Oh, Christ, here we go, he thought, no closer in his mind to a solution.

The doors swung open. Hurst was barely breathing; he dared not give away his presence, just in case this was a trap. But they knew he was here...

A second set of footsteps approached. Then there were voices.

'Lucas around, is he?' the van driver asked of his unknown companion in a cheery voice as he pulled the cart containing Hurst onto the tailgate and began to lower it. 'I've got a message for him. Best to deliver it in person, you know.'

'Yes, OK, I'll go and let him know for you right away,' the second, younger-sounding male voice replied, and Hurst heard the second man's footsteps retreating, before the cart he was in began to move. He was trundled away to who knew where, and then again there was silence as what were presumably the driver's footsteps retreated into the distance as well. This time the silence dragged on for a few minutes.

Hurst's mind was racing. Should he chance a look at his surroundings? Probably not. This had been such a bad idea. What had possessed him to think that he had any chance of escaping that place without being discovered? Better that he had stayed there and faced the consequences of what he'd done. At least he'd have died in the knowledge that he'd done what he could and that as a result of his help the Leader had managed to hold the vote. He wondered for a moment what the outcome had been. It had been heading for a resounding YES when he'd left poor Linda. Eighty-five per cent doesn't turn itself on its head.

The couple of minutes of voting that he'd witnessed had shown that it was likely to continue on to an easy and certain victory. The NO voters would hardly be likely to be saving themselves to vote en masse at the end. But you never knew. Anyway, more pressing matters were at the forefront of his mind right now, and he hardly cared at the moment what the result had been.

Despairing of finding a solution to his predicament, he was suddenly aware of a very low humming noise coming from directly underneath him. It sounded like a lift. Hurst frowned. What was it? The noise stopped. A second noise, equally quiet, came to his ears. It sounded this time like a floor tile sliding to one side. His eyes widened in fear. Hands... there were hands. Surely not, under the cart, it wasn't possible... he could sense them rather than see them, of course, but yes, they were there and they were doing something underneath the base of the laundry cart. Hurst gave a silent whimper, a frightened animal in his cage. Were they going to shoot him here and now, the sound of it nice and conveniently muffled for them by his covering of laundry?

The blood started pounding in his ears, and at the same moment, he realised that someone was again standing beside the cart. He hadn't heard them approach because he'd been so preoccupied with this new development. Whoever it was opened the front of the cart, pulling it free of Hurst's fingers which had been, hidden by their covering of linen, holding onto it once again, and spoke.

'Best if the heavy things are at the bottom,' said the cheerful voice. Hurst recognised it again as the same voice as before. The driver of the van. It was strange that he hadn't heard him come back. Even if he'd been preoccupied with visions of his own death, you'd have thought he'd have heard something. The driver put his hands into the metal cage and started lifting and rummaging through the pile of tablecloths and towels until his hand found Hurst's shoulder. He gave him a downward push, not unfriendly, and Hurst understood what he must do. The driver was creating a diversion for him to be able to move, by rummaging about in the laundry.

Wild eyed with relief, he scrambled to move the laundry he was standing on away from the bottom of the cart so that even more of it was piled up on his back, and as he did so he heard another voice, this time whispering from underneath him, which told him to move his feet to the edges of the cage. He did so, but it wasn't an easy position to be in, squatting like this in such tight confinement, and with a pile of laundry on his back.

He could now see the owner of the hands and the new voice. There was a middle-aged man with grey hair and glasses, wearing scuffed jeans and an ancient-looking faded blue T-shirt, looking up at him from the opening underneath the cart and the movement Hurst had felt just now had been him unclipping three sides of the middle section of the cart's floor with hurried hands.

'Jump down through,' the man half whispered, half mimed.

Hurst did as he was told, lowering himself down gently into the gap, bits of the laundry inevitably falling down with him. He saw that the floor tile under the cart had indeed slid away to reveal an opening just big enough to allow the passage of the cart's floor section, which had swung down into it, and he was now standing in a stooping position on top of what looked like a lift shaft.

'Help me stuff the things back up and clip it shut,' whispered the man now squatting in the space beside him into which he had descended, gathering up some fallen napkins. 'Quick.'

Hurst struggled. With the man's help, they pushed all the tablecloths and napkins back up, and between them they rammed the bottom of the cart back up into place.

The floor tile over their heads began to move quietly back into position. That done, the man sat down, took a torch from his pocket, and pulled the bewildered Hurst by the arm to follow suit and sit down beside him. They began to move slowly downwards. Where were they taking him? He was almost too fascinated now to be scared anymore.

While they descended, Hurst took the opportunity to take a closer look at his companion. It might be useful if he managed to get out of here alive and needed to give a description to the police. The notion was laughable, and he dismissed the thought from his head. Still… in the gloom, he could see that the man was about fifty to fifty-five years of age, tough-looking and weather-worn. He wore a deep frown on his face but, despite this, behind his glasses his dark eyes were wide and alert, which gave him a sort of crazed, almost humorous look. 'Are you…' Hurst began quietly, but the man put his finger to his lips and shook his head.

His lips silently formed the words, 'One minute.'

Chapter Twenty-nine

The moving platform came to a halt and Hurst and his companion stood up, bumping into each other uncomfortably as they did so. What the hell, he thought again? What was this place? Where was he being taken? Another layer of panic began to form, reminding him of the considerable amount already present and, as he started to imagine all sorts of unthinkable horrors once more, involving beatings, blindfolds and guns, the wall of the concrete shaft slid quietly open in front of them to reveal what looked like a very rudimentary office in an underground bunker. The walls were unpainted and showed the bare grey of the austere concrete blocks. A grimy metal desk with no chair and a twisted leg, as if it had had something extremely heavy dropped on its corner, stood abandoned beside the side wall on the left. Mutilated, it had been forgotten, no longer good for anything. It was covered in rubbish and a thick layer of dust. The place looked like a bomb shelter. Or an old secret service interrogation room. Hurst once again turned to the other man with a questioning look but was merely invited to step through by a gesture of the man's hand.

At the far side of the room a second man stepped through a doorway and stood waiting for them, neat and clean and ill-fitting in appearance in the middle of this cold, unwelcoming chamber and, Hurst still unmoving, the grey-haired man pushed him forwards out of the lift space without saying a word. As the door to the vertical passageway closed behind Hurst and his companion with a dull thud, the second man stepped lightly forward and held out his hand in greeting.

'Mr Hurst. Welcome. I wonder whether you realise just how lucky you are?' Reluctantly, and only because it was polite to do so, and being polite might be helpful to him, Hurst extended his own hand. The man shook it enthusiastically, with his eyebrow raised quizzically at the expression of incomprehension on Hurst's face, and made a grunting, 'Hm', sound. He spoke with crystal clear enunciation, which made him sound a bit affected. 'I wonder also whether you realise just how much danger you have put my mother in?' He shook his head. 'No. People don't, you know.' He continued to shake his head dismissively. 'No matter. One tends only to think of oneself when fleeing psychopaths with murder on their mind.' He smiled now, as if he imagined he'd made a joke. 'Understandable, really. But have no fear for my mother, she has already been evacuated from the facility by the talented and hard-working people on our side. They went in as soon as the voting had reached its conclusion.' He hesitated for a second, then said, 'Forgive me, dear boy. My name is Lucas. My surname is unnecessary, don't you think, and indeed unwise just at the moment, as I'm sure you are well aware. So please don't ask.' Looking Hurst straight in the eyes, and smiling as he read the words, "I wasn't going to", on his face, he said, 'I, on the other hand, and quite naturally enough, know everything there is to know about you, and you had better be grateful that I do, for it is the only reason that you are still standing erect and inhaling the rather stale air of this ghastly chamber.' Lucas turned to the grey metal desk and picked up a packet of cigarettes. 'Smoke?' he asked pleasantly.

Hurst gave a small cough to bring his voice to his throat. 'No thanks. I don't.'

'Good choice. Filthy habit.' Lucas went ahead and lit himself a cigarette, anyway, further contaminating the air. 'Please, won't you come this way?' He headed for a door, before stopping to add, 'I'm forgetting my manners. Perhaps you would care for a drink? Something to eat, maybe? It must be approaching lunchtime, and I for one am ravenous.' Without waiting for an answer, he flicked his free hand. 'Paolo, please see to it.'

The man who had accompanied Hurst on his strange and unexpected journey down into this frightening chamber in the bowels of the earth slipped away discreetly through a side door. Hurst had almost forgotten about him, so intrigued was he by this man Lucas, whose whole appearance and manner seemed bizarre to say the least. He looked like a well-preserved relic from the nineteen forties, and Hurst was willing to bet he knew it. An intentional nod to the past? An ally, after all? Or a clever ploy to appear as such?

Lucas was tall and thin with a head of dark hair oiled slickly down onto his neatly oval skull. He must have been somewhere approaching forty-five and was dressed casually in black trousers and a black roll-neck jumper, far too hot and quite unsuitable for the current weather, in Hurst's opinion, teamed with a pair of what could only be described as old-fashioned leather carpet slippers. He now led the way into a second room, larger than the first and, in comparison, the very last word in opulence and comfort. It wasn't really, of course, but compared with the bunker just now, well... The door slid firmly into place behind them, and Hurst could hear what sounded like a heavy shutter of some sort descending behind it.

At his jumpy glance towards this muffled noise, Lucas offered, 'Security, you know. It'll keep us safe for now.'

'What? What do you mean, for now?'

'Please, come through.'

Hurst let out a sharp breath but followed without further comment and looked around him with interest. There were two large sofas of shiny black leather in this second room scattered with fat white corded cushions. Several small antique tables were optimistically placed to be aesthetically pleasing, with vases of flowers struggling valiantly against the lack of natural light in what appeared to be Venetian glass upon them, and a huge wooden desk, on which sat the ubiquitous computerised controls for the large screen that adorned the wall above it, took up the space along the far wall. In here, the walls were painted pale blue, although were still un-plastered and unpleasant, and were hung with paintings in an array of uncomplimentary, mismatched styles. Somehow, the jumble worked well, and the room felt almost welcoming, in a sloppy antique shop sort of way.

'Er, sorry Lucas, but who are you?' asked Hurst. 'What is this place? Am I going to find myself being shot against a wall after this lunch? Is this my last supper?'

Lucas' brown eyes glittered with mirth, and he chuckled. 'My dear fellow, I would say you are safer now than you've been at any point over the last six years.' He stubbed out his cigarette in a crystal ashtray and indicated for Hurst to sit. 'But I do concur that I owe you an explanation.'

Hurst chose a sofa at random and lowered himself onto the edge of a cushion, still wary, and Lucas sat facing him at the opposite end, his hands resting on his knees and his torso leaning towards Hurst at a slight angle like a schoolteacher addressing a small child.

'Now then, you asked who I am,' he began. 'Well, I am the Leader's head secret agent.' Hurst raised his eyebrows, unimpressed by this ludicrous sounding title. 'Sounds thrilling, doesn't it?' trilled his host, misunderstanding his derision. Or maybe he didn't. Either way, he tutted. 'It's my job to support and to protect not only the Leader, but also those whom we feel have shown us unswerving loyalty at their own considerable risk.' He swept his hand towards Hurst. 'Such as your good self. My job, among other things, is also to carry out missions of rescue. Again, such as this. It happens more often than you'd think.' At Hurst's raised eyebrows and unspoken, "Does it?", Lucas' eyes glittered again with humour. 'Why, you don't imagine that our elaborate little entrance was built especially for you, surely?'

Hurst frowned. 'No, I…'

Lucas dismissed his words with a small shake of his neatly groomed head. 'Not everyone who disappears without trace has been thrust off this mortal coil by Agent Ward, you know. Sometimes we get there first and save people.'

'Oh!'

Lucas nodded. 'I do all this based on the fact that I am, without a doubt, the most informed man on the planet with regards to what the enemy are doing – for enemies are what they are, dear boy, as you know well enough and better than most. I'm also well informed on what our supporters are doing, of which you are now no doubt also becoming aware. That is not being big-headed, it is a fact. The Leader thinks I am simply marvellous!' He allowed himself a moment to preen camply at his own self-importance before quickly rearranging his face. 'However, there is no place for arrogance in this work. So... to continue, I have a network of spies, just as the World Administration do. Excuse me, ex World Administration. One of the most esteemed of these spies is my dear mother who, I'm sure you agree, looks most delightfully ordinary in a little apron and bonnet. To look at her in her darling little disguise you'd never imagine she was one of the United Kingdom's best secret agents, would you?' Lucas nodded, anticipating Hurst's question. 'Indeed, we still operate as such from the UK, still call ourselves British, and have always done so. For that is what we are.'

'Er...'

'Please, Mr Hurst. You don't imagine that the British would tolerate being dictated to indefinitely, surely? By the deranged successors of a nondescript Italian man who thought he could change the world with juvenile idealistic promises which even those with only a basic understanding of politics, had they bothered to utilise their brains towards the powers of debate with which at the time people were still blessed, should have known could never work? Please!' he said again and gave a sniffy inhalation of disgust at the thought.

'Well, I...'

'Now, onto your other questions,' Lucas interrupted, with a little waggle of his pointer finger. 'Firstly, the matter of what this place is, as you so eloquently put it. You will have gathered that we are underneath a laundry. I am employed as its manager.

You wouldn't credit it, would you?' Lucas' nostrils flared slightly as he said this, as though he found the idea more than a mite distasteful and demeaning. 'You will be happy to hear that we are positioned outside the jurisdiction of a certain Mr Ward.' He held up a hand to correct himself. 'I'm sorry, ex jurisdiction of Mr Ward. That is to say, we all know the entire world is under his control, but he can't have eyes everywhere. This area is watched over by someone else. One of the millions of dirty snitches who report back. You know how it works.' He blinked a few times in rapid succession, as if excited. 'Gosh, what chaotic times lie ahead for us all. He won't go quietly, you know,' he added conversationally, as if they were chatting over the garden fence.

'No.'

'But never mind, the law is the law and go he must, along with all the rest.' He tapped another cigarette out of its box and lit it. 'Anyway, I digress. Where we are, is inside my headquarters when I am in this part of the world. It's not much,' he ran his eyes over the room with the air of someone who knows they're worth more but is making a huge sacrifice for the cause, 'but it's safer than working from the Leader's offices, and I need to maintain a presence on site for my "job". And at least you can be sure there are no cameras down here. State of the art acoustic shielding is also in place, so no one up above in the laundry can hear a thing that's said down here. No one can hear you scream, and all that.' Lucas smiled. Hurst didn't.

'I don't understand. I mean, I understand what you're saying, but I don't understand how things have gone the way they have today.'

'Are you displeased with the day's events?'

'Oh, I'm enjoying myself immensely,' Hurst said. 'How do you think I feel? I can't say I particularly relish being yelled at in front of my colleagues or take any pleasure from realising I've been found out as a spy, and having my betrayal made known to me by the discovery of the dead body of my secretary or having to improvise a very shoddy escape as a result. So yes, I suppose you could say I'm displeased.'

'But you did manage to escape.'

'Yes… but I get the feeling that even that was engineered, and that somehow even my thoughts aren't my own. For all I know, I could still die down here.'

'Oh, come now, don't be melodramatic. Your options were merely thought about by us before they were thought about by you, and a contingency plan put into place to cover each one – nothing more sinister than that.' Lucas smiled. 'We haven't yet got to the point where people's minds can be penetrated in order to make them think the thoughts that others want them to. At least, not in the way you imply. If we could, then we wouldn't currently find ourselves here having this conversation, now would we?' Lucas stood up at the sound of a knock on a door at the far end of the room. 'This way. Our lunch is ready. Let's eat.'

As Hurst stood to follow him, his knees creaked inside his ruined trousers. It was a cliché, but he was getting too old for this nonsense.

'You didn't answer my last question,' he said, with more confidence in his voice than he actually felt.

'Are you going to be shot against a wall?' Lucas laughed. 'That depends, dear boy, on whether or not that tracking device you're carrying was successfully disarmed as you came through the trap door and down the lift shaft. I imagine that if it wasn't and it leads to your capture by our friend Mr Ward, then yes, you quite probably will be. Along with the rest of us.'

Hurst stared at Lucas, uncomprehending. 'What are you talking about? I'm not carrying anything.'

'Yes, you are.'

'No, I swear, I'm not.'

'Come, we could go round in circles like this all day.'

'I'd be inclined to be more worried about the cameras outside the kitchen.'

'They were the first ones we deactivated.'

'Ah. OK, good.' Damn it, if he'd known that before, he could have made a dash for his car and freedom after all. Instead, he was here, with this peculiar man who was insisting he was carrying a tracking device.

'Before we eat, I'd like you to go through into that room there,' Lucas pointed to a small door adjacent to the one they were about to go through to eat. 'And change into the new set of clothes that are there waiting for you. I ask that you change *all* your clothes. Everything. You must not keep on a single stitch of what you're currently wearing.'

Hurst, his mouth hanging open with incredulity, began to speak.

Lucas tutted irritably. 'Please just do it, Mr Hurst. I will explain over lunch. We do not have much time available to us.'

With a sigh, Hurst did as he was told and opened the door to a small room that contained nothing more than a table with a pile of clothes upon it. What in the name of all that's holy is this about, he wondered?

'I haven't got a tracking device on me. I even turned my CD off,' he mumbled petulantly. He could be irritable, too.

'Leave all your other clothes in there, including everything that's in your pockets. Your belongings will be returned to you shortly,' Lucas added, ignoring this last as if Hurst hadn't spoken, before disappearing into the dining room.

Hurst closed the door behind him and considered his predicament. Lucas had answered his questions, up to a point. He was still alive, so that was a good sign. Maybe he could trust this strange man, this oddly spoken throwback from another time, but who knew?

As there was currently nothing to be done about it either way, and given the fact that Lucas was waiting for him, and that actually he was so hungry he could eat a horse, he yanked off his clothes and put on the perfectly fitting new set, which consisted of a pair of rather expensive jeans, a white T-shirt and pale grey jumper. New underwear, new socks, new shoes… good God, why was this necessary?

He re-joined Lucas in the dining room after a couple of minutes, where a simple but very welcome lunch awaited him. He took in his surroundings but did not speak. It was a plain but functionally comfortable room, as much as an underground chamber ever could be, and contained only the necessary furniture for dining. The walls in here were painted black and silver and the table and chairs looked as if they just might be genuine mahogany antiques. Ornate silver wall lights surrounded the room and gave out a soft glow akin to late afternoon sunshine.

Scowling, and stewing over the fact that even his clothing sizes were somehow known to this wretched man, Hurst silently helped himself to a plate of pasta, as Lucas had already done, from the large earthenware pot that stood on the equally genuine looking mahogany sideboard, sat down opposite Lucas, and began to eat, still without a word, waiting for whatever it was that Lucas would say next. If he was going to be shot, he may as well have a nice meal first. It was a pity there didn't appear to be any wine forthcoming to go with it.

Chapter Thirty

The car reversed quietly out of the driveway. Sally knew better than to imagine any conversation would be private. Even though, with the winning of the vote, surveillance was now supposed to be legally forbidden, the new law was hardly likely to be respected so, while she kept her questions as general as she could, she wasn't too concerned about there being any legal repercussions for anything she said that could supposedly come under the bracket of dissent.

'What's going on?' she asked. 'Where are we going?'

The Leader didn't appear to know how to respond, so she simply shrugged her shoulders and spoke the truth. 'Kidnap is what is going on, Sally. It appears I was wrong to trust Frederick Lambert.' She pointed unnecessarily at the screen to the driver's seat, behind which sat the man in question. 'I was on my way to have a conversation with Robert Ward, to see whether there was any way we could get this changeover done amicably. There isn't, of course, but I was at least going to show willing and go to him as soon as the plane landed, and attempt to talk to him, show some good manners, common courtesy, and professionalism.

'On our way there, however, and bearing in mind my chief aide's and my tiredness after a long flight, Frederick Lambert here seemed to think that rather than do his job as instructed and as he's done for many years with no apparent problem, the better course of action today was to dispense with his colleague and mine on a lonely road over the other side of town by throwing them out of the car into a ditch in a hail of bullets like so much rubbish, and in so doing make it possible to get me to reverse today's vote and keep the WA in power.'

She looked tired and defeated, Sally thought, and hoped her aunt wasn't considering pandering to this man, giving in, and giving up on everything she'd worked so hard for.

'As for where we're going,' her aunt continued, absently picking at a loose thread on the seat beside her, 'I'm afraid I haven't got the faintest idea.' She looked across at Toby. 'How he's grown... Sally, I'm so sorry. For all of this. I should never have involved you.' She let out a long breath and shifted a bit to slump back into the corner of the seat, her restless fingers moving their attention to her shoulder length dark hair, so like that of her niece, which she twisted around and around.

She looked thin, Sally thought. The small contribution to the cause that she herself had made paled into insignificance compared with the strain her aunt must have been under for all these years, and she felt bad for her silent reprimand. Her aunt's unmade-up eyes were circled with dark rings of tiredness, and Sally wanted to hug her and tell her it was all going to be all right.

But *was* it going to be all right? Would that have been the truth?

Instead, she said, 'I chose to help you, Aunt, you didn't force me.'

'Yes, I know that, but I was talking about today. I probably shouldn't have involved you in any of it, but I definitely wasn't thinking straight when I asked him to go and get you today.'

'You *asked* him to come and kidnap me? You asked him to kidnap *Toby*?' she hissed.

'I'm sorry, I needed another brain to get out of this and you're the best there is,' she whispered. 'I wasn't thinking. I shouldn't have asked him, I know, but I didn't think he'd take any notice of me when I said I'd like to have you with me. I was just chancing my hand. I'm sorry,' she said again.

Sally shook her head, staring at her aunt. My God.

'Right, well, we'll have to see what we can do, won't we? I believe in the reformation of our old world every bit as much as you do. And we won, Aunt. We won. Things will be different now. We can't allow one man's stupidity,' she jerked her thumb at the screen of black glass behind her, as her aunt shook her head, her pale green eyes wide in a plea not to speak this way when she could so obviously be heard, 'to overrule everything we've worked so hard for, risked our lives for. So, we'll use his stupidity against him. Don't give up now. Please. But I swear to God, if you tell Anthony what you've just told me...'

Her aunt shook her head.

Silently, Sally mouthed the words, 'I'll help you.' Aloud, she said, 'I don't know what we can do.'

She then turned in her seat and banged on the glass. The Leader gasped and reached for her niece's arm.

'Don't.'

Sally shook her off. 'Why not? You wanted me here, so let's do it my way. What he's doing is illegal. Apart from anything else, there's an eight-year-old boy in the car, remember?' She banged again. 'Hey! What do you think you're doing? Talk to me!'

The glass slid down about an inch. 'Shut up,' came the gruff voice from within.

'I will not shut up. You are to stop this nonsense right now and take the Leader, your employer, to her office and then me and my son back to our house, do you hear?'

The glass slid back up.

'You're wasting your time,' the Leader said loudly. 'It won't do to try and reason with him. Do you think I haven't tried?'

'But what does he want?' Sally repeated desperately, solely for the ears of their kidnapper.

'I told you. He wants me to reverse the result of the vote, naturally. Make it null and void. No doubt he also wants recognition from the WA and particularly from Ward himself, along with a large cut of the ransom money he's demanded on behalf of the WA, for services rendered. I heard him make the call. Ten million is, I believe, the amount being asked for from our people.'

'Well, hard luck,' said Sally petulantly. 'Everything's done. Everything's in motion. It's too late for him to be making such demands. Not that they were ever acceptable. The WA is being dismantled as we speak. They might not like it, but it's a fact. We won the vote. It's written into law. Hell, it was written into law by Codardo himself. They have to concede defeat and move aside.'

'You know as well as I do that they won't go without a fight. If we don't stop it, there will likely be a war.' The Leader glanced across at the small boy, playing with his toy robot, oblivious to the danger they were all in. 'No, it's not worth it.'

'How can you say that, after everything? I won't let you say that. You're not making any sense.'

Sally's aunt smiled sadly at her.

'Even if there's a war, we have to continue to stand firm,' insisted Sally. 'Stand up for what we believe and know is right. You've done an incredible job, and I will not accept defeat, even if you do.'

The Leader simply continued to smile at her in an indulgent way, remaining silent.

Sally suddenly had a thought, a continuation of an idea that had struck her as she'd left her house, and she held up her hand to quieten any response her aunt might be about to make. Turning, she tapped again on the glass, this time all politeness. 'Excuse me,' she called. 'Would you mind if we stopped at my shop for a moment so that I can take my son to the toilet?'

Toby looked up at her and opened his mouth to protest that he didn't want to go to the toilet, but Sally put her finger to her lips to shush him, shaking her head. The child looked confused for a moment, but then went back to his robot without saying a word. For the first time in her life, she was glad that children were taught never to ask questions.

The glass partition slid down an inch again.

'Please,' Sally asked imploringly. 'Ms Lee and I also need the bathroom.'

'Hmph,' grunted the man. 'Yes, actually, that is where we were going. Because it suits me.'

The obvious schoolboy lie was amusing and gave Sally a glimmer of hope. He clearly hadn't thought this through. He didn't have a plan, hadn't known what he was going to do with them or where he was even going to take them. Yes, this was a good sign. Sally and her aunt looked at each other. Sally felt cheered. The Leader had perked up a bit, too, Sally noticed with relief, and the hint of a conspiratorial smile touched her lips.

Chapter Thirty-one

The man, Paolo, who had helped Hurst down the laundry shaft and produced lunch, came sidling into the dining room as they were finishing their meal carrying Hurst's belongings in a neat pile in his arms. He deposited them on a spare chair and placed a small item on the table before Lucas.

'It was as we thought, sir.'

Lucas picked up the little metal button and examined it closely.

'Ah, yes. Was the disablement successful upstairs?'

'Yes, sir.'

'Good. Thank you, Paolo.'

The man inclined his head and said, 'The pod is waiting, sir, so whenever you're ready.'

'Thank you. We'll just be a few minutes.'

Paolo turned and left the room.

Lucas looked at Hurst and held up the button. 'How did you come by this?' he asked.

Hurst put down his fork and wiped his mouth on a napkin. 'It's just a button.' He took a sip of water. 'It came off Ward's shirt collar as he was yelling at everyone this morning. He asked me to pick it up and give it to him before I left his office, but then he seemed to forget about it. I just put it in my pocket and left. It was actually very useful when I needed to undo the screws on the air vent. Why? What are you saying?'

'I'm saying that Mr Ward set you up. He intended you to keep this on your person. There's a tracking device on it. Look.' He slid the button across the table. Hurst picked it up and turned it around, examining it under the glow of the light on the wall beside him. Sure enough…

'Well, I'll be damned.'

'I have to say, Mr Hurst, that you really are far too trusting. After all this time. They always say that the easiest person to deceive is a deceiver. Did it not occur to you…'

'I didn't notice,' Hurst replied, with an air of panic now. 'I was more concerned with getting back to my office, and then with getting the hell out of there.'

'As he knew you would be. They were waiting for you to try and leave the facility. If you hadn't tried to leave when you did, if we hadn't arranged for you to be frightened out and pushed on your way, they would no doubt have confronted you and shot you by now.'

'Christ. You killed Linda?'

'Not personally.'

'For God's sake! Why? She'd done nothing to deserve that. She was innocent in all this.'

'Tell me, what method, other than something just such as that, would have frightened you sufficiently for you to get yourself out and to safety?'

Hurst drew in a breath and shuddered. But poor Linda... This was all supposed to be in the name of peace. But he knew Lucas was right. Seeing her lying there like that was the single thing that had indeed scared the hell out of him and spurred him into action. He looked Lucas straight in the eyes but made no further comment about the girl in his office, whose eyes he had closed...

'So, he knows where I am. Why wasn't I followed, then?'

'You were.'

'But...'

'You are not the only one who can plant devices, Mr Hurst. The person who followed you was dispatched as he followed you through the air conditioning tunnel.'

'What? I... oh God, I did hear...'

'A gunshot, yes. An automatic device set with a camera so that we could target any person who came through that air vent after you. All done from these offices.'

Jesus Christ.

'So, you were watching me come through the bathroom ceiling and along the floor spaces?'

'Of course. How else were we to let Mother know which route you'd taken?'

'Oh my God. But how do I know I can trust you?' Even as he said them, Hurst knew the words sounded ridiculous.

Lucas laughed appreciatively. 'Oh, for goodness' sake. Because otherwise, dear chap, you would already be dead, as I have already detailed. I can assure you that if I wasn't trying to help you, if *we* weren't trying to help you, you would have been left to your bloody fate. In both senses. Besides,' Lucas stood up and neatly tucked his chair back under the tabletop, 'I really don't see that you've got much choice.' He tilted his head, 'Do you? So, let's hear no more about it. It's getting rather tiresome, this lack of gratitude.'

Hurst sighed and also stood up. He supposed it was true. Lucas probably wasn't going to kill him.

'Fine.' He wouldn't apologise. For Linda's sake, he wouldn't apologise. 'So, what happens now?' he asked in a resigned tone.

'Now, we put a delightfully theatrical hairpiece onto your head…'

'What?'

'… And we take you to the Leader's plane so that you can travel to London.'

'London?'

'That's right, London.'

'But…'

'But what? Do you not want to return to your homeland? Would you rather stay here in this god-forsaken hellhole? That tracking device was active all the way to the laundry. If Ward is being vigilant, he'll notice it didn't stop moving in the air conditioning vent. His assassin will not return. They will be on their way here, and although we are ready for them and the place is guarded, there will likely as not be a rather vicious shoot-out commencing at any moment, which has been brought to the door of the people who work here, whether that be for me or for the WA, in the name of saving you. So, I repeat, do you want to stay? Would you perhaps like a gun so that you can defend yourself and help keep these others safe?'

'Well, no, of course I don't want that. I've never fired a gun in my life. Jesus, what the hell is happening today?' Hurst considered the irritated Lucas and relented. 'OK, look, no, I don't want to stay here, either here underground, or on this continent, and I'm sorry if my not recognising that a button was a tracker has brought danger to the people who work here, truly I am. But I didn't ask for any of this anymore than they did. I appreciate the help, and if you're offering me a way to leave, of course I want to go. Where is my wife, though? And my son is at school. I can't leave without them.'

'I'm just waiting on an answer to that very question. Sally does not appear to be at home, where you would expect her to be on a Monday lunchtime. At least, we sent a message to her CD, and she hasn't answered. Its tracking seems to be going round in circles. But I suppose it doesn't matter. We can always stop off quickly at your home and investigate. Perhaps your wife has had to go out for some reason. Did she mention anything to you about having to go out? To the shops, maybe?'

'No. Toby had the morning off to study for a test, and she had to take him to school for eleven thirty. Apart from that, she didn't mention anything.'

'Ah, well, in that case, we're in even more of a hurry,' said Lucas, looking at his watch. 'Because that makes it most unlikely that she wouldn't be at home right now. I wonder what could have happened to her?'

Chapter Thirty-two

They had to give the driver of the car, Frederick, directions to the salon. Both women took this to be a sign in their favour. However, there were added dangers to this turn of events. It was all very well thinking that if he was acting alone, it would be easier for them to overpower him, but the man was nervous, and that made him something of a loose cannon. Sally was armed, but so was he, and he had far more experience with using a gun than she did. Desperation to prove himself might well lead him to act more irrationally than he was doing already, especially if his demands were ignored, which of course they would be. No government had ever paid ransom demands in the past, and they wouldn't start now. At least, not openly. And certainly not to someone like Frederick Lambert.

They drew up outside the salon and the engine was switched off. Sally looked at her aunt. She was worried about her, too. This mission she'd undertaken, to put the world back to what it was two centuries ago, had taken years of planning and of co-ordinating dangerous intelligence missions, and it had clearly taken its toll, as it would on anyone. She imagined that the older woman was now uncertain of everyone she'd been dealing with. She looked exhausted. Sally knew that she herself was probably the only person her aunt could trust without question now, and she needed to keep her strong, keep her motivated, at least until they were sure the plans for the dissolution of the WA had been completed, because the situation was precarious to say the least. There would be plenty of time to give in to exhaustion later.

Perhaps if she, Sally, could somehow find out what was happening, she could take on more of the responsibility and help out a bit more? But first of all, they had to deal with Frederick. She had to do what she could to get them out of this situation first, before she could start thinking of anything else.

To think, a short while ago she'd been so excited about the result of the vote coming in so heavily in their favour, and now that joy had been replaced with a deep worry about the safety of all the people she cared about.

The driver's door opened, and Frederick appeared at the side of the car nearest the building. Toby, sitting nearest that door, unclipped his seat belt and slid away, closer to his mother. Opening the passenger door, Lambert said, 'Give me the keys,' and held out his hand towards Sally. She noticed a sheen of sweat on his palm. Disgusted by it, she fished in her bag, careful not to let him see the gun that lay there, and deposited the keys into his hand, taking care not to touch him. If she ever got them back, she'd make sure to douse them in disinfectant. He balled his fist around the keys, slammed the door shut on them again and locked it.

Using the few seconds it took him to cross the pavement and unlock the door to the salon, Sally hurriedly removed the gun and knife from her bag and stuffed the gun inside the waistband of her jeans, handed the knife to the Leader, who concealed it likewise under her suit, then said to her aunt, 'Follow my lead, OK?' Then she turned to Toby. 'Darling, listen, it's very important that you do exactly as I say and don't speak. Do you understand?' Her son looked at her for a moment and nodded his head, a flicker of fear underneath his obvious confusion. 'Good boy,' she smiled at him. 'Don't worry, everything will be all right.'

The car door opened once more. 'One at a time,' Frederick stated gruffly. He pointed at Sally. 'You first.'

Squeezing her son's hand encouragingly, she stepped from the car and calmly followed the man to the door of the salon.

'Give me your bag,' he demanded.

Without a word, Sally handed her bag and the two jackets over and stepped into the shop. Thank God it was Monday, and they were closed today. It was a gift. She waited just inside the door, thinking hard as she waited first for Toby, and then for her aunt to be led into the shop. Toby looked as if he was about to cry.

'He needs the bathroom,' she said, hoping Frederick would allow her to go with him.

The man jerked his head in a sort of nod and Sally grabbed her son's hand and led him, still clutching his robot, to the staff room at the back. Frederick followed them, pushing the Leader ahead of him.

The salon felt strange when it was empty. There was an aroma of hair products in the air and an echo as they walked across the tiled floor. Everything was clean and set up for the following day's appointments. They had a full diary, and Sally wondered momentarily whether she and her staff would be able to work as usual, or whether this man would render that impossible. She noticed the vase of flowers on the back windowsill needed some more water and made a mental note to see to it in the morning. She had to think as if things would be quickly resolved. It was the only way. Even if that resolution was positive enough to mean she'd be leaving to go back to the UK, and such trivialities as the flowers in the salon would be rendered meaningless, she couldn't allow herself to think about that yet. She had to stay focused on the here and now.

The staff room wasn't huge, and doubled as a stock room, with shelves full of hair colours and various shampoos, conditioners and treatments taking up most of the wall on the left, but there were chairs at least, and tea and coffee supplies in a little cupboard, with a fridge for milk and cold drinks. The toilet was at the back and Sally led her son towards it.

'He can go on his own, surely?' barked Lambert.

'Frederick,' Sally said pleasantly, stopping to turn and look at him, her hand on her hip and a look of mild reprimand on her face. 'May I call you Frederick, Mr Lambert?' He grunted what could equally have been consent or refusal. 'Have you got children?'

'What business is that of yours?'

'Well, just that if you have, then you'll surely understand that the circumstance of being taken from his home and put into a strange car by a man he's never met before and who is speaking aggressively to his mother is a very frightening experience for an eight-year-old child, and he needs the security of having his mother by his side. Even to go to the toilet.'

He grunted again. 'Get on with it, then, but be quick.'

'He will take as long as he takes,' she snapped, taking the robot from her son, passing it to her aunt and closing the door firmly behind herself and Toby, though not before ensuring the two women had made eye-contact.

Hardly daring to believe her luck, Sally whispered to Toby to ask him if he did in fact need the toilet. He shrugged. 'OK, well you try to go,' she whispered to him kindly. 'Mummy just has to do something, so I'm not watching you.' She racked her brains as her son did as he was told. There must be something she could do.

What was available to her in here? She looked inside the cupboard under the sink. Toilet cleaner, toilet paper, liquid hand wash and, yes, thank God, the stubby end of a long-ago abandoned lipstick. She grabbed it gratefully and turned to look at Toby. He had finished and had also turned to her to ask if it was OK for him to flush the toilet. How sensible her son was.

'Yes, darling,' she whispered. 'But just one second. I have to open the window a little bit, and I don't want that man to hear us, so you flush the toilet as I open it, OK? And we don't talk about this to the man.'

Toby nodded and waited for his cue. Sally uncapped the lipstick and nodded. Toby flushed the toilet, Sally indicated for him to wash his hands, and then she opened the window just enough that she could reach her arm out. She drew a big letter "L" on the wall outside, sent up a silent prayer, and hastily closed the window. 'OK,' she said, putting the lipstick into her pocket. 'Let's go.'

Chapter Thirty-three

As Hurst stepped from the covered launch pad into Lucas' pod, he felt like an absolute fool. They had indeed placed a wig onto his head – a wig of thick brown curls, that made him feel as effeminate as Lucas looked. Not to mention that it was disgustingly hot and sweaty and smelt of the ancient cheap nylon that it was. What was the point of this pantomime? To test his resolve? To satisfy some theatrical urge in Lucas?

'Why must I wear this stupid thing?' he grumbled.

Lucas let out a sharp breath. 'Do you know who it was who discovered your misdemeanours and shopped you to Ward?'

Hurst was thrown. 'Of course not. Why, do you?'

Lucas rolled his eyes. 'Yes, of course. Who in your group of colleagues has hair like this?' He pointed to the offending prop sitting on Hurst's head.

'Oh! It was Charley? Charley Greenway?'

'It was.'

'But Charley! Surely not? How do you know?'

'The girl in the office who goes by the name of Jane. She's one of ours. She was suspicious when he went back into the room after this morning's nine o'clock meeting and started closing all the blinds. Thought something funny was going on. Wouldn't have been difficult to deduce, by the sound of it, because apparently, he made far too much of the fact that she was to remain silent upon the matter. They always have to remain silent on every matter, so why the need to reiterate it this time? Naturally, she contacted Paolo about it and sent him a recording of their conversation.'

'But he's still there at the facility, working, isn't he? Greenway? How can I get away with this?' He waved his hand at his head. 'There aren't two of him. If anyone sees me, they'll know it's a ruse.'

Lucas gave Hurst a withering look and urged him into the pod. 'You'll need to take the controls, if you would,' was all he said in answer.

But Hurst persisted. 'If this is true, then why wasn't I challenged straight away?'

'I imagine because he had to speak to Ward first, and by that time the Leader's speech had begun. It's probably what saved you. There was suddenly too much else going on. The button was probably Greenway's idea. He knew you'd try to run, and Ward doesn't have the intelligence to come up with a trap like that himself. I'm surprised he managed to pull off the part he did have to play.'

'But why ask me to decode the security around the Leader's speech if they suspected I wouldn't do it? It doesn't make any sense.'

'No, I agree. Perhaps they were just trying to isolate you while they thought about what to do with you? I can't think of another reason.'

'Jesus.'

'Hm, quite.'

The two men sat down in the confined cockpit area of the pod. There was no time to ask any more questions, even if Hurst had been able to formulate the jumble of thoughts and resentments swirling around in his head into such, because as they were about to leave, the man Paolo came rushing up to Lucas, waving his arms, stop, and gave him the news in an urgent gabble that a message had come in to say that the Leader had been taken hostage on her way from her airstrip into town. She'd managed to send a hurried message to the office while the violence was unfolding outside the car to say that her chief aide and the kidnapper's colleague, one of her security team, had been thrown from the car and shot at, possibly dead. The office, already watching the location of the car, said that it had then stopped off at Hurst's home, and a check of Sally's CD showed that he must also have taken Hurst's wife and son. The car was being driven by a man called Frederick Lambert, who worked in the Leader's office and who was one of her usual drivers when she was in this part of the world, said Paolo. A security guard, if you could believe the irony.

The question as to why he was currently driving the Leader around the city was both obvious and answered before either of them could open their mouths to ask, but quite why he'd taken Sally and Toby was anyone's guess.

'Lucas,' Paolo continued, dispensing with his usual "Sir" in his harried state. 'Your office in London has received a ransom demand for ten million dollars. However, the WA has denied making any such demand,' said Paolo.

'So little?'

'Apparently so.'

'He's working alone, then,' Lucas said, happily matter-of-fact, as they fastened their seat belts and prepared to leave. 'Too unsure of himself to request anymore than that. How very fortuitous. Unusual though, for one of our lot to turn their back on us and move over to the dark side. And strange about Sally and the boy, too. Yes, well... Thank you, Paolo. Keep me informed.'

Paolo inclined his head, formality resumed, and stepped back as Lucas closed the pod door with a press of a button and a small smile. Lucas then muttered to himself, repeating what they already knew and ticking off the points on his fingers as he made them. 'Right then, Lambert's using his own company car, driving around in open view, and the WA deny any association with him. Don't worry, the car is still being traced, so they'll be easy enough to find.'

'How can you be so calm? This Lambert person has got my son, for God's sake. The kid's only eight. He's clearly unstable. Lambert, I mean,' he added unnecessarily. 'He could do anything. And if we can trace him, so can the other lot. In making that ransom demand, he's alerted the WA – and specifically Ward – to exactly where the Leader is and, also, by association, my son! We need to get to Lambert before they do.'

Lucas put up a hand to stop Hurst from talking. 'Yes, I know. Hang on a moment, if you please.' His attention had been drawn to a flashing green light on the control panel of the pod. He popped an earpiece into his left ear and pressed the button. 'Oh… Yes.' He frowned as he listened. 'Well, that makes things more complicated,' he said as he removed the earpiece.

'What? What's happened?'

'Our evacuation of you, turned rescue mission of the Leader and your family, just became more urgent. Robert Ward has gone missing, and so has his pod. I imagine, as you suggested, he's on Lambert's tail. Let's go.'

Hurst fired up the engine and the pod took off almost noiselessly from the launch pad. They shot off into the early afternoon heat. Ordinarily, Hurst would have loved this rare chance, not only to ride in a pod, but to actually fly one. He couldn't afford such luxuries himself, of course, and had to make do with a car, a boringly old-fashioned land vehicle, and had only ridden this way a few times. It should have been thrilling.

From up here, the town below looked almost normal. Were it not for the heavily guarded fortifications around the perimeter it could have been any old town at any point in history, with its parks and shopping centres, and rows of houses slumbering contentedly in their gardens against the heat of the day.

But it wasn't any point in history. It was now, and now was a dangerous time, especially at the moment, for himself and his wife and child. And of course, the Leader. The view from the air highlighted how true it was that the only problem with the world was people. People ruined everything. But they needed to find that car and save his son, and therefore there was no time for taking in the view or philosophising, even for a moment.

'Do you really think he'll go after them?' Hurst tried to keep his voice level as he grasped at straws. 'Ward's disappearance doesn't necessarily affect our tracking down of the lunatic who's got my kid. Ward's likely to go into hiding, surely? He's not going to want to do anything stupid personally. He's not really likely to go after the Leader himself, is he? He's got people to do that for him, surely.'

'Dear boy, don't be so naïve. You betrayed him. Do you imagine he's going to allow you to get away with that? I imagine he thinks you're already dead, courtesy of Greenway, because so far nobody's come looking for you as a result of that button you were carrying – most lax of them, really, not to be paying closer attention to it – but the Leader is being dished up to him on a plate, with the wife and child of the man who betrayed him as a nice little added extra. A side dish, if you will.'

Anthony glowered at him. 'Stop being so flippant.'

Lucas coughed in apology and tried to move smoothly on. 'We have to hope he doesn't know about that yet, about Sally and Toby being with the Leader. But yes, as you rightly pointed out, if we can trace that car, then so can he. It's not going to matter to him whether he takes the Leader, your wife, your son, or all three of them into custody. Or indeed me. He wants to make his point, show the world he's in control. So yes, he is very likely making a charge towards the town right now in a spitting rage.' His head gave a small involuntary twitch. 'Hm. We need to make haste. I suggest that first we go to your house and see if we can find any clues as to where Lambert's taken them, while we wait for an update from Paolo on the location of the car.'

Hurst was about to speak, but Lucas pressed the little green button, which had started flashing again.

'And here it is. It appears the car has come to a stop at your wife's salon. Also, my team have detected a sign from her.'

'A sign? What are you talking about?'

'A big pink letter "L" has been drawn onto the wall outside a window at the rear of the shop, alerting us to her presence,' Lucas chuckled. 'Takes a lot to faze your wife, I will say. Were I ever to be inclined to take a wife, I rather think I should choose one such as she.'

'Christ Almighty,' said Hurst. 'Take her. I imagine even you would love her more than I do right now. I never want to clap eyes on her again after this.'

The pod swerved in mid-air and Hurst hurtled along in the direction of the town centre. He sat there unable to think straight, gripping the controls and heading for the salon. How did Lucas imagine nobody would identify this pod as belonging to the Leader's office, and shoot the damn thing down? The public might not think anything of it, looming in the sky above them, trained as they were not to notice or comment on anything, but the WA would certainly know whose it was and would be after them like a shot.

'To answer your earlier question in a more rational fashion, we have to hope,' said Lucas, 'that Ward has called off any agents he may have instructed to deal with Lambert, and that he really is heading into town himself. He, of course, wants the Leader more than he wants the rest of us, so we will have moved down his hit list, so to speak. But he intends catching up with us eventually. All of us. The only difference is that his agents would shoot first and ask questions later, whereas Ward needs the Leader alive. At least for the moment.'

'How comforting. She lives until he gets what he wants, and we die immediately, with me being first in line once he discovers – if he hasn't already discovered – that I escaped Greenway's assassination attempt. Oh yes, I can't wait to see him again. What a happy little reunion that'll be. I need to rescue my son,' he growled. 'I'll never forgive Sally for this.'

Lucas smiled reassuringly. 'I wouldn't worry if I were you. I'm certain he doesn't intend killing anyone, let alone a child. He wants a public U-turn on the vote, and he can't get that if the Leader's dead and he's in prison. No, no, it'll be OK. Besides, the Leader and Sally are both more than capable of looking after themselves. Who knows, Lambert may even be dead by now. We just have to get to them before Ward. Avoid all the nastiness. Taking her and making threats is just going to cause the public to get jittery, and we desperately need the rest of this day to go as smoothly as possible. It'll set the scene for the tone of the transition, don't you see? Smooth people's nerves.' He paused and Hurst gave a non-committal grunt. 'Damn nuisance, all this lone ranger crap, don't you think?' he added conversationally, as if they were having nothing more than a friendly chat over coffee.

'I thought surveillance was supposed to stop. How come all this tracking hasn't stopped? Didn't the Leader win the vote?'

'Yes, of course, but it takes time. We start at the top and work our way down to car tracking when we can get to it. A couple of weeks will probably do it. However, right now, that car is sitting there outside the salon like a big black signpost.' He nodded his dark head. 'I'll be glad when we no longer have to think about these things.'

'You and me both. You're not exactly making me feel any better, you know, Lucas. And you didn't say that he doesn't want *me* dead enough to try again with another hitman.'

'No, I didn't, did I? He undoubtedly does want you dead, yes. But look, his fear of prison still holds, and employing the services of a hitman, as you put it, is just as bad as pulling the trigger himself. And anyway, Sally has no doubt had plans in place for months to deal with a situation such as this.'

'Has she?'

'Very probably. You continue to underestimate her.'

'Don't tell me what I think about my wife.'

Lucas smiled again. Hurst wished he'd stop doing that. 'No, you've actually made that very clear yourself, but forgive me,' Lucas conceded. 'I am here to protect your life and deliver you safely back to your family. Your safety is everyone's priority. As for dealing with the situation, I imagine that Sally and the Leader, and also your son, are probably all safely tucked up in Janine's house by now. I'll send a message to tell them about Ward and to say stay put.'

'Who the hell is Janine?'

Hurst knew that Lucas was right about his wife, and he didn't like it. There was so much he still didn't know about Sally, so much he'd never known. It didn't sit well with him that other people – people who were strangers to him – knew her better than he did. After all these years. She had a whole other life, a life of subterfuge. Of espionage. The life of a spy.

He'd more or less come to terms with the bigger picture, but it was the details of it that vexed him the most; the fact that whenever there was a vital development, he was always the last to know about it. And even when he did find anything out, it was only ever snippets that he needed to be told for his own safety, or because keeping him in the dark was no longer an option. In his opinion, the best thing Sally could have done to ensure his safety was to have told him everything, from the start, and by missing out no details. When all this was over, things were going to change. He would leave. He'd had enough. He'd take his son and leave. And that would be an end to it. A quiet life away from everyone except his son. Away from other people's egos and manias and dramas.

He gripped the controls so tightly his knuckles turned white, and he chewed on the inside of his mouth in order to stop himself vocalising anymore of his thoughts that could lead to confirmation of his apparent status of expendable pawn in Sally's game.

'Janine is my mother,' Lucas said.

Hurst was jolted away from his thoughts and back to the conversation. 'What? Janine is the tea lady? Huh. I never knew her name.'

'That doesn't surprise me. Don't berate yourself for the lapse.'

'I wasn't.'

Lucas chuckled. 'Fair enough. She's good at fading into the background and making herself invisible, though, wouldn't you say? She's turned avoiding scrutiny and questions and not volunteering information into an art form.'

'Yes, well, it's become clear to me how little I know about more than one person today. Your mother is the least of it.'

Chapter Thirty-four

Sally and Toby emerged from the bathroom to discover the Leader standing over the prone form of the man, Frederick, and holding Toby's toy robot, club-like in a firm grip.

'Christ, what the hell have you done?' Sally's voice was a strained squeak.

At the small boy's widening eyes, the Leader announced, 'What I thought you intended me to do, of course. Don't worry, darling,' she said to Toby. 'He's just having a little sleep.' She met her niece's eye and held a set of car keys aloft. 'A bit old-school, but quite effective, I thought.'

Sally stood there dumbfounded. It hadn't been what she'd intended at all. She'd sent a message to Lucas herself. That's what she'd intended her aunt to understand.

'I meant... I thought you'd... I've sent... oh, Aunt, really!'

'Well, I mean, come on,' continued her aunt. 'You didn't seriously think I'd given up, did you? After all these years? How would you have been able to execute your plan to call for help which, from what you've just gabbled, I'm sure you did magnificently, unless he'd,' she pointed towards the body on the floor, 'believed that I'd lost my nerve? To paraphrase your words back at you, really, Sally! Where is your faith? I persuaded him to take you with me for this very reason – to help me escape. It would have been more difficult alone. Everything I've worked so hard for blown to pieces by the pathetic amateur efforts to intimidate me by a creature such as that? Someone so daft as to have no plan and then to actually turn his back on me while I'm holding a big hunk of metal? Honestly!' She shook her head in disbelief. 'Now,' the Leader rinsed the robot under the tap, wiped it dry on a paper towel, and handed it back to Toby, ruffling his hair and winking at him, which made him giggle. 'We need to get out of here.'

'And do what, exactly? Go where?' Sally's relief was enormous, even within the confusion of the situation. And her aunt was right. She shouldn't have doubted her resolve and was daft to have done so and not seen through her aunt's plan, even if right now her own resolve was taking a bit of a bashing and she was scared to death of what Anthony would say if he ever found out about this little development. She had to hope Toby didn't understand, or would keep quiet about it if he did, that's all.

'I'd suggest that first of all, we deposit our friend here in the driver's seat of the car, we leave the driver's door open, and we drop these keys down the nearest drain. After that, we make a bloody quick dash for it and hope to God Janine's home.'

'Who the hell is Janine?'

'No time to explain. Help me up with him. He's heavy.'

Sally let out a short breath and pinched her lips together but didn't argue. Together, the two women took hold of the man, Frederick, one under each arm, and hoisted and yanked him up into as much of an upright position as they could. Both of them being quite short, the man's feet dragged along behind him like a drunk as they staggered through the shop.

'Is he armed?'

'Not anymore, I hope. I found a small pistol in his pocket, standard issue.'

Sally nodded. 'Right. Are you sure he's not dead?' she asked, with more than a mild look of concern on her face.

'No.'

'No, he's not dead, or no you're not sure?'

The Leader shrugged lopsidedly under Lambert's weight. 'I've never done that before and I'm not sure how much force it takes to kill someone as opposed to knocking them out. Can't say I've ever tried checking anyone for a pulse.'

'Oh, that's just great. Marvellous.'

'Regardless, we'd better get a move on. If he's dead, we can deal with it later.'

'Jesus Christ, Aunt.'

'Yeah, well, what can you do?'

On reaching the front door of the salon, the Leader said, 'Toby, open the door for me please, darling,' then poked her head out, grateful for the drawn blinds, and announced that the coast was clear.

'Wait,' gasped Sally, struggling for breath from the exertion of propping up the dead weight of the man. 'Isn't it better to put him in the boot and drive the car away from here a bit, so that when he's found it's nowhere near the salon and therefore less incriminating? That way, at least at first, anyone watching the car will think he's still driving it.'

Her aunt considered this for a moment, then nodded assent. 'Yes, you're quite right. OK, quick.' She pressed the unlock button on the keys. 'Let's get him in. Stay there,' she told Toby. Obediently, Toby stayed where he was, watching in fascination from the open door as his mother and this strange woman he'd never met but who seemed to know all about him dragged the unconscious man to the car and heaved him into the boot.

It turned out to be a tricky task. Lambert was, by necessity, big and burly and realising after a couple of unsuccessful attempts that it would be too difficult for them to lift him, even though there were two of them, they opted for a different approach and tipped his torso into the cramped space, and then hoisted his legs up and in after him. They both stood back, hands on hips, gasping for breath.

'We'd make useless gangsters,' commented Sally.

'Uh-ha,' wheezed her aunt.

Toby had stood in the doorway of the salon all the while, watching them curiously, but had stayed quiet. A final push and shove of the big man's frame allowed them to close the boot with a bit of a shove. Sally told her aunt to lock it, before going back for her son, picking up a couple of towels, and locking the door of the salon.

She rushed the boy over to the car, helped him on with his seat belt in the back and then joined her aunt in the front, where they lowered the dividing screen so the child could see them, and shot off down the road in a cloud of dust. Toby remained silent.

'What's the best thing to do?' the Leader wondered aloud. 'We can't take the car all the way to Janine's place, or it'll make it too easy for them to track us. Equally, we can't just get out and walk.'

Sally thought about the dilemma for a moment before she spoke.

'Maybe we can.'

'How?'

'How far is this Janine's place?'

'On foot, I suppose ten minutes.'

'Well,' said Sally. 'If you tell me the address then we can split up. If the WA are looking for us, they'll assume we're all together.'

Her aunt looked sceptical. 'You can't imagine they're that stupid?'

'Right now, I don't see that we've got much choice, do you? Also, we haven't got much time. At the very least, they'll be looking for Frederick. Everyone will.'

With a sigh, the Leader nodded. 'Right. OK, the address you need to head for is one-two-two, Twenty-fourth Street.'

'The number of the martyr,' Sally said darkly.

'What?'

'Twenty-four. The number of the martyr.'

'Oh, for heaven's sake, you don't believe in all that mumbo jumbo, surely?'

Sally, who did believe in these things, smiled but said nothing other than, 'Come on, Aunt, we need to hurry.'

Her aunt nodded again and swung the car around into a narrow lane behind a row of shops.

'We'll leave the car here. You know where you're going?' she asked quickly, as they got out of the car and Sally handed her a towel.

'Fingerprints,' she explained, at her aunt's questioning expression. 'He didn't bash himself over the head and climb into the locked boot, did he?'

'Right. Good thinking. But we can't wipe them all. He abducted us, so our prints would naturally be all over the car.'

'But not in the front. Not on the boot.'

'Yes, you're right.'

'You know where you're going?' the Leader repeated, as they finished the task of cleaning the relevant bits of the car.

'Yes. I'll take Toby into the toy shop and out the other entrance on the main road. Then it's just a matter of turning left to the end of the street, crossing over and walking a minute or so to the right, and it's there on the left, yes?' The Leader nodded. 'What about you, Aunt? What will you do?'

'I'll continue on down this lane and cross over into the park. I'll skirt along the right-hand edge between the trees, then I can approach the house from the other end of the street. If there's anyone around, I can use the back lane.'

'Right, let's go. Be careful, Aunt. Give me the towel.' Sally stuffed both towels into her bag.

'You, too. If you get to the house before me, don't hang around waiting because as I said, I might use the back door. Knock three times, pause, then knock twice. Janine will come.'

Sally nodded and the two women parted company.

Chapter Thirty-five

Cerys Lee strode down the lane and didn't break pace as she rummaged in her bag for the thin blue scarf which was nestled at the bottom. She pulled it out and wrapped it around her hair. Not much of a disguise but, at the moment, it was the best she could do. If anyone saw her, it meant they wouldn't immediately recognise her – or at least, she hoped they wouldn't. Tying it securely under her chin, she then dashed across the road at the end of the lane and turned right into the park where, as she'd said to Sally, if she stayed as much as possible under the cover of the trees at the park's boundary, it would hopefully provide her with a safe and quick route to the far end of Twenty-fourth Street. As she walked, she sent a message to alert Janine to the fact that they were on their way.

Mercifully, there weren't any people around in the park at this time of day, because to get to the upper end would take a minimum of ten minutes. Everyone was at work, which was good. Ordinarily, not that there was such a thing as ordinary anymore, a walk in the park would have been a thing of pleasure. It was all manmade, of course. Well, there was hardly anything left on the planet that wasn't, these days, but yes, all the greenery had been brought in and fashioned into a big spacious park for the oh-so-grateful and happy residents to pretend to enjoy on their days off. False, is what it was, but even so, it would have been lovely to be in a position to spend some time taking in the sight of the peaceful little ducks in the pond or listening to the chirping of the birds in the trees, while walking along the ornate stone pathways between the, albeit yellowing at this time of year, grass.

But under the current circumstances none of those detours were possible and the emptiness that surrounded her was not in any way relaxing. It was in fact both good and bad for her. Good, because there shouldn't be anyone around to see her but bad, of course, because her presence was so unusual. All it took was one person looking out of one window to decide to report the presence of a walker in the middle of the afternoon darting along from tree to tree, and the WA would be onto her in a flash. If indeed they weren't already. Relaxing it was not.

She speeded up almost into a run as she saw the top of the road she was heading for come into view and, with her shoes now covered in dust from the dry earth, she darted out from between the trees at the edge of the park and onto the pavement. There was no one around. Right, over the road, she ordered herself, and don't look round. Just go. Almost there… try not to run… easy, now…

Chapter Thirty-six

Sally hurried Toby across the bit of waste ground that doubled as an ill-kept customer car park between the lane where they'd parked the car and the very useful back entrance to the big toy shop and ushered him through the door.

'Are you going to buy me a new toy, Mummy?'

'Not today, Toby, I'm sorry. Tell you what, at the weekend we'll come back, and you can have something then for being such a good boy. Maybe even that toy pod you've been looking at so much.'

The child's eyed widened in delight, and he grinned and hugged her arm as they walked. 'Really? Wow! Thank you, Mummy.'

Christ, thought Sally, please let us be in a position to come back at the weekend. I'd buy him ten toy pods for that chance.

'That's all right, but shush, now, OK?' she quietened him, and he nodded. 'We really shouldn't be here.'

'Yes, Mummy, I know.'

'Good boy. Come on, then.'

She tried not to walk too fast through the shop so as not to draw attention to them. It was highly unusual for a child to be out of school and wandering around a toy shop, and even if it shouldn't have been the business of shop workers, there were those who would make it their business. But there was nothing to be done about it except keep walking and try to look as natural as possible.

Their route through the shop needn't have taken more than a minute or so, but Sally was watchful of the staff and steered her son around a wavy path like a couple of disorientated bees, in order to avoid having to speak to anyone. Getting stopped and questioned, even if it was in such an innocent way as asking if she needed any help to choose a toy, would draw unnecessary attention. Even if the staff in the shop were unconcerned, Toby should have been at school by now after his morning study break and no doubt the relevant authorities had already been alerted to his absence from the mandatory test, and an alert would have been put out for people such as shop workers to look out for him. And so, Sally was very careful to duck and dodge her way around the shelves and displays and make slower than desired progress towards the front doors.

Eventually, they reached the front entrance, and after waiting a few extra moments behind a stack of soft toys in the shape of zebras, giraffes, elephants, and tigers – their inspiration all long ago extinct, of course, just as much so as the dinosaurs, which were also still popular toys – they slipped out onto the busy street at the front of the shop, timing it as someone else was coming in so the door opening gave the staff something else to focus on. Hurdle number one had been cleared. Sally now took a firmer hold of Toby's hand and, with a casual glance up and down the road, said again, 'Come on', and they scooted down the street towards the address her aunt had given her.

Her training before being sent on this mission had been intense, and not only because she'd had to keep it secret from her husband, although that had been hard enough. In one part of the training, she'd undergone hours of instruction on how to spot whether she was being followed and how to follow others without detection. She'd become proficient in using her peripheral vision and in noticing and remembering details. At the time, she'd wondered whether it had been necessary to spend such a long time over this one point, going as they had over and over the same thing. But now she was grateful that the methods had been drummed into her so hard, because now it was second nature, and she needed it to be. She noticed everything, and it appeared that today no one was following them. She certainly hoped that was right and that her instincts and training techniques had not let her down.

Nevertheless, she tried to formulate an excuse as to why she was marching her son at speed through the middle of town when he should have been at school. Of course, it all depended on who stopped her. If it was her own people, that was all well and good – also unlikely, because her own people didn't follow and interrogate the citizens. If, on the other hand, it was the WA, then the obvious solution was the dentist. She would make up a story about Toby complaining of a toothache and she thought she could take him to the dentist on her way to do a bit of shopping on her day off. If they mentioned the fact that she had been located in the moving vehicle belonging to Frederick Lambert, she'd say he'd released her and her son out of the goodness of his heart and she didn't know what had happened to him or to the Leader since. Ludicrous, but it was all she had.

When she simplified all this to give her son the heads up so that no look of puzzlement gave them away, he looked at her in a strange way and said, 'But Mummy, why don't we just tell the truth? That man came to the house and took us away in the car. The WA will be angry with him and not with us because he works for the Leader, and they didn't tell him to take us. It's not your fault I didn't do the test, it's his.'

'Yes, Toby, you're absolutely right,' she said, smiling at him. 'You're very clever.' Sometimes, she did overthink things rather.

But now she needed to concentrate. It was all very well explaining her son's absence from school in Toby's simple and easy way, but as they'd obviously escaped the clutches of the madman Lambert, the question would then become why were they walking in this direction and not in the direction of the school? She quickly explained this scenario to Toby as they hurried along the road. He nodded his head in solemn agreement, and she went back to her observations. She needed to pay attention because they weren't out of the woods yet.

They turned into Twenty-fourth Street and Sally slowed her pace slightly to look at the numbers on the doors of the houses. It was a long street with wide pavements, and mature trees stood like dusty sentinels at unnaturally precise intervals up its length. On the house closest to her was the number one-three-five. Good, that meant they were at least at the correct end of the road. She realised she'd been holding her breath and let it out in a nervous puff. She wondered how her aunt was getting on and hoped she wouldn't be spotted coming down the long length of the road from the other direction. She hoped she was all right, because she couldn't see her. Sally quickened her pace again a bit, more nervous by the moment. It all seemed a bit too easy for her liking.

Much like the houses in her own street, the buildings here were spaced widely apart and sat in large gardens. Everything was neat and tidy, as you'd expect. Neglect of property was not tolerated in this town or anywhere else, but especially in this town. The outward pretence of gratitude and delight at being here had to be maintained at all times. Fines were issued against anyone who didn't maintain their property, keep the paintwork fresh and the garden neat, regardless of whether or not they could afford the expense or even had the time to spend on the task, and while it was a good thing to look after your house, the way these rules were enforced was yet another reminder of the controlling nature of the system they were up against. Every aspect of life was interfered with.

Sally sniffed in distaste and quickly darted across the road to the correct house. One last furtive glance up and down the street, and she hurried up the path, pushing Toby in front of her, and knocked in the way her aunt had told her.

The door was opened instantly by a small woman with curly grey hair and a sharp look in her eyes. Upon seeing Sally and her son standing on the doorstep, as she had no doubt known they would be, she opened the door wider to grant them access.

'Come through,' she invited, and led the way towards the back of the house without a backward glance, leaving Sally to close the door herself. Whether this was down to trust or bad manners, Sally couldn't tell. Either way, Sally wasn't sure she liked it. 'Ms Lee told me you were on your way.'

Sally and Toby exchanged a look and followed.

The hallway of the house was typical of that of many other houses owned by old ladies everywhere. It played host to a small table inside the front door, on which stood a potted plant in a blue and white china saucer, and there was a long, woven rug that ran from the front door almost to the staircase. Sally couldn't help thinking that such an item would be downright dangerous in her own house, what with an eight-year-old boy charging about all over the place. Well, an eight-year-old boy playing. Toby didn't charge.

The walls were painted a sugary pale pink and on them hung clusters of elaborately framed family photographs, notably all of an older generation and none of present-day living people, and several watercolour paintings executed by an obviously amateur brush of the London skyline, whose colours clashed frightfully with that of the walls. Sally thought of her own house with its tastefully modern decoration and resisted the urge to wince. Three sturdy, white-painted wooden doors, one on the right before the stairs, and two on the left, presumably led into what must be a lounge and a dining room, and who knew what else, but they were all firmly closed to prying eyes.

The old lady opened a fourth door at the far end of the hallway and, smiling now, ushered them through the kitchen and on into a large bright conservatory, which had on its floor a thick-piled white carpet – something which must have cost a fortune and been very difficult to get hold of, since carpet had been deemed horribly old-fashioned and unhygienic by most people for at least a hundred and fifty years – from edge to edge, and large glass floor-to-ceiling windows around its three outer sides, each one individually flanked by long silver velvet curtains, including the door in the middle that led into the garden. She settled them onto a plush pink sofa, one of two, with a coffee table between. The effect was like being enclosed in a miniature theatre designed by a six-year-old girl. Either this woman was colour-blind, or she had no sense of style whatsoever.

Apparently misunderstanding the look on Sally's face as her sense of vision was assaulted, the older woman told her, 'Don't worry, we can see out, but no one can see in. Very useful.' She smiled again as if she didn't have a care in the world. 'Now then, as you will have guessed, I'm Janine. It's very good to meet you after all these years. I've heard a lot about you.'

'Have you? I'd heard absolutely nothing about you until about twenty minutes ago,' Sally said.

Janine smiled more broadly, showing wonky teeth. 'Well, that's the way it should be. It's better if we don't know the identities or whereabouts of too many of our agents.' Her manner was business-like. 'You'll be pleased to know that your husband has been brought safely out of the facility and that he's now in the company of my son. That's all the information I've got for the moment.'

'Oh, thank God, I was so worried about him.'

'Were you?'

'Yes, of course. Why wouldn't I be?'

'Oh, no reason. Lucas said he seems a bit angry with you, that's all. Spitting hellfire, was the phrase he used in his last communication. Maybe you'd like to talk about it? Sometimes this work can be extremely taxing, as you well know and don't need me to tell you, and warring couples can be something of a security risk.'

'Oh, well, excuse the hell out of me! Anthony being angry with me is none of Lucas' goddamn business and, forgive me, but it's none of yours, either. And for your information, even if he is angry, it doesn't mean I wasn't worried about him. I didn't come here for marriage counselling, Janine. Let's be clear on that. I've got a job to do, which I'm doing and doing well. As is Anthony. I'm grateful that you've given us this refuge, but apart from that and our mutual concern for what's happening in the world, we've got no connection. Our private life is none of your concern.'

'OK, fair enough. Forgive my presumption. Let's not get off on the wrong foot, eh?' Sally raised her eyebrows – really? 'In any case, I'm happy to have been able to put your mind at ease over Anthony's welfare. I'm pretty sure nobody followed you here either, you'll be pleased to know.'

'I know. I haven't just walked in off the street as a random houseguest, I've been trained for this.'

'OK, Sally.' Janine shook her head and changed tack. 'The streets are very quiet as usual, but there's an air of waiting out there, of everyone hiding away but peeping out of windows in expectation, wouldn't you say?'

'I suppose so. I hadn't really thought about it.'

Janine considered her. 'Can I get you anything? A cup of tea, maybe? Juice for your boy? A biscuit?'

'Where's my aunt?' she asked, both nervous and angry now, and ignoring the offer of refreshment for the moment, even though Toby had looked up hopefully at the word "biscuit".

There was a second knock on the door, but this time the sound came from the back of the house.

'Right there, with a favourable wind.' The old lady's crooked teeth bared at her in a smile once more, she said, 'I'll put the kettle on.' She hummed happily to herself as she left the room, presumably to admit entrance to the Leader on her way to the kettle, and utterly unconcerned at Sally's rebuke.

Sally got up from the hideous pink sofa and paced anxiously around the expanse of the conservatory, scowling, and not entirely convinced of the safety of the windows or of anything else, anymore. Who the hell was that interfering old bag, Janine, and where did she get off speaking to her in that way? She peered out of the glass at the garden beyond, but all did in fact seem empty, calm and normal. She wondered what the large metal structure was that stood against the outside of the conservatory doors like a big metal picture frame, but there was no time to look further or be nosy as, a couple of minutes later, her aunt entered the room. Sally breathed a sigh of relief and rushed across to hug her.

Chapter Thirty-seven

Howard Dyer opened his eyes. It took him a few moments to focus on his surroundings and a few more after that to become aware of the throbbing pain in his shoulder. With some difficulty he pulled himself into a sitting position and winced. His eyes swam with the pain of the movement. Glancing at the source, he wasn't surprised to see his sleeve saturated with blood and a puddle of it where he'd been lying. Frederick Lambert's image slithered back into his mind, and he cursed. Shit, the bastard had taken Cerys.

He didn't think the wound to his shoulder was deep, but the pain was fierce. He needed to get it treated. Obviously.

For now, though, it would have to be an exercise in mind over matter, because that clearly wasn't going to happen any time soon. He shrugged himself out of his jacket and, holding it steady between his knees, ripped out the lining with his good hand, bound it tightly around the injured shoulder and then, with some difficulty, put the ruined jacket back on. Best not to leave anymore trace of his presence than necessary.

He looked around, wondering what had become of his companion, and noticed a trousered leg sticking out from the scrub at the bottom of the ditch they'd been thrown into, some twenty feet or so to his left. The irony of this, given his conversation with Cerys before they'd left London, was not lost on him.

He began to crawl towards the other man, not trusting his feet to hold his weight steady quite yet and not wishing to be seen, either. He wasn't sure whether there had been any buildings in the vicinity when the man Frederick had begun his violent assault, but assumed not, otherwise his choice would have been madness. Nevertheless, it was with deep caution that he slowly raised his head to chance a quick glance over the scrubby grasses that stood between him and the road.

Nothing. He let out a shuddering sigh, winced against the pain in his shoulder, and resumed his agonisingly slow progress towards the other man, his eyes blurring with the severity of the pain. The sun's burn was intense, which didn't help matters, and the air was dry and dusty, abrasive against the soft inside of his throat as he made his awkward advance. He took a quick look at his watch. He must only have been unconscious for a matter of ten minutes or so, but Lambert had had time to get away to God alone knew where.

However, worried as he was about Cerys, he must for now concentrate his efforts on getting himself and his colleague to safety. Assuming the other man was still alive.

As he reached him, the trousered leg twitched. Thank God. Alive, then. He hoped he wasn't badly injured. The lack of houses or buildings of any kind meant, of course, that apart from there being no one around to report their whereabouts, there was also no one around to offer them any help. Lambert had taken both his and James the security guy's CDs from them, so they had no means of communicating with anyone unless they got to safety. He remembered that he'd hurriedly told Cerys to send an alert using hers and then hide it under the seat if she could, and he wondered whether she'd managed to do so.

Howard cleared his throat and spoke. 'James? James, are you all right?' He pushed back a dusty mass of scrubby thorny bushes with his foot and the elbow of his good arm to better see his companion.

The man James was at last coming to his senses, but he looked dazed and confused as he pushed himself up into a sitting position. 'Who are you? What happened?'

'I'm Howard Dyer, the Leader's chief aide, remember? Frederick Lambert threw us out of the car and fired at us as we fell into the ditch.' Howard indicated said ditch with a pointless wave of his uninjured arm.

'Ah. Yes. Of course. That was a very potted and simplified explanation, Howard! Raving mad murderous nutcase traitor takes two highly trained men by surprise, tries to kill us and makes off with the World

Leader who was supposed to be in our charge and being kept safe, really says it better. Christ, I feel terrible.'

'Have you been shot?' Howard asked the bodyguard. 'Are you in pain?' He couldn't see any blood on the other man.

James gave himself a cursory shake and pat down and seemed content with his findings. 'No, not shot. But my head…' He turned to one side and was promptly sick. 'Concussion, I suspect. Nothing more,' he said practically. 'I've suffered worse in my time.'

'OK, well, that can still be serious, though, so we'll need to be careful. Do you think you can walk?'

'Probably,' said the younger man. 'I don't suppose you've got any water?'

Howard shook his head. 'Sorry.'

'Can't be helped. From what I remember, we're not far from town. We'll head back the way we came, take it slowly.' He hauled himself unsteadily to his feet, holding the back of his head where a huge bump was visible under his short red hair from the hard contact it had received from the rock against which he'd been flung. 'Well, we can hardly run.' He then seemed to register the injury to Howard's shoulder for the first time, which was now leaking through its improvised bandages and trailing a stream of blood through his jacket sleeve and down his arm to the cuff, where it dripped darkly onto the ground. 'It looks as if we need to be more concerned about you. We need to get you to a hospital.'

Although the ditch wasn't particularly deep, the two injured men made heavy work of getting themselves out of it and up onto the road. The ground was full of loose stones and, for Howard especially, it was hard to get a foothold when he couldn't steady himself with both hands. But after a lot of ungraceful scrambling and with the concussed James pulling him up by his good arm, they made it out.

'Thanks.' Howard clutched his shoulder and was almost sick himself.

'You OK?'

'Not really. I've had better days. You?'

'Ditto.'

There weren't any cars around, which wasn't so unusual, but it was odd that there weren't yet any signs of life after the result of the vote. No doubt people were still afraid to go out, not yet trusting that it would be safe to do so, and who could blame them? This caution was in fact probably a good thing for the two men, as it meant they didn't have to answer any questions or explain themselves but, had they been observed, they would have made an odd, post-apocalyptic sight as they shuffled slowly along the dusty road with their injuries and ragged clothes, retracing the route of the car, one dazed and unsteady on his feet, the other nursing an evidently far deeper wound than he'd originally thought.

'He shoved a syringe into my arm,' said James. 'Must've been something to shut me up before he dealt with you.'

'I wondered why you didn't put up a fight. Shit, where do you think he's taken her?' asked Howard.

'No idea. Assuming we get ourselves to a medic before one of us dies, we'll have to try and contact Lucas. I don't think her life is in danger. She's worth more to him alive. But you never can tell, I guess, with a lunatic. And it's turned out that Frederick Lambert is a lunatic. Makes me feel a bit of a prat for not noticing it before.'

Howard nodded in sympathy and bit back his fear of what was happening to his boss to ask, 'Will it be a problem, do you think, going into a hospital? Aren't they run by the WA?'

'I'm not in so much of a concussed state,' James grimaced, 'that I would be so stupid. We'll go to my office. The Leader's office. There's a private hospital wing.'

'OK, good. And in the meantime, let's hope the WA aren't looking for us.'

'Unlikely, I'd say, at least for the time being. I reckon they've got bigger fish to fry.'

'We shouldn't blame ourselves for this, you know,' said Howard.

'Not you, maybe, but I work with Lambert, day in, day out. I should've noticed the signs.'

'Were there any?'

'I don't know.' James thought about it for a while. 'I really don't know.'

The two men looked at each other for a long moment and continued along the road.

Chapter Thirty-eight

His safe house would have to wait. Ward had had an idea. He raced as fast as his heavy frame would allow to the landing station where he leapt and bounded towards his pod, praying to a god he didn't believe in that there weren't as yet any of the Leader's staff in that area. They'd started their takeover alarmingly fast and were already in the process of dismantling surveillance equipment and removing his agents from their jobs. There was nothing he could do about it, legally speaking, over which he was still berating himself and would always do so, mercilessly, for his failure to change the law while he'd had the chance. It was an unforgivable lapse. Illegally speaking, however, he was armed, and if anyone got in his way, he wasn't afraid to press home his authority that way.

However, luck was on his side for the moment because it appeared that while this work to remove his staff went on in his facility, no one had as yet reached the landing station. How very remiss of them, he thought to himself with a ghoulish smile. He opened his pod and clambered heavily inside. He'd barely sat down before he started punching information into its control panel. The information took but a few seconds to process and then he was away, grinning maniacally.

His surveillance systems may have all been shut down, but there were still methods of tracking vehicles, and they didn't seem to be affected yet. He knew what the Leader's driver, Frederick Lambert had done, and he knew he'd gone to Hurst's wife's salon. If the car moved from there, he'd know about it. That's where he'd get the so-called World Leader. That's where he'd get her. Anymore updates on the position of the car and he'd know about it via the computers in his pod.

The recruitment of Lambert by the WA had clearly been bungled and the man had ended up with delusions of grandeur and had started issuing threats and making his own demands. Foolish man. He'd have to be dealt with severely for this crime, of course. Just who the hell did he think he was? He'd been told to keep track of the Leader's movements, nothing more. Really, if you wanted anything done properly in this life, you had to do it yourself.

God, he was sick of being surrounded by treacherous incompetent fools. There were plenty of those in his own party. This being done by someone in the Leader's employ, albeit someone the WA had been trying to recruit, just went to show how useless and clueless she and her so-called agents were, and how little he needed any of them, and of how little use they were to him. He would stop his recruitment programme immediately.

The cheek of the man, botching his own kidnap attempt and claiming to be working on behalf of the WA when all he was supposed to be doing was gathering information! People were so slapdash and unprofessional. This is what happened when you didn't watch people and control them properly. He would remove Lambert from the picture without further ado. How dare he!

As for Cerys Lee, well, fancy being kidnapped by your own employee! The public had no idea how stupid she was. They had no idea what the vote meant and what they would be going back to – a world of governments arguing and countries fighting each other because no one was taking proper charge of the world – and he needed to stop it; he needed to stop the Leader in her tracks. The sooner people realised that his word was the only word the better.

He'd get her. He'd put an end to this. He'd have her arrested so that the world could see she was just a crazy middle-aged woman acting illegally and without a clue of what she was talking about, or any idea of how adversely her actions would impact the world. His world. And then he'd resume control. Proper control. His control. His way. He was so angry his face contorted. His nostrils flared and his top lip curled itself upwards in the manner of a horse braying. His pale grey eyes widened in urgency.

A light flashed. Ward punched a button to listen to the automated message. The car had moved. New location. Damn it. Then, as he was waiting for the new location, the connection went blank. He pushed a few more buttons, trying to restore it, but nothing happened. Damn it again.

He slowed to a stop and hovered while he thought about what to do. The car had moved from the salon. Where would Lambert be likely to go? Why had he even gone to the salon in the first place? Perhaps if he, Ward, headed there anyway, he'd be lucky enough to spot them.

He hunched forwards over the controls, grinding his teeth and growling out loud, and set off again, wishing he could whip his chair like a jockey, to get there faster, faster, go, go.

Chapter Thirty-nine

'Look,' the Leader was saying as she came into the room with Janine, who was carrying a heavily laden silver tea tray in front of her like a servant. 'I really think we're blowing this out of all proportion. I mean, it's the law. Here, let me help you with that.' After disentangling herself from her niece, she cleared a space on the small side table and relieved Janine of her burden. 'We won the vote, the WA is being disbanded as we speak, and that's that. It might take some time to reorganise things, but that's to be expected. We've got a solid plan, which is being sent out into the world for all to see. We're being as transparent as it's possible to be. OK, so Ward has disappeared off the face of the earth, but so what? What do you think he's going to do? Form a one-man army against us and blow the world to pieces? People don't have to be afraid of him anymore. Nobody followed me here. I even took the back lane as an extra precaution, so I wasn't seen coming down the street. It's all fine. We just have to stick to our plan.' She sat on the sofa next to Toby, cradling a cup of tea in her left hand and, smiling, passed him a biscuit, which he munched with enthusiasm, grinning toothily back at her.

I wish everyone would stop grinning like idiots, thought Sally grumpily, as she accepted a cup of tea herself from Janine with a cursory, 'Thanks.'

'I hope you're right,' Janine was now saying. 'Just because we don't know where Ward is at this moment, doesn't mean he's not a threat. You know better than anyone how it works, Ms Lee. As soon as Lucas knows anything he'll let me know, but just because you weren't followed on foot, it doesn't mean anything. The man is a law unto himself, and you know how unpredictable he can be. We have to put everyone's safety first, more so now than ever. My son has left his office and intends putting Mr Hurst, who's with him, just to catch you up, on a plane back to London. They received your message at the salon,' she told Sally. 'But they already knew Frederick had got you all with him, and were on their way to your house, the last I knew. No doubt they'll find a way to come here and collect you before taking you all to your aunt's plane. I wonder what's keeping them.' She shook her head. 'It'll be fine. Lucas can land the pod securely right here in the back garden, believe it or not. Isn't technology wonderful, even with all its imperfections?' She looked wistful and dreamy as she said this.

'Hang on a minute. London already?' interjected Sally. 'If everything's now as safe and easy as you say, then don't we at least get the chance to pack?'

'We'll send your things on to you,' her aunt said as she shrugged.

'This all seems a bit odd to me,' Sally said. 'You just said it yourself, we held a vote, and we won. That's it, surely? What's the need for all this running around like fugitives? We haven't done anything wrong.'

The Leader stood up and walked across to the window, then turned with a short sigh to face the others. 'Janine's right. Unfortunately, it's not as simple as that. Ward is a dangerous and unpredictable man. Yes, we all know that we won with a large majority, but there are still many supporters out there of the WA and many people who could, and probably will, start to cause trouble. They know, of course, where Ward's facility is, and that your husband is being accused of helping to bring this about. There will be severe repercussions for all of us if we don't handle the situation with care. The WA's supporters are baying for Anthony's blood. There will be unrest and it will likely start right here and here is where it will be worst and where it will have to be got under control with a swiftness that could be extremely violent unless we take preventative measures to avoid that. Our victory needs to be firmly established, reiterated, and compounded by our next actions. And it needs to be done immediately. We can't risk the people who've voted for us today being caught up in a situation which makes them doubt their choice. Speed is paramount. If you're all safely back in London, it's much easier for us to keep an eye on things here before they get out of hand.'

'If you don't have to worry about Ward trying to kill us, you mean?'

'Yes, that's exactly what I mean. Sooner or later, he'll be after you – or after Anthony at least.'

Sally's jaw tightened. 'So now we've served our purpose, it's best if we leave and let the adults get on with their job? Is that what you're saying?'

'If you're going to react like that, then yes. Stop being ridiculous.' Her aunt let out a breath. 'Look, it's not safe for you here at the moment, Sally, and I thought you wanted to be back home in the UK? I'm just trying to protect you. As it is, my chief aide and my other security man, my bodyguard who's been with me for years, are probably already dead. I don't want to risk anything happening to you. And if we're talking about adults protecting children, I have to bring your attention to the one sitting right there.' The Leader's eyes rested on the small boy who sat listening intently before returning meaningfully and uncompromisingly to Sally.

'Of course I want to be back in London,' said Sally, ignoring the point about the two men, and the hint that she was being negligent towards her own son's safety. 'But I assumed you'd be implementing the changes from there, from London, and would be there with us. In fact, I thought you were there now, to be honest. I had no idea you'd recorded the speech and flown over here.

My running away at this time is like admitting some sort of culpability, Aunt, can't you see that?'

'No, not at all. Let me handle it. The camera footage isn't a problem. Even if the cameras in the WA facility picked up any incriminating evidence against Anthony, which we know they must have done, because they at least showed him escaping the facility through the bathroom, those cameras are being removed in front of the WA's staff and destroyed. And anyway, even if they manage to save any, or think they've got archived material that can be used against him, they're wrong. For all her ditsy blonde persona, the girl Jane who I had working there, is actually an extremely good actor, as well as one of my most highly regarded special agents. It was easy to get her a position in the facility, given Ward's rather old-fashioned attitude towards secretaries having to be female. His sexism worked in our favour for once. Getting her in there meant that she had the opportunity to use one of our most powerful new pieces of technology, that enables the erasing of any footage that was downloaded from those cameras, wherever and however securely it's kept. I'm very proud of that technology. It was developed by my team in London, you know.

'Anyway, she, Jane, headed that team and knows better than anyone how it works. She activated the deletion of all the facility's surveillance footage on our signal before we brought her out. The activation device was concealed in the click mechanism of a pen she kept in her bag. Wonderful, isn't it? It also contained a recording device. We've been able to keep track of her every movement and have the details of every conversation she had in that place. She will by now have gone through this morning's information with my team at the office and the details of how she managed the situation. She was one of the first people to be evacuated and taken back to the central office. I can't wait to see her report. The girl is worthy of an Oscar, should they ever come back. We owe her a huge debt of gratitude. The removal of the cameras by our staff is simply being done for effect, primarily because there are still people in the WA who know about Anthony's involvement, and they need to think the evidence against him is gone and, with it, any opportunity of trying to have him prosecuted. I'd rather you were all out of harm's way.'

'But'

'But nothing. And to answer your other question, yes, for the most part, I will be in London. I'll be travelling back as soon as possible, but I need to show a presence here first. The people need to see I'm serious about their safety and that they can trust me. Besides, it'd be something of a security threat for us all to travel together like one big happy family, even in the most peaceful of times, don't you think? But for now, we need to concentrate our efforts on your husband and Janine's son before we can do anything else. If we're quick, you, Anthony and Toby can be halfway across the Atlantic before they even give you and the boy a flicker of thought, and, yes, that will mean we'll have less people to worry about. That's always assuming Lucas is successful in his current mission to complete the liberation of your husband, that is. They seem to be taking rather a long time.'

'Janine just told me he'd escaped the facility…'

'He did, but they have to get from Lucas' headquarters to here. It's quite a way out of town, but even so. I just hope Ward hasn't caught up with them.'

Janine interjected, 'Actually, going back to what you were saying about Howard and James, it was in fact they who alerted Lucas to the fact that you'd been kidnapped by Lambert, Ms Lee. Evidently neither of them was killed, but they were both injured, and they made their way to the medical facility at your offices in town.'

Sally was surprised to see, along with the look of relief on the face of her aunt, some other emotion which, unless she was very much mistaken, showed that her aunt had an interest in the safety of Howard Dyer that went beyond the professional. She smiled, despite herself. Good for her.

Shaking herself out of these musings, however, Sally said, 'I'm glad the two men are safe, but I'd like to make a couple of points. Firstly, I'm wondering why, if it's as dangerous for us as you say, because of there being a bounty on my husband's head, you're suggesting we all three travel together? I'm not happy about Toby being on the flight home with Anthony. I do actually put my son first, by the way, which is why I got involved with all this in the first place, and I'm getting fed up with people suggesting otherwise.'

'Sorry to interrupt,' said Janine, looking at her communication device, 'but the men are about to land out the back.'

Cerys nodded. 'OK.'

'Secondly,' continued Sally, not about to let the others get waylaid, 'have you forgotten that there's possibly a dead body in a car parked behind the shopping centre? Once it's found, they'll be after all of us, me included. I'm not going anywhere until I know it's safe to do so, and until I know that I'm not an accessory to murder.'

'Yes, I agree that that particular issue might be a bit of a problem,' Cerys conceded. 'However, please just trust me, OK? I'll get someone to deal with it and we'll talk again later. I haven't got time to argue about it now, I need to get down to my office. There are people I need to speak to. Janine, I'll borrow your car, if I may?'

The old lady nodded. 'Of course.'

'What are you doing? You can't go out! Are you insane?' Sally hissed.

'Quite the contrary. Don't worry. I shouldn't be gone for more than a couple of hours, then I'll come back, and we can talk again.'

Sally nodded. 'Fine.'

'Mummy, I don't think the man is dead.'

'What?' Everyone turned to look at Toby as he sat on the awful pink sofa eating another biscuit.

'Oh, well yes, you're probably right, darling.'

'But I felt his arm, Mummy.'

'What?' Sally repeated, all the adults now giving him their undivided, astonished attention.

'The lady you call Aunt,' he said, pointing at Cerys. 'She said she hadn't felt anyone's pulse, but I saw it on a police show on TV, and I know what to do, so when I opened the door and his arm was just sort of hanging there while he was looking asleep, I held his wrist and I felt something ticking in it like a little clock.'

'Oh, Toby!'

'Did I do something wrong, Mummy?'

'No, no, you did something very right, my little angel.'

Toby grinned proudly while the adults continued to stare at him, stunned.

What the hell have I done to my son, thought Sally.

The Leader chuckled. 'Well, it looks as if we've got ourselves a new recruit,' she said. 'Janine, if this is true, he'll either be running out of oxygen or kicking and banging and making a scene. Could you please get someone to go and deal with the situation? He's in the boot of the car in the lane behind the big toy shop. I have to go.'

'Of course, right away.'

'Please don't go out, Aunt,' begged Sally. But the Leader headed resolutely for the door, without stopping to listen to anymore of Sally's arguments and closed it behind her with a decisive click.

Chapter Forty

'You will notice, dear boy, that as expected, we are indeed being followed. Your acting skills are about to be put to the test, I fear.'

Hurst turned his uncomfortably be-wigged head in the direction in which Lucas was pointing.

'Perhaps,' Lucas pondered, 'it would have been better if we'd taken the scenic route, and not drawn attention to ourselves. But no matter, what's done is done. Besides, we've planned for it, so perhaps they can be shaken off.'

'I'm not your dear boy, Lucas. I'm thirty-eight years old. And while I appreciate you've got a flair for acting a part, I haven't, and I haven't planned for any of this today, so I really don't know what you expect me to do. I've never had the slightest desire for or leanings towards subterfuge, let alone improvisation, and all this is, quite frankly, getting a bit too much to be borne. We're not pratting about between the footlights on a stage, you know. This is real, and it's dangerous. And, on top of all that, there *is* no scenic route! This is a God-forsaken arse-end of a place with nothing scenic about it and, while I understand you were just using a turn of phrase, it's annoying. Besides, we're in the air in a damn great flying machine and, wherever we are, we're just about as obvious to spot as obvious gets.'

Lucas chuckled. 'Quite right. I'm glad to see you offering a spirited argument.'

'Don't laugh at me,' Hurst snarled, almost at the point of punching Lucas in his miserable face. 'I hate today, I hate this place and, right now, whether you've saved my hide or not, I also hate you.'

'Forgive me. Let me explain my plan. I think the best thing we can do is send a message to Mother and get your wife and son ready to board as soon as we can manage it after landing. As a result, Mother's house will no longer be safe, of course, but then again, after this is done, it won't have to be. But for the moment, you are right; we must take extreme care.' He reached out towards a button and, pressing it delicately, and without the slightest sign of any adverse reaction to Anthony's tearing him off a strip, announced that they should be expected to land in the garden in a couple of minutes. It sounded absurd. *He* sounded absurd. 'In the meantime, *Mr Hurst*,' he said pointedly, and Anthony tutted. 'I'd like you to make eye contact with that person and make some sort of sign to them to indicate that you've captured me and that shortly you'll be heading back to the facility.' Lucas craned his neck. 'Gosh, I do believe it's Ward himself.'

'What?' Hurst's own neck spun on his shoulders like that of an owl.

'Yes. Come on, get on with it, we haven't got all day. I'll set the autopilot for my mother's garden.'

'Seriously?'

'Yes, yes.' Lucas started pressing buttons.

I really am getting too old for this, Hurst thought again, but he nevertheless positioned his face to look out the window, making sure not to get too close to it in case his features were easily distinguishable, and did indeed catch Ward's eye. He pointed at Lucas and made a waving motion with his hand in the direction of the facility.

Ward's face displayed several emotions in quick succession. First came shock. Then approval, as he nodded to what looked like Greenway, and finally, a confused hesitation. In this momentary pause, as both Hurst and Ward wondered what to do next, Lucas had plunged the pod forwards with the autopilot, and they headed with pinpoint accuracy and terrifying, whiplash inducing speed for Janine's back garden. Ward only hesitated for a moment before he was speeding along in their wake.

'I knew it wouldn't work,' yelled Hurst, as the pod brought itself to a jolting hover over the landing area.

'He believed it for a couple of seconds. It was all we needed. Land,' Lucas yelled back. 'Land! Now!'

The pod descended between the trees and even as it was passing between them, before it had settled on the ground, a screen was moving quickly into place above them, slicing into place between the trees.

'It'll prevent him trying to land,' Lucas explained a bit more calmly now as they opened the door of the pod closest to the house and ran down a short tunnel that someone had pulled out into place like the bellows of an accordion between the landing area and the conservatory door. 'Whereas this stops him seeing us if he happens to penetrate the screen.'

'Penetrate the screen? What the absolute blazes are you going on about? He knows where we are, whether he can see us or not!'

'Just get inside, will you?' Lucas shoved him unceremoniously through some tall glass doors into the house.

Janine finished her communication about Lambert with head office and welcomed the two men with relief into the conservatory where Sally and Toby still waited. Hurst headed straight for a shocked looking Toby, hugging him hard with relief. He'd thought he was never going to see him again on more than one occasion today. Pointedly ignoring Sally, he turned his attention to Lucas. Toby looked quizzically at his father's head.

'Forgive another stupid question, theatre man, but how exactly are we supposed to get out of here?'

Lucas pursed his lips.

'Don't worry,' Janine answered for him. 'It's being taken care of.'

Hurst looked across at the old woman. 'Janine, right? You're the tea lady.' Janine nodded confirmation that yes, she was. 'I understand that I have you to thank for saving my life today,' he said.

'Oh, well…'

Sally interrupted this exchange. 'Being taken care of? Aunt didn't have to do anything at the office at all, did she?' she said, realisation dawning on her with a tardiness she was ashamed of. 'She's drawing him away. She's acting as a decoy. But she can't! He'll hurt her.'

Anthony Hurst rounded on his wife with fury. 'Wait a minute… What? Aunt? Who is your aunt?'

'The Leader. The World Leader. I'm sorry, Anthony, I… I thought it was best if I didn't… I thought it was safer if you didn't know. Besides, I was sworn to secrecy.'

'Secrecy? Safer? Let me get this straight, the World Leader is your AUNT? And you thought I couldn't be trusted to know this minor little detail about your life – about my WIFE? Do you really think I'm that untrustworthy? Or that I would have somehow given her away? Do you? You really are the giddy limit, Sally, do you know that? Bat-crap crazy, that's what you are.' He shook his head in incredulity. 'All this time, and I never knew. No wonder you were so damn keen to help. She was, is, your family! I didn't know you had any family. You said you didn't. Jesus, I always wondered how you knew her, how you had access to her. No wonder you had access to her if she was your AUNT!' He stood there shaking his head at her in disbelief. 'I've never felt so let down in my entire life. I'm trying to get us out of here, doing all this stuff to help you, without even having been consulted as to whether I wanted to be involved, but doing it anyway because I HAD NO CHOICE. Doing it to get us out of here and get us to safety, and all the while...'

'All the while that's exactly what I've been doing, too,' she shouted at him.

'No. You've been playing a game of intrigue. That's what this is to you. To all of you.' He glared pointedly at Lucas. 'It's a game. Well, let me tell you that I happen to think our son's safety comes first, above your games, above everything, and I'm disgusted that you don't. In fact, I'm disgusted by the fact that you've got us involved with any of this. In fact,' he turned to point at Janine, 'I was just in the middle of thanking the woman who saved my life today – something she had to do because *you* put me in danger – and you care so little about that, even about common courtesies, that you *interrupt* me? I've had enough. If your precious aunt gets herself killed trying to ensure a safe passage for Toby, then so bloody be it.'

Chapter Forty-one

At that very moment, meanwhile, Ward was congratulating himself heartily. After the frustration of chasing the pod as far as the house and watching with fury as it landed where he couldn't follow, and contemplating setting the rockets on the place and blowing it sky high, he'd spotted something else. Something entirely unexpected. The World Leader appeared to be getting into a car outside the property. Alone and in broad daylight. The arrogance of the woman knew no bounds! He could hardly believe his eyes. Or indeed his luck.

As she calmly drove away, Ward tailed her, a hundred questions sparking around his brain like an electrical circuit gone mad. Had they been using this house all along? If so, how had it not come to his attention? Who was the man in the pod that the badly disguised Hurst had been pointing at? How had Hurst got away from the facility? What had become of his, Ward's, agent, Charley Greenway, who'd been sent to deal with him, to kill him? Had Hurst killed the man? If so, how? Did he really think Ward was so stupid as to fall for such a rudimentary ploy as a curly wig? And the biggest question of all: where was the damnable Cerys Lee going?

The answer to that last question scarcely mattered. She was buying time, allowing the others the opportunity to escape, that much was obvious. But it didn't matter that he'd fallen for it and tagged along behind her as she'd hoped because he could stop the others easily enough and there would be time to deal with them later. And boy, would he! He'd throw every last one of them in jail. Including the kid.

He tried to put a call through to his office in order to send word that the Hursts weren't to be allowed to leave the town, let alone the area, but the lines he tried were all dead. His communication had been cut off even from his own staff! He threw the headset roughly to one side. They'd have to wait. He'd track them down himself – follow them to the ends of the earth if needs be. But that would have to be later. For now, the most important thing was that he get hold of the Leader and force her to retract everything she'd said and done today. Reverse the damn vote and reinstate his party as the true leaders. Reclaim his power. Then he'd show the lot of them what happens when you double-cross Robert Ward.

He followed as she drove down the narrow backstreets. Trying to lose him wouldn't work. Stupid woman. Sooner or later, she'd have to either abandon the car or take it out onto the wider roads, either option making it inevitable that he would catch her. She knew it, too. She thought she was so clever, buying time for the traitor Hurst, his traitor wife, and whoever the others were that were helping them, but she was nothing but a naïve fool. She was done for. He'd take her to his safe house and force the retraction. He'd keep her there as long as it took.

He hovered menacingly, ever closer to the car below as it finally turned out onto the main road out of town. The road led in the opposite direction from her headquarters, and therefore from her plane. Blasted woman. He hated being forced to choose between taking her and dealing with Hurst. But he hated her more. She had to be his main target, so yes, he must forget the others for now. She was the only means of getting his party back into power.

God, how he hated her. He'd get her, just see if he didn't. But he must be careful, because she would be no good to him dead, and tempting as it would be to shoot her – oh, how he wished he could have the satisfaction of shooting her – he needed to resist the urge and control himself. He let out a regretful whine like a dog in pain as this realisation hit home. Such a shame. However, there were other means of serving justice. He hurtled forwards and pressed a button to activate the small gun on the outside of the vehicle, set the back wheel of her car as his target, and fired.

The technology in his state-of-the-art pod meant total precision. He was glad of it because who knew how steady his own hand would be. The car below him swerved violently but the damn woman kept it on the road, screaming along but more slowly now in a cloud of dust and sparks, as the tyre burst, and the wheel rim carved vicious lines in the surface of the road. Ward's mouth stretched into a wide grimace, and he laughed. He would get her. Almost… she was almost in his reach, almost his for the taking. He was going to win!

He set the gun on the other back wheel. She was already slowing considerably, but he fired anyway. He was enjoying himself.

What a state for the supposed World Leader to be in, thought Ward. Not so high and mighty now, are you? Out here alone, sacrificing yourself in some pathetic antiquated land vehicle for people whose only aim is to flee, not to help you. Where is your security? Where are your staff? Where is your protection? Hahaha… Where is your dignity? Yes, this is all going very well. You'll see just how much you've underestimated me. I'll get back what's rightfully mine and I'll see to it that no one can ever oppose me again.

The car ground to a halt in a shriek of metal and smoke a short way onto the start of the main road out of town. It was the perfect place for Ward to land his pod. Stupid woman, he thought.

Cerys had known she couldn't fend him off for long. She hadn't intended to. Just enough time to lure him away from the house and for Lucas to get Sally and her family to the airstrip. Not that Sally or the boy would be leaving, so it would only be her husband, but at least that was something. She understood Sally's reluctance to leave, she really did, and her harsh words had only been spoken out of fear for her, but she did wish she'd agreed to go. Still, it was what it was and there wasn't anything she could do about it. Right now, she had the problem of Robert Ward to deal with, and he was not an easy customer.

He'd blown one of the wheels of the car clean off with his first strike, if the hideous screeching sound of metal on tarmac was anything to go by. She'd kept the car on the road, of course, but the game was up. She'd slowed down and there was nothing she could have done about it. He'd fired at her again and taken another wheel out of action, bringing the car to a standstill. This second strike had been out of pure spite, she knew, because she was stopping anyway. Cerys was shaking at the thought of this confrontation. This was it.

It was unlikely that he'd kill her, she knew that. He needed the retraction. However, taking her by force to his safe house, even though her people knew where that was, was problematic. Who knew what lay in store for her if she refused to do what he wanted? She would be more difficult to rescue, and her team's luck was bound to run out at some point. He'd be stronger on his own territory. She had her gun, of course, but then she fully expected that Ward did, too. And he was, without a doubt, more than a match for her.

In her mirror she could see the door of the sinister black pod slowly swinging upwards into the open position. Yes, this was it. All her powers of mediation and reasoning were about to be called into action and she couldn't afford to fail because if it came to a battle of physical strength against this man, she was finished. He could crush her like a baby bird.

Others would take over her work, of course, in the event that he killed her, but who wanted that? Who wanted to die at the hands of a thug, and with the realisation of their dreams so close, at that? They weren't only personal dreams; she genuinely cared about the people and their lives and the state of the planet.

To say she was nervous wasn't even scraping the surface of how she felt.

No. She couldn't allow all her work to be handed over to a colleague. Even one she trusted implicitly. No, she wanted to do this herself. Wanted to live to see the results of all her effort. She could, and she damn well would. She would not let a man such as Robert Ward get the better of her and she certainly wouldn't let him and the WA dismiss her life's work like so much rubbish. Dismiss *her* as so much rubbish.

Mental strength, she told herself. Come on, pull yourself together. Think of your training, think of your thirty years' worth of darned hard work, then look at that man in the pod, for God's sake. Buck up. You won the vote. And you're no pushover when it comes to defending yourself, either.

She and her agents were all highly trained and skilled in self-defence, as well as at their jobs, using a system that had been devised by a team of the absolute best secret service agents and the cream of hand-to-hand combat teachers, and her methods had so far worked for those agents. Now, if it turned out that her diplomatic skills were left wanting, it would be time to practice what she preached, and she could do it.

But he was younger than her, physically larger and stronger...

No, Cerys, she told herself harshly. Age, size, all that stuff means nothing. You know that. It's what you do, the methods you use, the way you exert your strength over your opponent, that's what matters. Use your mind. Do your job. And while you're at it, for God's sake try not to kill him.

Ward took up his gun from where it lay on the seat beside him and stepped calmly out onto the baking, scarred tarmac. A heat akin to opening an oven door greeted him, but he hardly noticed it. The Leader was herself getting out of the car, apparently putting up no resistance. His puzzlement at this registered only momentarily on his face as he lumbered towards her, with the gun held joyfully out in front of him, almost laughing. Finally... finally...

'Good afternoon, Mr Ward.' The Leader's voice was steady and clear, betraying no sign of her fear. If anything, he thought he detected pity in her tone as she spoke the few words. How dare she pity him? 'What is it you want from me,' she was saying, 'that must be demonstrated in such a violent manner? You could have just picked up your communication device and had a conversation, spoken to me like the civilised human being you claim to be.'

'How dare you? You know what I want. You will come with me, and you will make another public address. Live, this time, and you will tell our good citizens that you made a mistake and that I am not only still in charge with the World Administration, but that I will also be taking over as World Leader.'

The Leader didn't make any move to walk towards him. She shaded her eyes against the sun and pointed at the gun, her own only a second's grasp away at her hip. 'Is that really necessary? It's not conducive to helpful talks, you know.'

Ward ignored her and indicated his pod. 'Get in,' he ordered.

'No. If you want to talk, we talk right here. And I repeat, lower that gun. Threatening me won't achieve anything. I must also point out that whatever you do with me, nothing changes. The WA is being disbanded and replaced as we speak. It's the law, Mr Ward. The party may still want you as their leader, but that's for them to decide. As for the role of World Leader, that's my job. The public have indicated in no uncertain terms who they support and which way they want things done from now on, and there's nothing you can do to change that. If they'd voted NO, I would have kept my word and resigned, and who knows, you could have been in with a shot.' She shrugged. 'But as it is, they voted YES. Eighty-five per cent voted YES, Mr Ward. Even if you kill me, my deputy assumes the role of temporary World Leader, as you well know, and your situation doesn't change. Except, of course, that as a murderer you're hardly likely from a prison cell to be able to lead anything more than a jog around the yard, let alone your party. And you certainly won't ever be able to contest my job which, as you know, will no longer exist anyway after we've got everything running normally again.'

Ward growled and took another step towards her, not lowering his gun even by an inch.

Chapter Forty-two

'You two standing there glaring at each other like schoolchildren isn't going to help anyone.'

Toby giggled at Lucas' words and pointed at his parents. 'You're schoolchildren!'

Everyone turned to stare at the child, not so much because they'd forgotten him or forgotten to be discreet in front of him, but because he'd dared to speak in such a way. Not only was it unheard of for children to voice an opinion, any opinion, but the idea of a child laughing at their parents was shocking indeed. Sally's heart swelled with pride. Her son would not live in fear. And that's what this was all about.

'Toby, why don't you come and help me make a sandwich?' Janine held open the door into the main house and, reluctantly, Toby followed, turning first to his mother, wide-eyed and with a quivering lip. He appeared to be as shocked as everyone else at his behaviour and was wondering if he was about to be told off by this strange woman he barely knew.

'It's fine,' Sally reassured him with a smile. 'You go and eat something.' Without another word, he reluctantly allowed himself to be led from the room.

The moment he was behind the closed door, Lucas spoke again.

'You two will have to put aside your differences and pull together. We need you on a plane and out of here. Then we have to help your aunt, Sally, who's out there putting herself in danger just to give you the time to get away, and we're wasting the time she's buying us with you two squabbling.'

'I already told Janine and my aunt that I'm not going anywhere. I'll return to London once I've helped my aunt out of this situation and seen a safe removal of the WA with no ill effects for her or anyone else.'

'Really?' Hurst's words were filled with contempt. 'Your aunt and your precious System of Nations bollocks is more important than the safety of your son?'

'Of course not! Don't be a moron. They are one and the same.'

'Oh, so I'm a moron now? Funny, but I was deemed intelligent enough to almost get myself killed planting bugs for you lot.'

'I'm not arguing with you, Anthony. We can talk properly later. It's extremely important that we help my aunt, as you well know. Or have you changed your mind? Do you want to live like this forever? Do you not want people to have their freedom back? You do realise that if Ward gets his way and finds a path in to discrediting the vote, overpowering my aunt, or forcing her to retract today's statement and the result of the vote, things will not only go back to how they were before today, but they'll be far, far worse. It will mean our freedoms will be completely extinguished. Probably forever. Are you suddenly not with us on this? Perhaps you've changed your mind and would like to go back and work for the WA for real?'

'You know what, Sally? Insulting me isn't going help. And to be perfectly honest, at the moment I couldn't give a rat's behind who's in charge of the world. I didn't ask for this crap. I didn't want to leave my home, my job, my friends...'

'Well, there you are! Do something about it, then, so we can go back to that life, to a better one.'

'... Don't interrupt me. As I was saying, it was all you. It was all done behind my back with your plotting and scheming and your perverse power trip, without a regard for anyone else's feelings, thoughts on the subject, or of your own son's safety. And I'm sick of it. The WA wouldn't even have noticed me if you hadn't put them onto me and arranged it all, with your contacts and subterfuge, and... and your equally conniving aunt. I just want a quiet life. Why can't you get that through your head? And you call me stupid.' Years of pent-up anger burst out in this torrent, like a long-dormant volcano spewing its accumulated boiling contents, and now he'd started, he had so much more he wanted to say but, as he stood there shaking with the release of the tension and the anger, Sally cut him off.

'OK, look, if that's how you feel, do what you want.'

'I bloody well will! You can't keep telling me what to do. I'm not your child.'

'Fine. Go, stay, it's all the same to me if you're going to stand there and yell at me like this in front of a stranger. But as for Toby, of course I care, and I resent your saying otherwise. That's why he stays here with me until all this is over. Travelling with you isn't safe for him right now.'

'Because of YOU!' Hurst bellowed, lifting a hand in an unconscious move to drag it through his hair and encountering the wig. He ripped it off and threw it on the floor. 'This is all such shit.'

'We can talk later.'

'We cannot.'

'Please, Anthony, be reasonable.'

'Reasonable, she says.'

'OK, look, you can go if you want to. We'll join you when it's safe to do so,' she said calmly.

'Thank you so much, but I don't need you to sign a permission slip. You'll join me only to hand over custody of my son,' he barked back.

'I will do no such thing. Have you lost your mind?'

'You know what, I really think I must've done. I should've told you to go to hell when we had that ridiculous conversation in the bathroom years ago. That was me losing my mind – agreeing to go along with you – not this. This isn't me losing my mind. This is me standing up for myself at long last and regaining my mind.'

Lucas coughed delicately from the opposite side of the conservatory. 'We really are wasting time.'

'Now look...' Hurst began.

'Yes, I'm sorry,' said Sally, interrupting him yet again. 'We're being indiscreet and I'm sorry for embarrassing you. I'm coming. Just tell me what you need me to do.' She looked back at her husband. 'I really am sorry if I've done anything that's hurt you,' she conceded. 'I never meant to. Toby and I both love you very much. And we really could use your help.'

Hurst glared at her with daggers of pure loathing in his eyes, and said, 'We? Ambiguity at its finest, Sally. And manipulation. Again. Well done. I accuse you of blackmailing me with my own son, telling me I have to do as you say because he needs me to. You counter that with a denial, saying that that's not what you meant and the "we" referred to you and your Democratic Party cronies. How can you be so cold? So false? So fake? You don't love me, you love the fact that I'm useful to you, that's what you love.' Then he turned back to Lucas. 'Frankly, I don't know what my wife thinks I can do about it. And I don't *care* what you think I can do about it. I want nothing more to do with any of it or any of you. The sooner I'm on a plane and out of here the better.'

'I understand your distress, dear fellow, and I agree that the safest course of action for you is to leave as soon as possible, as we had planned.' He then addressed

Sally. 'If you insist on staying, we need to hurry up and get on with it, finish the job.'

'And you know where he is, do you? Ward?' asked Hurst, curious despite himself. 'Where are the proper authorities? Why don't you simply call the police?'

'Ward has got a safe house, just as we have this one. Well, ours is not so safe anymore, but he thinks his is and my guess is that he will have found a way to stop the car and will have taken the Leader there. The police work under the laws put in place by the WA, as you know. Or at least, they did before today. They'll be working with us from now on, of course, but I think it's a bit soon to expect any help from them today. Therefore, we must do this ourselves. It'll be faster and more efficient. So, if we approach Ward's safe house from all sides, we should be able to get in.'

'Yeah, because he'll never notice that, will he? What, have you got invisible cars now? Stealth cars that I haven't been told about?' He was becoming half-crazy with everything that had happened today; he could feel the madness taking over his brain. Perhaps Sally was right.

Lucas tutted. 'Of course not.'

Outside the door, upon hearing this exchange, Janine hurriedly made a call. 'Activate Plan B,' she said. 'L delayed. Danger of capture C.'

Hurst, attempting to prove to himself if not them that he wasn't the crazy one, asked a more rational question. 'Well, anyway, how come you know where this house of his is, but he didn't know about this place?'

'A reasonable question, with a simple answer.' Lucas spread his hands in a wide gesture. 'He was fed false information as to the location of ours – we weren't. Now, if you won't help us, are you ready to leave? We need to get on with it.'

Hurst stood there with his face twisted into an expression that could have been disdain or contempt or a dozen things in between. He thought about leaving without Toby, and it nearly floored him. But perhaps it was his easiest option if he wanted a free ride out of here. He would get his son back once he was home in London. Once again, he found himself being manipulated into doing something he didn't want to do, into appearing to the child to be the parent who was abandoning him, just to please other people. Negotiating and bartering for his own peace of mind. He almost wished they'd left him to his fate at the hands of his boss. Almost.

'Fine, let's go. But I want your word that this is it. I'm going home now, and I want no more to do with any of you people, I want my safety guaranteed, I want watertight immunity from arrest, should the WA regain office, and I want a home in London that's the equivalent of the one I had there before. And I want all of it at no cost to me. For free, do you understand? I think I've earnt it.'

Lucas inclined his head.

Hurst crossed the small room to Lucas, holding out his hand. 'Shake on it.'

Lucas, hiding a smirk, shook on it.

'Right, let's get it over with. What's the plan? How do I get out of here?'

'We'll take the pod and head straight for the Leader's plane. Sally, you wait here. I'll come back for you, and Mother can look after Toby for a little while. The Leader has got her CD with her, so she's easy enough to find, as long as Ward doesn't think to take it off her. We were lucky on that score earlier, that Lambert didn't. I've been watching and monitoring her position while you two have been arguing,' he said in a disapproving tone. 'Currently,' Lucas consulted his own device, 'she's stationary, on the road out of town. I just hope, what with your wasting time yelling at each other, that it's not too late and we're not going to discover that Ward's taken her and left her CD on the road or, God forbid, find her dead body lying there. She's been there for rather a long time, I fear.'

Chapter Forty-three

If she could keep him talking, thought Cerys, as she stood facing the profusely sweating figure of Robert Ward, they would come. She had assumed that Lucas at least would have understood what she was doing and followed her. Where were they? Didn't they understand? Had something gone wrong?

Apart from the two of them, her and Ward, the road was eerily deserted. No cars drove by, no people were on the streets, not that there were pavements beside this road out of town, anyway, because there was nowhere for them to go, and there weren't even any birds visible in the sky overhead. She strained her ears for any sign of a vehicle on the road and put her peripheral vision to work trying to spot airborne traffic, but there was nothing. Somewhere in the distance, a dog barked. She listened to the noise of it echoing hollowly into the emptiness. Ward loomed over the scene like a desperate and hungry bear, snarling at his prey through his small yellowing teeth. My God, she thought, he really believes he's going to win.

For some reason, he looked more ridiculous than threatening, but Cerys wasn't going to drop her guard even for a second. Desperation, of course, didn't always know any boundaries. Quite the reverse, with a man such as this.

However, to her relief, he was now saying, 'Don't worry, killing you is not on my agenda, Cerys,' as if he was doing her a favour as well as reading her mind, while also trying to undermine her position by the impolite use of her first name. 'You're no good to me dead, even if I truly and wholeheartedly wish you were, for the trouble you've caused me. And not just today.

'How you dare… how you dare go over my head in front of the entire world, conning people with your promises of a freedom which has never existed, no better than Codardo in his day, with your proclamations of peace and love like yet another ageing hippy. Planting spies and bugs in my headquarters, and in God knows how many of my other offices. Oh no, my dear, I'm not going to spend my life rotting in jail for killing you. You're not worth it. What I want from you, as you well know, is a reversal of that confounded vote. And that is what you're going to give me.'

Cerys sighed. 'Mr Ward, please, be reasonable. You know I can't do that. And even if I could, I wouldn't. It was a democratic vote and the law states quite clearly that the WA are no longer in government. A new interim government formed from the Democratic Party will be set up to oversee the transition back to the old countries… you know all this. You're not a stupid man, Mr Ward, so do please try to accept it.

Governments come and governments go. You made it extremely difficult for anyone else to have a voice during your time in power, even those who are on your side. But now I've found a pathway through your dictatorship and the people have spoken. It's out of your hands.'

'The vote was illegal.'

'The vote was not illegal. Don't accuse me of gathering intelligence in an underhand way when you do the self-same thing. I was just creating a more level playing field. And don't compare me with Codardo. His idea was madness. It has been two centuries of madness. He didn't think it through. All he was doing was setting the world up to be controlled by people like you, whereas I'm taking the world back to a system that works. I grant you it's not perfect, but what is? Neither my system nor yours has anything in common with Codardo's vision. I'll say it again: his naïve idea of democracy was crazy and could never have worked in a million years. Ultimately, all it meant, all it could ever have meant, was an easy way in for those who wanted to control.

'What I'm doing is returning to a way of doing things that allows people to live their lives free of fear, while it seems all you want to do is create more of it and become ever more extreme in your domination. I can't keep saying the same thing over and over.

'But I repeat, the world has spoken. The vote we held today was legal and it stands as such in law. Just because you don't like it and weren't expecting it, and just because you found out that some of your staff were less than loyal to you, and because you've lost control, you're throwing a tantrum. I am World Leader, and my authority overrides yours. I do not and did not need to ask your permission. And I repeat again, one last time, just to make my position on the matter crystal clear: the vote was legal and the result of it stands. You'll just have to accept it. Your time in power is over. It's finished.'

Ward growled in the back of his throat again and took a final step towards her. He was now within reach, and he made a heavy blundering move to grab her. She dodged out of his way. She knew she'd gone too far, but he needed to hear it. Sometimes the plain truth, in all its brutal honesty, was the only course of action. How else was she supposed to get the message through his thick head? It had been difficult to stand there and tell him she thought he wasn't stupid, because in a lot of respects – in most respects – he clearly was. But this last, she saw, was too much. As she'd said her piece, she'd known her words were too strong, and antagonising him in this way was counterproductive. She needed to keep him talking to allow help to come to her, and she'd just blown any hope of that, big time.

Damn it, where were they?

As he made another lunge at her she managed to dodge out of his way a second time, but he quickly came at her again and this time grabbed her tightly by the arm, shaking her roughly in his rage. Her head shook with the vigour of it.

'A tantrum, is it? We'll see about that. We'll see whose authority overrides whose.' He began to drag her towards his waiting pod. 'You will do as you are told.'

Chapter Forty-four

Dyer was in the room when the call came from Janine. Someone was to be sent to deal with a situation on behalf of the Leader in a lane behind the shopping centre. The man Lambert was there, apparently locked in the boot of his own car and there was reason to believe he was still alive. Thank God for that, but he needed to be dealt with, and as soon as possible.

'Let me go and see to it,' he said. 'I have to go out anyway. I have to find the Leader.'

'The Leader is safe,' his colleague told him. 'She's at Janine's house. But Lambert needs to be taken care of safely. We can't have you shooting him. Or doing anything else fatal,' he added as Dyer opened his mouth to speak. 'We can't have this thing made personal, Howard. Think of the impact.' He waited for a nod of agreement. It was a long few seconds in coming. 'But equally, I concur that he's as much of a nuisance to us roaming around alive. He needs to be brought into custody asap.'

'I'll sort it out.'

'I'm really not sure you're the best choice.'

Howard raised his voice. 'Oh, come on. I'll bring him alive, OK? You have my word on it.'

'That's not the only problem, though, is it? How can you challenge the man when it's likely to require physical restraint? You're injured, man.'

'OK, well then get me some backup. Police, if you can.'

His colleague paused for a moment and considered this request. They were wasting time, and he knew Dyer well. They'd worked together for years, and he knew he wasn't going to give in any time soon. 'All right, fine,' he said at length. 'I'll see what I can do, see whether there's anyone high up enough in the police who's on our side and willing to help. But don't hold your breath.' He left the room at speed, shaking his head at Dyer's stubborn insistence and muttering to himself about the pointlessness of speaking to the police.

As it turned out, he was wrong to doubt, and the chief of police was only too glad to help. He said it would give him the utmost satisfaction to personally help them out. Within five minutes, he and a colleague had collected Dyer from the office, and they were flying across town in the enormous black police pod at full speed, like the proverbial bat out of hell, while the chief cheerfully relayed the story of how every member of the force – or at least every officer in every location they'd heard from so far – had voted a resounding YES and been delighted to do so to support the Leader.

Howard wondered whether this help was being given because of a genuine wish to help, or whether it was to boost the chief's own popularity within a workforce who were, he'd told Howard, thoroughly sick of the system. Did that mean they were sick of him, too? He also wondered whether, aside from the chief's evident excitement at bolstering his own importance, he fully grasped the seriousness of the situation. He supposed it didn't matter either way. At least they were on side. At least they were helping.

Frederick Lambert's car was exactly where they'd been told it would be. They landed on the waste ground behind the shops and the three men leapt out and ran towards the car. Howard's colleague back in the office had been right. If they could take Lambert alive, arrest him for the kidnap of the Leader and her niece and the boy, and arrange for him to be thrown into jail, it would save a lot of very awkward questions, not to mention the reputation of the Leader and the credibility of the vote.

If in fact it turned out that he was dead after all, the Leader would be finished. This day would be a disaster in every possible way. Understatement. It would go down as the biggest disaster in recent history, for the Leader to be involved in or responsible for the death of a man, even if that man had kidnapped her and she pleaded self-defence. And, even if it didn't affect the changeover of government – the Leader would take no part in that government, after all – without the Leader to oversee the changes as she'd promised, there would be chaos. So, to protect her, lies would have to be told, someone would have to be framed, or a situation would have to be staged... God, what a mess. It didn't bear thinking about.

They approached the car from three different directions and slowed their pace. Caution was the key.

Dyer's CD buzzed in his pocket. Great timing. He hesitated, not sure if he should take his eye off the ball even for a second to see who it was. But then again, if he ignored it and it turned out to be urgent... that would never do. So, he pulled it out of his pocket, tutting, with annoyance, one eye still on the car as they advanced, and quickly looked at the message from his colleague back at the office.

"Plan B has been activated in relation to the decoy. Possible capture. You're on site, so are you able to deal with it?"

Oh hell.

Dyer called to the police in a loud whisper as they crept towards the car.

'We need to get to the Leader. She took one of our cars and Agent Ward has found her. I've got the location.'

A nod from the chief of police. He held up his hand. Five minutes. Dyer hoped to God they had five minutes.

He responded:

"On way 5 min"

They reached the car and, with weapons trained on the boot, the police chief easily clicked open the lock with an automatic device that swung the lock mechanism round to open with nothing more than the click of a button. He threw the boot open. Howard and the other officer leapt forwards, muscles tense and guns at the ready.

It was empty. The boot was empty.

They all looked at each other. Howard Dyer's head span.

'No time to discuss this now,' said the chief of police urgently, all joviality suddenly gone. He slammed the boot shut and ran back towards the pod, indicating for the other two to follow him. 'We need to find Cerys Lee. Hurry.'

Chapter Forty-five

Janine took a call on her CD and burst into the conservatory without any concern for manners or for interrupting the conversation that had been going on in there, or for the fact that Toby, sitting at the table in the kitchen eating his sandwich, would be able to hear everything. She spoke urgently to the room at large, her face as white as paper.

'Something bad has happened.' Agitatedly, she waved her CD in the air.

'What? What is it? What's happened?' asked Sally.

'He's gone.'

'Who's gone?'

'Lambert.'

'Lambert's dead? Oh my God, no... What does this mean for my aunt?'

'Not dead, no.' Janine shook her head. 'He's disappeared. The car was empty.'

'Then what's the problem?' snapped Hurst. 'All that means is that you and your precious aunt,' he glared at Sally, 'won't be up on a murder charge and I can get out of here as planned. It doesn't make any difference to any of us what's happened to this bloke Lambert. I thought we all understood that nobody, neither the WA nor the Democratic Party wants to be affiliated with him.'

'Perhaps,' said Lucas.

'Perhaps what? I don't understand what all the fuss is about.'

The four of them stood in a circle and regarded each other.

'We need to track him down,' said Lucas. 'He's still got the capacity to cause a lot of trouble. He's still after the Leader, of that I have no doubt.'

'Although,' added Janine, 'Mr Hurst is right in that it doesn't affect our plans to return him to the UK. Lambert couldn't care less about him, so we should still make a move to get him out.'

Lucas nodded. 'Yes, OK, you're right. Come on then, let's do it. Let's go.'

Chapter Forty-six

So loud was Ward's voice as he huffed and hollered in Cerys Lee's face, that he didn't at first hear the low hum of the approaching pod. But the World Leader did and, praying it was someone from her own office, someone who was coming to help her, she moved to give whoever it was more time to get themselves closer before he noticed, by shrieking loudly and aiming distracting kicks at the meaty shins of her captor as he dragged her along.

By the time he was aware of the visitors, a shot had been fired, and he sank to his knees with a look of surprise on his purple face, his grip on the Leader's arm loosening to nothing, before sliding gracelessly to the dusty ground, like an enormous mound of bread dough being dropped into a pile of flour. Cerys shuddered and instinctively made a wiping motion on her arm, to rid herself of the feel of his fingers that had gripped so tightly at her flesh and stood there staring at the massive body on the ground, shocked, her head spinning. She continued to rub her bruised arm. Her overriding thought was to wonder why, as he'd obviously been shot, there was no blood.

The pod landed neatly on the road a short distance from that of Ward, and Cerys' head jolted round to look at it, still terrified, but hopeful. After all, she wasn't the one lying motionless on the road. She held her breath as the doors opened upwards with a quiet hiss, the shiny black metal of the machine glinting in the sunlight like a giant metal beetle.

She waited, motionless, almost blind with fear for what seemed a terribly long time, and by the time her brain registered that the pod belonged to the police, she had almost stopped breathing. Could they really want to help her? How did they know where she was? How did they know about any of this?

She was stunned, but as she slowly came back to herself and reasoned that someone, maybe Janine, had called them, she began to calm down a touch, and moments later, she was even more stunned to see Howard Dyer step out of the pod's door with two other men she didn't recognise. She stood rooted to the spot, sure she must be hallucinating. Why was he getting out of a police pod? What had happened? Was she about to be arrested for what she'd done today?

Howard rushed towards her. 'Are you OK? Janine sent word to the office that someone should come and look for you. We took a chance on the police because I thought it was the best way. There must have been some sort of problem with the Hursts that caused a delay with Lucas.'

Cerys nodded. Ah. Thank God. She wasn't going to be arrested then. But she was too traumatised at the moment even for the relief to show itself. It was just a problem with the Hursts...

Breathe, she told herself. She took a deep breath and shuddered.

'I'm not in trouble with the law?' she asked anyway.

Howard shook his head. 'Of course not.'

Cerys felt herself relax by a few degrees. She was by now shaking like a leaf.

'I thought you were dead,' she whispered. 'Until half an hour ago, I honestly thought you were dead.'

'No, I refuse to die in a ditch and have you say I told you so.' He grinned.

'But you're injured.' She pointed unnecessarily at his bound shoulder and his arm, now supported in a sling.

'It's nothing.' He shrugged as if it was an everyday occurrence to lose cupsful of blood from gunshot wounds. 'They patched me up nicely at your clinic. Hardly hurts at all now, the number of painkillers they pumped into me.'

'Good. That's good... And James?'

'Concussion. He's under observation.'

Cerys nodded, saying no more. Her head was spinning.

Dyer turned to the two policemen who stood watching their reunion with interest by the open door of the pod. 'Cerys Lee, may I present the chief of police and one of his very skilled marksmen?'

The Leader shakily tried to pull herself together and walked the short distance to where they stood, taking another deep steadying breath. She shook their hands and thanked them profusely, and with her tone as professionally cool and relaxed as she could force it to be, asked matter-of-factly, 'Is he dead?' She turned again to look at the figure lying in the road. 'What will happen now?'

The policeman shook his head. 'It was just a dart. Only a tranquiliser. He'll sleep for a bit and then wake up nice and cosy in a prison cell, where he'll no doubt stay for rather a long time after we've compiled the extensive list of charges against him. He's looking at ten years before he's even considered for parole, I'd have thought.'

Cerys nodded. 'Yes. Yes, quite. Well, thank you again, both of you.' She looked at Howard. 'Now, if you're feeling up to it, I think we should get to the office as soon as possible. There's much to do.'

'We'll take you back into town,' said the police chief.

'Very kind.'

Howard smiled. Always the professional, was Cerys. She'd satisfied herself that he was OK, allowed him to see that she was both professionally and personally happy about that, and now it was back to the grindstone for both of them. Even if he knew better than to believe that she was so quickly recovered. He could see every quiver of fear in her as she began to calm down and it ironed itself out.

'Of course,' said the policeman.

'We should be able to fend off any serious unrest now, at least,' said Howard. 'I think a well-timed news interview, confirming the arrest of Ward and repeating a few of the promises made in your speech would go down well.'

The chief of police nodded. 'I'll set it up.'

'I agree. But first, what I really need to do is have a nice cup of tea. And a biscuit. Janine had some really rather nice ones, and I didn't get to eat a single one.'

Howard put a hand on her arm and indicated for her to hang back and let the police go on ahead and get into the pod first. He turned to her and spoke in a low voice.

'That might have to wait, I'm afraid. I hate to dump more on you at a time like this, but Lambert's disappeared, and if it turns out that he's dead and someone other than us has removed his body, then I'm afraid you and your niece may have got yourselves into a bit of a mess after all. I went to the car you left him in with those two.' He pointed at the policemen. 'So they know he's disappeared. It won't take long for them to start thinking along the same lines.'

'Ah. Yes. That would be a problem, I agree. But I'm sure he's not dead. Besides, if anyone found a dead body they'd report it, wouldn't they? Especially if they're against me. They wouldn't be likely to carry it off as a trophy.'

'That's true enough, I suppose. But we need to find him as a matter of urgency.'

'Yes, let's hope he turns up quickly. We'll put someone on it straight away.' She didn't have the energy to think about Frederick Lambert and the consequences of his possible death right now, but as she climbed into the police pod, Cerys said with a weak smile, 'I'm sure he's alive. And by the way, Howard, if you'd died in a ditch, you wouldn't have been able to hear me say I told you so.'

Chapter Forty-seven

As Lucas and Anthony were about to leave, Lucas' CD rang. Hurst and Sally stood watching him, avoiding each other's eyes as he took the call. He smiled. The first genuine smile either of them had seen on anyone's face for a very long time.

'We did it,' he exclaimed. 'Howard Dyer and the police have caught Ward, he's been arrested, and the Leader is on her way back to her office as we speak. She's fine. She managed to keep Ward talking until they arrived. The chief of police helped out personally, by all accounts.'

'That's such fantastic news,' said Sally, turning to her husband. 'Isn't that great?'

'Yes, it's absolutely bloody marvellous. I'm happy things went the way you wanted them to. You must be very pleased with yourself. I hope you think it was all worth it.'

'Of course it was worth it. Please, Anthony, don't turn this into another row. I never wanted any of us to be put in danger.'

'How else was it going to go?' He turned to Lucas. 'Congratulations. Good for you. Now, please, I'm going home to pack a case, seeing as the streets are now an apparently safe place to be, and then I want you to keep to your side of the bargain and put me on a plane back to the UK.'

'The streets are not a safe place for you to be. You heard that message just now. Lambert's on the loose. He could be anywhere.'

'I'll take my chances. While I'm getting my stuff, you can sort out that flat for me and tell me where to collect the keys.' He turned on his heel and headed for the door, where he paused to look back again at his wife. 'I'll take you to court for custody of Toby if I have to. I'm only leaving him here with you now because I'm not a total bastard and I don't want to upset him anymore than is necessary. Anymore than you've done already.'

With that, he went to the kitchen, hugged his son, told him he'd see him very soon, and then he marched out of the house, leaving all the doors open in his wake.

Sally ran up the hall calling after him to come back, but even as she did so she knew it wouldn't do any good. He was right. She'd done this to them. She was responsible for damaging their family. But what else could she have done? She'd acted with the absolute best of intentions from the start and continued to do so. And, frankly, she'd rather live as a single parent in a free world than as a family under the conditions they'd been living under all their lives. Her son's freedom was worth everything, even the sacrifice of her marriage.

However, she understood Anthony's anger. She wasn't completely devoid of feeling. She sighed deeply and closed the front door, resting her forehead on it for a few seconds. When she turned round, Toby was standing in the kitchen doorway staring miserably at her. She gave him what she hoped was a reassuring smile and led him back into the conservatory.

Chapter Forty-eight

The unlikely little group sat in the conservatory absent-mindedly drinking the now tepid tea. No one thought to replenish it. All of them were silent, the adults each deep in thought and the child playing with his toy robot.

No one had any idea what to do about the turncoat traitor Lambert. The only thing they knew for certain was that, dead or alive, he was still in the vicinity. If alive, it would be impossible for him to leave town, just as it would be for anyone else, without all and sundry finding out about it. The Leader's office had put out alerts to their guards, of course, who were stationed around the border fences. The irony of this, that there were border fences, was not lost on any of them. What had the world become?

Still, that was all about to change and, although borders would be re-established, they would be fair, the way they used to be in the civilised countries of the past. There would be security checks, passport control and, if you were doing something wrong, you'd be stopped. If you weren't doing anything wrong, you'd be allowed on your way, in and out of other countries for holidays or business, as you needed or wanted, the way things used to be. The way things should be. Without let or hindrance, as it used to read in the old British passports.

In the meantime, even in this phase of transition, the same held true for wrongdoers, even without passports. Frederick Lambert could not leave, and that was a good thing. He was, at the very least, making a nuisance of himself. The police had been alerted to what he'd done and would be keeping a lookout for him. If he tried to leave, there *would* be hindrance.

'Anyone got any ideas?' asked Lucas after a time.

'Well,' said Janine. 'Ms Lee is safe, we know that. I suppose we should just wait here until we get word that Lambert's been caught.'

'That could take hours... days. If he's even still alive.' Lucas stood and started to pace up and down. 'I'll send a message to Paolo, see if he's heard anything.' Paolo would have contacted him by now if that was the case, but it gave him something to do.

No one spoke for a long moment. Both the women knew it was pointless. What was there to say? Lambert could be anywhere.

'But if he's dead,' said Janine, 'that'd mean...'

'He's not dead, I'm certain of it, or we'd have heard about it by now. Chances are someone from the WA is hiding him,' said Sally, shaking her head. She put down her empty teacup with a rattle. 'This is all a bit disconcerting, actually, sitting here talking like this at this late stage. We usually have a plan. Why haven't we got a plan?'

They all looked at each other and no one spoke. Nobody had any answers, and one by one they retreated back into their own musings. Lucas resumed his pacing of the room.

Suddenly, the door swung open behind them.

'Well, what a miserable little gathering this is.'

The four people in the room raised their heads from their thoughts in surprise to see a swaying, wild-eyed Frederick Lambert standing in the doorway to the kitchen brandishing a small penknife.

'You really should lock your doors, you know. You never know who could wander in.'

Chapter Forty-nine

It was the last thing anyone had imagined.

Lambert was right, thought Janine. They should have locked the door. And Sally was also right. They should have had a plan. This could end in disaster. How on earth had they not anticipated that he'd turn up here?

Frederick Lambert remained where he was and leant against the door from the kitchen. He looked terrible. His clothes were dishevelled, there was dirt all over his face, most likely from having had it thrown against the filthy car paraphernalia in the boot, and it was as puffy and blotchy as a storm cloud, which was strange, Sally thought, because he hadn't sustained any injury which could have caused it. Not at their hands, anyway. It was plain for all to see that he was rallying himself before he spoke. His face suddenly turning white, his eyes didn't appear to be properly focused. They were wide and fearful. He continued to sway, even with the support of the door frame.

'What, did you forget that I knew where your safe house was?' he said eventually. Lambert's hulking frame almost filled the doorway as he slurred his words at them. He looked as if he'd been drinking. Perhaps he had, because his demeanour certainly supported it, and his general state couldn't be totally down to what the two women had done.

To our shame, thought Janine, yes, we did forget that.

'Weren't you expecting me? What, isn't anyone going to speak? Welcome me? Don't say you've drunk all the tea?' He looked at the table. 'And eaten all the biscuits, too. How rude.' The room remained silent while the three adults tried to figure out how to handle him. 'Well? Isn't anyone going to ask how I got out of the car, at least? No? Is no one curious?'

'With the penknife?' Toby shrugged as if it was the most stupidly obvious question ever.

'Oh, so we've got ourselves a little smart mouth, have we?' Lambert took an unsteady step towards Toby.

Sally leapt to her feet to block his path. 'One more step towards my son and you won't live to see another dawn.'

Lambert laughed, looking down at her. It was a croaky, forced sound, almost as if it was something he was doing for the first time and wasn't really sure how it worked. As he stood before her, she could indeed smell strong alcohol on his breath. Sally barely reached his shoulder, but she stood firmly in front of him, issuing her challenge, and he clearly thought it was hilarious. 'What, you think you can take me on?'

'Want to try me, Frederick? You want to underestimate me? I really wouldn't do that if I were you. Unlike you, I paid attention during my training, and I promise you that if you lay one finger on my son, I can have that knife off you and through your neck in approximately one and a half seconds.' The cogs of his brain working, trying to process her words and decide whether he believed them, were almost as visible as if his head had been transparent. 'The only reason you're not already dead, threatening Toby like that, is because I'd hate to make a mess of Janine's carpet in front of him,' she said. 'But go ahead, try me.'

'Sit down.' He gave Sally a dismissive shove but when her only movement was a backwards motion of her shoulder, he looked surprised and seemed to think better of it, glancing at his knife. He took a small step back towards the door and tried to exert some authority another way by saying to Lucas, 'You sit down, too.'

Lucas did as he was told and sat, poised, waiting, ready for him if he dared to make another move. Legally speaking, it was better if they waited. Walking in through an open door waving a little penknife wouldn't in itself be enough to have him arrested. There was the charge of kidnap, of course, but you never knew. The police might still take some time to adjust, despite their help with rescuing Cerys, and at this stage, if you got the wrong judge, getting a conviction could be difficult, even with the tracking information of the car and the testimonies of Howard and James against him.

So, it was best to make sure your own moral high ground was covered with an immaculate layer of metaphorical tarmac and didn't have any unsightly stones in it. They'd already knocked Lambert on the head and locked him in a roasting hot car boot like a chicken in an oven. Yes, there were stones enough already upon their moral high ground. They needed a decent lawyer and the reinstatement of unbiased jurors. He coughed.

'Do as the man says, Sally.'

Sally looked at Lucas and frowned, but she caught the small shake of his head that meant don't antagonise him. She sat, wondering why Lucas was being such a wimp. Perhaps he had an idea? She looked at him from her chair, waiting.

A second man silently opened the well-oiled door into the hall from the dining room and crept the few paces along to the open kitchen door, which he slowly pulled closed and soundlessly locked, before returning to the dining room. He checked the screen on the table that showed what was going on in various rooms of the house and clicked on the conservatory to make the image bigger. For now, the coast was clear, so he moved to the side of the window and then very slowly swung it open and climbed noiselessly out onto the path beside the house. It was a good job there was no gravel out here, he thought, or any other noisy encumbrance underfoot. The low maintenance garden was of great benefit to him right now.

He ducked down behind some bushes in a flowerbed the other side of the path and assessed the situation. He could see into the kitchen from here and all looked quiet. They were all still in the conservatory. He darted to his right and turned at a right angle, pressing himself against the wall of the kitchen. In case his help was needed, surprise would, as always, be key.

In one hand he held a pot of pens, his fingers curled tightly around them to stop them rattling. A bad choice, but it was the first thing that had come to hand. In the other, he held a gun – only ever to be used as a last resort, of course – and on his shirt was a concealed camera, cleverly camouflaged into the design of the fabric. He knew well enough what he was doing and how the situation needed to be dealt with from here. He had experience. He was the wrong side of seventy-five years of age but was nevertheless still quick on his feet and had good reflexes. And he'd handled far worse situations in his time than this. This was like a first-level training exercise. Rather fun, in fact. It sort of brought back the old days. Nevertheless, he still had to watch his step. Complacency had been the undoing of better men than he, and now was not the time to be getting nostalgic.

The reason for the pot of pens was to signal, because the issue he had was with the conservatory windows. Not being able to see in, while everyone inside could see out, was a problem. Therefore, he couldn't go in that way. He couldn't go anywhere near the outside of those windows.

Added to the problem of the windows was the fact that there was a pod in the garden, connected to the conservatory entrance by a tunnel. It meant the only thing to do was to go in through the kitchen, through the back door.

He moved closer, slowly, silently, ducking as he passed the first kitchen window and moving quickly past the door. Standing between the door and the second, open, window, he reached out his hand and carefully placed the pot of pens on the ledge outside and hoped it would be enough. He waited with his back to the wall, listening intently, and trying to catch what was being said in the conservatory beyond.

Inside the conservatory, Lambert stood over the little company as they sat. Lucas waited to see what Lambert was going to do next with a raised eyebrow and small smile. His hand, nevertheless, rested on his gun, which he'd removed from his pocket while Lambert had been arguing with Sally and slid down the side of the chair between the cushion and its frame.

'Where is Cerys Lee?' Lambert addressed his question to Sally.

'I don't know.'

'Don't lie to me.'

'I'm not lying. She left, took the car, Janine's car. She said she had work to do. I suppose you could try the office. I imagine you'd receive quite a welcome there, after what you've been up to today. Yes, there's probably a party being planned for Frederick Lambert the traitor. Yes, they're probably drinking celebratory shots and chucking your crap out the top floor window as we speak.'

Lambert considered her. 'Sarcasm, Sally? That's not a great idea, now, is it? She tried to kill me. The woman tried to kill me. And you helped her.' He poked the knife in the air in her direction.

Sally looked him straight in the eyes. 'You kidnapped her. And nobody tried to kill you, Frederick. We just got ourselves out of a situation, nothing more than that. If the tables were turned, you'd have done the same. And what about Howard and James? You tried to kill them.'

'Who?'

'Your supposed colleagues who you left for dead.'

'Pf...' He waved his hand dismissively. 'Irrelevant both. Where is the Leader?'

'I told you, I don't know.'

'And I told you don't lie to me.'

For a time, nobody spoke. Sally sat and continued to stare at him. What an imbecile. What did he imagine he was going to do? She wondered how he'd ever got through his training to do the job he was supposed to do. What if he'd been loyal to the Leader and something had happened where he'd had to defend her? He'd have been worse than useless. A blundering liability. Hell, even Toby, an eight-year-old child, was more observant than this man.

However, he had a knife, albeit a small one, and Toby was here in the room. Hold your tongue, Sally, she told herself. For Toby's sake. Lucas is right. See what he intends to do. Then act.

The good thing, in Sally's opinion, was that as before, he didn't appear to have much, if anything, of a plan.

'Frederick,' said Janine at length. 'Could I please go and get a glass of water?'

'What, you think I'm an idiot?'

Yes, thought the assembled company.

'Of course not. I just need a glass of water.'

Lambert hesitated.

'Come with me, if you like.'

The large man wavered, in both senses of the word. He touched his free hand to the bump on his head. He shot an evil look across the room at Toby and his metal robot. He'd learnt his lesson about turning his back on anyone.

'Look, the kitchen's just there, as you well know, having walked right through it uninvited. There's a glass on the draining board, so I haven't even got to open any cupboards. No surprises. Stand inside the door to the conservatory, if you must; that way you can still see all of us. You only have to move a couple of feet.' Janine only just stopped short of rolling her eyes at him. Here she was, detailing to him the obvious moves he had to make, when she herself could probably take him out with one punch. It was a tempting thought. Not a serious one, but it amused her, nevertheless.

'Slowly, then,' Lambert told her. He pulled Sally by the scruff of the neck from her place on the sofa beside Toby. 'You'll come too.' He curled his arm around her throat and indicated to Janine that she should get up.

God, he's stupid, Janine thought as she got to her feet. Before starting towards the kitchen, she looked across at her son, who gave an almost imperceptible nod. She walked through into the kitchen. Lambert followed her to just inside the door, with a firm grip on Sally, whose feet, now Lambert had straightened from pulling her up, were suspended about six inches from the floor as she dangled by the chin from his forearm. She held onto it as if she was doing a bizarre sort of pull-up, in order not to be throttled by the tightness of it, while he vaguely pointed the knife at her, oblivious to or not caring a jot about her discomfort and her reddening face.

As they watched from the sofa, Lucas whispered very quietly to a frightened Toby, who had gripped his robot in both hands and moved forward on the sofa as if he intended trying for himself what Cerys had done earlier, that he didn't have to worry. Toby looked as if he didn't believe him, but stayed put.

Janine immediately spotted the pot of pens teetering on the ledge outside the kitchen window. OK then, we're about to have some action, she thought. Good to know.

Slowly and calmly, she picked up the glass from the draining board, glad it was there, although she supposed she could just as easily have used a teacup, and filled it with water.

'Frederick, what are you doing with that knife?' she asked, her face still pointing towards the window.

'If you don't give me what I want, I'll kill her,' he said.

Janine nodded. Yes, the man was very stupid.

'But Frederick, we've told you that we don't know where the Leader is. We *can't* give you what you want.'

'You can get me the money, then. Ten million is my price.'

'Hm… I see.' She then did three things at once. She took a step to her left to fling open the back door with her left hand, hurled the contents of the glass with practised accuracy over Lambert with her right, and called Lucas.

Lucas sprang towards the door to the kitchen like a panther, pulling the gun from the sofa. At the same time, his father burst in through the outside door aiming his own gun at Lambert.

'Drop the knife.'

Lambert, soaked with water and momentarily disorientated, and already woozy from the bang to the head and the drink, was easy to disarm. He dropped both Sally and the knife without a fuss. Both the woman and the small blade clattered to the floor. She grabbed it and stood up, seeing stars, and gasping for air.

'What are you doing?' he mumbled, wiping water from his eyes.

'Defending ourselves,' said Janine. 'I told you that's what we do, remember?'

Father and son restrained the big man with minimal effort and an air of almost disappointed anticlimax, by tying him very firmly to a kitchen chair, which they placed in the conservatory where they could keep an eye on him until the authorities arrived. Janine put through a call to the very helpful chief of police. He was on his way.

'All recorded,' said Lucas' father happily, tapping his shirt. 'Although not much to show in the way of footage, I'm afraid. Still, at least we've got proof of what he was saying, eh? Are you OK?' he asked his wife. 'Sally?'

'Yes, I'm fine,' Janine told him. 'We're all fine.' She looked at Sally for confirmation, and she nodded, coughing. 'I'm glad you were at home to help, Gregory. I don't suppose we'll need as much security or the little camera gadgets anymore after this,' she said, hoping the fact that they would soon be moving home, and that this life of creeping about doing God alone knew what would be over, would start to sink into her husband's head. He, like his son, enjoyed the life of a spy rather too much. 'It'll all be over soon,' she reiterated. And thank goodness for that, she thought. The sooner he stopped messing around with those blasted gadgets and the sooner he stopped staring at the security cameras in the house on those blasted screens, and the sooner the dining room could once again be used for eating in, the better. The sooner they could go home, the better. Maybe he would find a nice sedate hobby, such as gardening.

'We should send word to Ms Lee,' Janine said on a long-suffering breath, and took her CD from where it lay on the table. Without further ado, she called the Leader. It was over. They'd done it.

Chapter Fifty

Cerys Lee sat at her desk with her longed-for cup of tea and let out a long sigh. She placed her CD down in front of her and relayed Janine's message. 'My God, what a day.'

'Yeah,' Howard Dyer laughed. 'That's the understatement of the century.' He rubbed his eyes, exhaustion sweeping over him now that he'd finally sat down to relax for ten minutes. His shoulder throbbed dully as the painkillers began to wear off. He was starting to get a headache. 'You made a good call, Cerys. You did the right thing at exactly the right time. If you hadn't done what you did there would probably have been another war. I don't see how we could have avoided it. Nuclear destruction. It's a hideous thought. You saved the world from that, and the world will thank you for it. I know I do. No one will ever forget what happened today. You should be proud of yourself and all those years of hard work.'

'Yes. Though I rather fear it's been at the expense of my niece's marriage.'

'Nobody forced her.'

'Mm, true. Anthony was forced, though, and I do feel responsible for that. He didn't get any say in the matter, did he? He didn't get any of the training that she did. And he didn't get any warning. It must have been like living for six years in a relentless nightmare for him. Like a prison sentence.'

'He would never have agreed to do the training.'

'Probably not.'

'And we couldn't have missed the opportunity of having Sally on board. She was one of our best agents. So was he, as it turned out. We did what we had to do.' Howard rubbed his eyes. He was worn out.

'I know, but you can't blame him for being angry, feeling used. He could easily have died today. And don't try to share the blame, Howard, it was my doing. Mine and Sally's.'

'We're all members of the Democratic Party, Cerys. We stick together.'

'Yes, that's true enough. But what about poor little Toby?'

'I'm sure poor little Toby will be fine. And Anthony will work it out in time.'

'I hope so. But I still wish there was something I could do for him, for them.'

'They're adults, Cerys. They'll work it out for themselves.'

Cerys sighed again. 'Yes, I suppose you're right.'

Howard stood up from where he'd been sitting in the chair the other side of Cerys' desk and walked across to look out the window at the harsh landscape. It would soon be dark. Dark dust instead of light. The mountains turned to silhouettes, still restraining them, however prettily. He hated it. 'I was thinking about getting myself a nice little place in the Sussex countryside when I get back to England.'

Cerys smiled. 'That sounds nice.' She poured more tea. 'Where, exactly?'

'I don't know yet. Somewhere green with oak trees, and houses built from red bricks or faced with flint. Chalk in the earth, blackberries in the hedgerows. You know the sort of thing, somewhere that makes your soul sing with joy and at the same time cry with the relief of being home.' He turned away from the window to face her, pulling himself together. 'Perhaps you'd like to help me choose? I'd value your opinion.'

Chapter Fifty-one

Once the media was allowed to start reporting actual news events again, it didn't take long – in fact it was only a matter of hours – for the story of the Hursts' involvement in the downfall of the WA to get out and be known around the world. Consequently, by the time she and Toby arrived back in the newly reinstated United Kingdom, Sally found that she was almost as much of a celebrity as her aunt.

This state wasn't something she'd anticipated or that she particularly relished, and she had shuddered to think in those first few days back in England how Anthony was dealing with it, but she had to admit that, for her own sake at least, it was useful.

She'd long since planned to go into politics properly herself, whether her aunt had been successful in getting rid of the WA or not, and her newfound celebrity meant that pathway was now easy for her to traverse, laid out before her as it was like a red carpet, and so her earlier than expected leadership campaign – she'd only thought of becoming a local MP, but the possibility of heading the party was practically handed to her on a plate – was conducted without as much as a single obstacle to be overcome. That's not to say that she'd been waiting for an easily cleared passage, she hadn't. She'd definitely thought to start at the bottom and work her way up. The only other thing she'd been sure of was that if her aunt had failed, she, Sally, would have had to take over or at least be part of a new strategy to get rid of the WA, and that could potentially have taken years more work than her aunt had already dedicated to the task. It wouldn't have been easy, because Ward would undoubtedly have tightened his grip on the world to the point of suffocation.

Still, as it stood, that situation had been avoided and Cerys Lee had succeeded in opening up an amazing chance for her niece. And so, cheered on by the people of the United Kingdom, she immediately ran for leadership of the Democratic Party.

This leadership campaign to head the Democratic Party had been anticipated, expected, and almost demanded of one of the Hursts, not only by their adoring public, but also the existing members of the party, so much so that their current leader took a timely early retirement in order to give the public what they wanted. He'd stood openly in the House of Commons, the first time in generations that anyone had been able to do so, and declared his intention to step aside into retirement so that one of those marvellous two could lead their party into the future, if it turned out that that was what his colleagues and the public wanted. He would give his total support to whichever of the Hursts was elected, he said. A couple of other people put themselves forward as candidates, but nobody took them very seriously, and everyone knew it was only being done for the benefit of giving a choice in the way of the old leadership campaigns. It was a way of getting back to the old ways, of going through the process in a manner that none of them had done before and had only read about, of being able to use words such as hustings for the first time in two centuries. The whole process was conducted with the air of intense anticipation, like excited children rehearsing for their Christmas play.

So, it was a good thing, Sally had thought on numerous occasions, that she'd actually wanted to do it, to take on the role of party leader. It meant the pressure had been taken off Anthony who, if confronted with a bank of journalists, would have got off that plane from Nevada, which in the end had been just a week before her own flight, spitting venom at the very thought of it. Sally's enthusiasm for the job had meant he'd been able, more or less, to skulk away into the shadows to nurse his wounded ego in peace.

Perhaps that was unkind, but it was certainly Sally's view of what she saw as a massive overreaction. Not to the danger he'd faced, because that, of course, had been very real, but to Sally's role in getting him to join her in her mission.

Had it been manipulation? A bit too much pressure? Possibly. Maybe she hadn't had a right to involve him. But she knew it was better that they'd faced the WA together rather than her trying to keep it a secret from him as well as from everyone else. By necessity, there had been enough things she'd had to keep secret from him already – imagine if she'd had to work alone, without his help. It would have been impossible. Getting him into the WA facility had been the only option. There would have been next to nothing she could have done to help her aunt if she'd had to stay in London. They'd needed to be on site, she and her husband together. He'd been the one with the suitable qualifications and talents for working in the facility. He really had been the best person for the job. It was as simple as that. It had been the only way.

Anyway, she hoped he would heal quickly from his pain, for Toby's sake as well as his own.

If she hadn't gone for the job of leader of the Democratic Party herself, Sally would have probably tried to persuade Lucas to stand. She would have supported that amazing man wholeheartedly and no doubt so would the public. But she *had* wanted the job, desperately, and she received no challenge or objection from him or anyone else. And anyway, Lucas decided the Secret Service suited him better.

He and Paolo had also returned to England, but split their time between a plush penthouse in Mayfair where, when they weren't working, they enjoyed a busy social life involving the theatre and copious amounts of champagne-drenched parties, and a villa high up in the hills of Campania looking down over the Bay of Naples, which was a wonderful place to relax and revitalise the soul, while looking back on his own theatrical role in the downfall of the WA with pride and satisfaction. He would dine off the stories for the rest of his life.

Robert Ward showed no remorse for his long list of crimes and was given, as predicted by the chief of police when arrested, a ten-year prison sentence. He stood in court and calmly told the judge that he'd do it all again. His situation wasn't helped by his calling the judge a snivelling jobsworth. The judge promptly ruled that Ward was in contempt of court and that as a result he would serve every minute of his ten-year sentence, with no parole hearing, and he was to think himself lucky that his impertinence hadn't cost him another year or two. Ward spat on the floor and laughed as he was led away.

He spent his time of incarceration in a high security prison in Carson City building plans in his head and waiting for the day of his release with a calculated patience. When he got out, he would return to his home in west London and start again. His wife had left him when he'd been arrested, but he'd replace her easily enough. This time, he'd start with a clean sheet and do things properly, do things his way. Meanwhile, he went over and over his plans in his mind, perfecting every minute detail.

Frederick Lambert argued unsound mind and duress as extenuating circumstances for his actions. Extreme stress relating to the pressures of his job with the Leader's office, but especially from Robert Ward, whose agents' relentless attempts to recruit him had made him lose his sense of reason, he said. He'd snapped. He understood that he'd been used and that he'd been stupid, and he was sorry. Robert Ward and the agents in question had denied it, of course, but the judge believed his story, and therefore his own ten-year sentence was reduced to four.

Lambert's lawyers asked for a change of identity and location for him. They didn't want there to be a risk of Ward's people dealing out their own justice in jail, or of their finding Lambert when he got out. He was afraid for his safety, they said, and they believed that fear was justified. To his relief and surprise, this request was granted, and he was sent under a new name to a rehabilitation facility in Paris, where they offered all manner of different types of counselling, including therapy through art. Lambert discovered he had a talent for painting and spent hours by himself watching and painting the boats on the river. His future would be a quiet one.

Sally's subsequent election as prime minister a couple of months after she took over leadership of the Democratic Party was a mere formality. The Democratic Party, *her* Democratic Party, won the first general election after the downfall of the Free World system with a landslide majority, the like of which, save for the result of the vote to return to the System of Nations, had never been seen before.

The only cloud hanging over her happiness was the fact that she missed her husband. He hadn't as yet filed for divorce so she took that to be a small glimmer of hope that at some point in the future they could perhaps be reconciled, but in the few months since she'd got back from Nevada, she hadn't seen him at all. She hadn't expected to. The only contact they'd had was through a solicitor to make the necessary arrangements for him to see Toby. Sally never objected to his suggestions. She had no wish to separate father and son, so always agreed to whatever Anthony's plans were without the least argument.

He would, as a rule, pick the boy up from school on a Friday afternoon and take him back there Monday morning, from where Sally would collect him that day after school. He'd wanted things arranged this way, she knew, because he was still too angry to see her or speak to her in person. She couldn't say she blamed him, not really, but wished he'd understand that what had been done had been done the way it had for everyone's benefit, for the greater good.

She was sure that one day he'd understand. After all, he'd been on board there for a long time in Nevada. He'd agreed with her that what they were doing was for the sake of their son, as much as for the world at large. He hadn't wanted Toby to live in a dictatorship, away from his true home and being afraid of everything his whole life, anymore than she had, and she was certain that one day, after he'd worked through the trauma of that dangerous day back in May, his feelings on the matter would come full circle. They had to, didn't they? She hoped against hope that he was receiving counselling.

Meanwhile, Sally had no choice but to go along with doing things the way he wanted them done if she didn't want him to start threatening custody battles again, and if that meant going through a solicitor to talk about Toby, then so be it. It was far from being an ideal situation and it made all three of them miserable.

But in Sally's head the seeds of another plan were germinating…

Chapter Fifty-two

Six months to the day after the vote to return to the System of Nations, Cerys Lee resigned her position as World Leader. She had done everything she'd set out to do and, although there was still much work to be done, and many thousands of creases yet to be ironed out all across the world, she decided the time had come when the role of World Leader was a superfluous one. The day she resigned was a magical one because it signified victory, freedom and success on a level that no one could have foreseen as being even remotely possible just six short months ago. She was proud of herself, and she was proud of the people of the world. She was humbled that they had trusted her and thankful that she'd been able to deliver on her promises. She'd had help. Everyone had pulled together. The thing of which she was most proud was the agreement that she had set up between nations to reinstate without contention all borders at the locations they had been two hundred years ago. Who knew how long the peaceful situation would last, but it was a start – and it was a very promising one. Perhaps lasting peace, or something close to it, would now be achieved at last? On that point, the world was holding its breath.

Another very exciting vote was held in the United Kingdom, put forward by her niece, the new prime minister, to ask the public's opinion on whether or not there should be a return of the British royal family. Cerys thought this was a wonderful idea. The public were living in happy times, and this was something else that could reinforce their nation's identity. It was something else to be celebrated, and the public agreed.

As a result, the closest descendent of the previous king whose family there had no longer been any place for under the so-called Free World, and who had been forced into mainstream if not subservient roles along with everyone else, was returned to the Palace as Queen Elizabeth III. It seemed right that the most loved and inspirational monarch ever known, the longest reigning monarch, no less, be succeeded by her namesake, to become the symbol of a whole new world. Other countries quickly followed suit.

Unsurprisingly, after this quick reinstatement of the royal family, Cerys Lee's name was first to go onto the honours list, for services to her country.

Chapter Fifty-three

Sally Hurst was a competent and popular prime minister, but the regret she felt at the way she'd manipulated her husband was always there in her mind, increasing every day and hanging over everything she did. It was a permanent fixture, eating away at her, always there to take the edge off the happiness she should have been feeling as she slowly built her country back up.

She still loved him, after all, and wanted more than ever for him to come back to her and to the family home. Not that she exactly had a family home, living, as she did, in Downing Street. There hadn't been a spare second to think about buying another place yet. Any spare time she got she spent with Toby.

Six months had passed since she and Anthony had last seen each other face to face, and though she could now admit that her actions had been less than fair at times, she'd had enough of feeling bad. And of him feeling bitter. She decided that now was the time to do something about it. She would go and see him. What was the worst that could happen? He could yell at her and throw her off his property. Well, his yelling was nothing she hadn't experienced before, so...

Her government was in need of a foreign affairs minister, and Sally knew her husband would be the perfect man for the job. MPs could be chosen in different ways now. If there was someone who was suitable to do a job, then why not? The only proviso was that that person needed to be a fully paid-up member of the party, but that was just a minor formality. The problem was going to be in persuading him to take it on. The only way to persuade him was to go and see him, talk to him face to face, and hope that he accepted. If he did, then who knew, maybe one day the two of them could become friends again. Or maybe he'd even come home. Kill two birds with one stone. But perhaps that was too much to ask.

One thing at a time.

Her car came to a stop outside Anthony's apartment building and Sally shook her head in bewilderment. He'd stuck to his guns and insisted on a flat similar to the one he'd been forced to leave, even though Lucas had tried to offer him something better. No, he'd said. He wanted his old life back. Just without his wife. And so here it was, an ordinary looking block on an ordinary looking street, from where he worked remotely, designing software for his old company. Bland, unnoticeable, grey, generic. Not just the apartment building, but his whole life. She didn't know whether to feel ashamed that she'd done this to him, to them, or whether to be thoroughly, unutterably irritated by his stubbornness. To be honest, she was more inclined towards the latter. There was no need for him to live this way.

'I shouldn't be too long,' Sally told her driver, and got out of the car onto the wet pavement. Her bodyguard got out and stood beside her. 'It's OK, James, I'll go in alone. I'll call you if I need you, but this is my husband, it'll be fine.' James nodded, but remained standing by the car, arms folded, watching.

It was now late autumn and there was a chill in the air and the threat of more rain to come. It didn't rain much these days, so she enjoyed it when it happened. There was exciting new technology coming, which was in its later stages of development in a huge research facility in Oxfordshire, that would mean artificial rain being produced all over the globe, and such was the state of the climate now that in Sally's opinion it couldn't come quickly enough. She'd pumped millions upon millions into the project, as had many other contributing countries, and she couldn't wait to see it in action.

However, that was something for another day. Today's objective was to snap her husband out of his pit and back into the real world.

There's only so much feeling sorry for yourself that people can take, she thought irritably as she crossed the pavement and pressed the bell. It was time for her husband to get over himself. If he didn't want to come home, well then, she'd just have to learn to live with it, and she would, but as far as his sitting around wallowing in self-pity went, she couldn't stomach another second of it. They had a child together, for God's sake, and they didn't even speak to each other. How long before his woe is me attitude started affecting Toby, turning him into someone who wanted to hide himself away from the world? No, that was exactly the fate she'd fought so hard to avoid for him and she wouldn't allow it.

'Yes?' came the voice answering her ring.

'Anthony, it's me. Can I come in and speak to you, please?'

Chapter Fifty-four

Anthony Hurst had written a book. He hadn't bothered to try and find a publisher, even though he knew he wouldn't have any trouble doing so. People would be only too eager to read all about his experiences over the last several years and his role in the downfall of the World Administration. Yes, he knew it would be enthusiastically lapped up and that he could no doubt become very rich as a result of its publication.

However, in the beginning at least, he'd only written the book as a sort of private therapy. He'd thought that if he made a detailed account of all of it, of everything he could remember since that fateful day when he'd been approached by the four men in the car park of his old workplace, then he could come to terms with everything that had happened and maybe start to find some peace. He didn't like the use of the word "closure", but he supposed that had also been a big part of it. He'd hidden himself away from the world, from the now different sort of prying eyes, the vulture kind, and had worked on the book every day that he hadn't had Toby with him. For six months he'd toiled. The words had spewed out of him through his fingers, and now the book was complete. Three hundred pages of anger, regret, nostalgia, fear, betrayal and hurt. All done in the name of therapy.

It had worked, too, up to a point. He was far less angry now than he had been six months ago and, also, writing about Sally's role in his ordeal had served to help him understand her better and almost to sympathise with her situation. He'd made himself be completely honest in his writing, and this was why he'd never followed through with his threat to sue his wife for custody of Toby. His honesty in the pages of the book had brought with it a new clarity. She loved the boy every bit as much as he did. He could now, if still slightly grudgingly, understand that her motivation had genuinely been to create a better world for their son to grow up in. She'd felt that she hadn't had a choice. Perhaps she'd been right, and she hadn't had a choice. He wanted the best for Toby, too. So, yes, he could understand it more clearly now.

Part of his anger with her had been because of the shock of the situation that had been so suddenly sprung on him, and his inability to react to it, to do anything about it. His initial shock and anger had had to be repressed by necessity and had ended up festering away in the corners of his brain while he got on with the job of living the life of a spy and surviving. He could acknowledge that now and, with the acknowledgement, came a release.

He also understood that another part of his anger had been down to the fact that, although he hadn't realised it at the time, he'd been almost envious that someone could be so passionate about something that they would pursue the end goal whatever the cost. And Sally had always kept Toby safe. Or as safe as she was able. His life hadn't been so different in Nevada from what it would have been here in London, after all.

Would Anthony himself ever have entertained the idea of doing something so dangerous, so seemingly impossible, to follow something he believed in? Even for family? Even for his son? The answer was no, he wouldn't, because he'd never felt that strongly about anything. Anything, that is, until now. Now, he wanted his marriage and his family back and to have a normal life.

He glanced across at the old family photo from just after Toby had turned two, which stood in a prominent position in the middle of the mantlepiece and sighed regretfully. Yes, he understood. He'd been jealous of his wife's drive and ambition.

The need to consult her and get her permission before submitting the book for publication, was another reason he hadn't done so. Even if he didn't have a problem now with the thought of contacting her, embarrassment meant he hadn't yet done so for any other reason than to make the necessary arrangements to see Toby and, even then, that was all done through his solicitor. That conversation, if he wanted to consult her about the book, would by necessity have to be one constructed mainly of digging up the past and reopening old wounds, and he wasn't sure he was quite there yet. A lot of pride swallowing would need to be done. Besides, on a purely practical level, he wasn't sure it was fair of him to ask the prime minister of the country to agree to the publication of such a book.

Maybe it was time to dispense with the solicitor, however, and make his visitation arrangements directly? Baby steps. He went through to the kitchen and put the kettle on for a cup of tea. He would actually quite like to get the book published, now he came to think of it. It felt like it was his brave step, his thing to believe in.

The doorbell rang.

'Yes?'

'Anthony, it's me. Can I come in and speak to you, please?'

Chapter Fifty-five

It came as a complete shock to the ex-World Leader to find out that she was going to be the first recipient of the newly reinstated Nobel Peace Prize. When the phone had rung to notify her of the honour, she'd thought it was a joke. It had taken a ten-minute conversation and a promise of written confirmation to follow to convince her otherwise.

Howard smiled at her over his shoulder as he made the coffee that morning in their newly acquired Sussex home. 'Seriously? Come on, Cerys, who else was it going to go to? Quite honestly, I think they probably only brought it back so quickly for this reason, for your benefit. It's no more than you deserve, after all, and it would have been a travesty if they hadn't. A travesty if it had gone to anyone else, come to that. Especially the first one of modern times.'

'I don't know what to say.' There were tears in her eyes as she thought about the recognition she was shortly to receive, for the work she'd done. She'd been quite teary and emotional lately, as her life had relaxed and softened into something she'd thought would never be possible. From her new vantage point of after-the-event deep exhaustion, she wondered how she'd ever managed it and got through it, that massive thirty-year task. Intelligence, counterintelligence, spies, lies, subterfuge and scheming. Gunpowder, treason and plot, but in reverse. 'It *has* been a lot of work.'

'A lot of work? That's the biggest understatement I've ever heard in my life. You've been fighting this thing, battling against a mountain range of problems and dangers, for decades. And yet you did it, you pulled it off, when only a handful of people ever seriously thought you could or would, and when the WA were so powerful. You never gave up on it, and I'm so proud of you. The world is proud of you.'

Chapter Fifty-six

Cerys Lee stood on the stage in Oslo looking out at the assembled audience and, biting back the nerves, prepared to give her acceptance speech. It had almost been harder to write than the speech she'd prepared for the vote to revert to the System of Nations, which had come naturally to her, even if at times as she'd been recording it, she'd thought it had just sounded like a middle-aged woman ranting.

For this speech, however, she'd spent hours hunched over a computer writing, deleting, and rewriting it until in the end she'd given up, deleted the whole thing and decided to just wing it. It was something that should be natural, off the cuff, candid. It needed to be all her. It needed to be real. Spontaneous. It needed to be from the heart. So, she waited for the applause to die down and then took a deep, steadying breath.

'Thank you. Thank you so much to the Nobel Committee for this exceptional honour.

'World peace is something we all dream of. Something people have dreamt of for thousands of years, and it's something I, like everyone else, believe we have a right to. And world peace starts with democracy, with fairness. Democracy does not, should not, and cannot mean a free-for-all. Democracy, as our recent history has taught us, needs to be managed by sensible minds that can look at all sides of the argument and handle the balance. When democracy becomes too loose, it becomes easy for the wrong people to pick up the reins, which they invariably pull too tightly, and in this way, democracy and fairness are strangled.

'My contribution to our current situation took three decades to prepare, but it was, perhaps, made a little easier in its execution because its completion came at the right time. People were ready for change, more so than ever before, and so I like to think I helped to keep the transition process peaceful by acting, as I say, at the right time. The world was facing a very unpredictable future at the time we held the vote to return to the safer and trusted System of Nations, with unrest building by the day and ever more ferociously, and the threat of another world war was looming large over us.

'Thankfully, we managed to avoid that fate, because you don't need me to tell you it would have been disastrous. Every war is disastrous, of course, but with the first press of the nuclear button, our planet's fate would have been sealed. It would have been over. Humanity wiped out.

'And yet here we are. We are very lucky, and I hope the people of the world will take a moment to contemplate just how lucky.

'There are many creases still to be smoothed out, of course, in the running of our new world, and that, quite naturally, will take time. But we are on the right path.

I'm excited to see how the world now develops from here. We are now repaving the path of true democracy for all.

'Credit for what has happened in the world over the past months, for this achievement, cannot be given to me alone, however, for there are many other dedicated men and women without whose help I could not possibly have managed to achieve half of what I did. Their support was invaluable and at times it was what kept me going.

'Yes, it's true to say that I couldn't have done half of it without them. And so, although there are too many for me to mention them all personally, there are some people that I *do* need to mention by name.

'First of all, I'd like to thank my niece, our wonderful and dedicated prime minister, Sally Hurst, and her husband, Anthony Hurst, for their bravery, their loyalty, and for doing whatever it took to help me in my endeavours to restore peace to our planet, regardless of what it cost them and the danger they put themselves in.

'I'd like to thank Lucas Blackmore and his mother, Janine, along with their team in Nevada, for doing likewise. At times, their job seemed an impossible one, but their commitment and dedication, and their constant attention to detail was the rock to which the rest of us clung.

'And last but not least, my partner, Howard Dyer, and my team in London who, with one or two notable exceptions, did all they could to keep me safe and to help with the complex business of getting that oh so important vote out there to the people.

'I truly could not have done any of it or managed to achieve anything without these people, and so this award, this honour you've bestowed on me today, I dedicate also to them. I share it with them equally. It belongs to us all.

'I'd like to say, that if anyone out there has a dream, a belief, or a desire to fight an injustice, then you should never give up. Because sometimes, the little people do win. The seemingly impossible will always be so unless you try.

'Before I finish, I'd like to remind you of something that I feel – I hope – has become newly relevant in these times. It is unnecessary to make any comment on the politics of the time, but in 1979, on the fourth of May, Margaret Thatcher was elected prime minister of the United Kingdom. One of the headlines in the National Press read: May the Fourth be with You. A reference, of course, to *Star Wars* and "May the force be with you". The Americans quickly picked up the phrase and the fourth of May became "*Star Wars* Day". Now, whatever your feelings on Margaret Thatcher, or indeed *Star Wars*, everyone must surely be familiar with the phrase.

'But ancient, redundant politics and science fiction aside, I'd like to remind you that the vote we held to rebuild our world after its almost total destruction, was on the fourth of May. So, perhaps this phrase will now resonate with us all more than it ever did before, its meaning reinvented to forever symbolise our freedom. I hope so.

'Therefore, with a little humour, because we're allowed that now, but truly from the bottom of my heart, and to each and every citizen of each and every country of our wonderful planet, I say thank you for trusting me, thank you for your courage and your support, and May the Fourth be with you.

'Thank you all so much.'

Chapter Fifty-seven

Twenty years later

The children burst into their classroom for the start of the spring term and the second term of the new school year. Toby Hurst allowed them a few minutes to find their seats and settle down. He didn't mind their noise, their enthusiasm. It always made him grateful. Grateful for the opportunities they now had, the lives of opportunity that lay before them and, as always, he was most grateful of all for the contribution made by his parents and his great-aunt to this happy environment.

When he thought back to how things had been for him at this age, the memories made him sad. Not angry anymore, just sad. He had been angry for too long as a young child, without even realising it until he was brought back to London at the age of eight. It had been a London he didn't remember and it had all seemed very strange to him, but he had begun to be allowed to live in a whole new way, he remembered that clearly, and this had opened his young eyes to the terrible time everyone had been having before. It was as if something magical had happened in his world, which, of course, as he soon learnt, it had.

Not only his generation, but many before, had been subjected to the kind of repression and control that was unthinkable now. It should always have been unthinkable. He had sat in silent classrooms with serious-faced classmates, while their questions and opinions and characters and spirits were systematically drummed out of them as the lies of that time were drummed in.

He hadn't known any differently or any better at the time, of course, but after the overturn of the New World regime's World Administration in the early twenties, he'd begun, little by little, to understand, and he'd been happy since coming back to the UK. There was no good to be gained from dragging the baggage of the past into adulthood, anyway. Toby felt it wouldn't have been respectful to those who'd fought to change it.

In his new London school, he'd begun very quickly to be taught all about the World Administration and Codardo's original vision, and all the things that had happened as a result of that man's election to power. He learnt about the politics of the Democratic Party, and what they stood for. This sudden change in teaching methods and content had been a revelation to him. As he'd got older, his family, and in particular his mother and great-aunt, had told him of the involvement of his own family in the downfall of the WA, and he was incredibly proud of them, of their sacrifices, of their strength and of their determination. But saying he was proud was an over-simplification of his feelings. There had also been a lot of confusion and bewilderment in his young mind at how such a small group of people could have been so instrumental in changing the world. He could remember things that had happened to him as a child in Nevada, things that had been so scary and confusing at the time, but about which, through habit, he had never dared to ask. His father still didn't like to talk about it, even now.

The stories Toby had gradually been told, in answer to a lot of his questions, were full of intrigue, suspense, and danger, particularly in relation to his father who, in these stories, was always cast by his mother in the role of brave and conquering hero. Perhaps that was why his dad stayed quiet on the subject. He was a very private and humble man. So, Toby didn't push it, and never directly asked his dad questions.

There were also some humorous aspects to the stories he was told, but perhaps these had been added for the benefit of the telling to a child.

Of course, their work in Nevada had almost meant the end of his parents' marriage. They'd had some difficulties that had meant they'd lived apart for a while when they'd returned to England, but the details had largely been kept from Toby. He supposed that was only to be expected.

One day, they had all started living together again in the same house. Toby had been over the moon, he remembered. Of course he had. And while to suggest they lived happily ever after was probably overdoing it, they seemed OK, and life for Toby regained its stability. Others hadn't been so lucky. Others had lost more than their marriages; they'd lost their lives in the fight for change. Another reason to be grateful for what they now had.

Toby had decided at around the age of fifteen that he would go into teaching, do his bit to make sure that the ideals and the rights for which his family and so many others had fought were never lost in such a way again. Of course, his subjects were history and politics.

The process of reverting back to a System of Nations had been easier than his parents and great-aunt had expected. The vote that had been cast that momentous day in the spring of 2222 had unleashed a tidal wave of support for his great-aunt and the Democratic Party. In just the same way that the desperation after the pandemic in Codardo's time had meant people had rushed forward to accept his new ideas and accept the World Administration into their countries, the people of two hundred years later had also rallied in support of their own freedoms, and most countries now had their own version of the Democratic Party. The difference was that they existed within sovereign states. There was no more central control.

Ward's behaviour, and the behaviour of many before him, had caused chaos, of course, but there had been many who, after the downfall of the WA, had remained steadfast in their support of the party and of Ward himself, even during his ten years behind bars. A lot of these people still remained firmly in his camp even now, but, generally speaking, the WA around the globe had peacefully left office and the members of the Democratic Party had taken charge of the transition, replacing borders, issuing passports, and taking care of all the other issues of any other regular parliament. Little by little, the job had been done, and each country, rejoicing in their newfound nationalities, had gone on to elect their own members of parliament and prime ministers from their own political parties – in many cases from their newly formed Democratic Parties.

There were, true to Cerys Lee's promise, many international laws that remained in place, but these were now laws that helped people, rather than controlled them. If anything, the return to sovereign states brought the citizens of the world closer together. There was more tolerance between once-warring nations, and an appreciation – a genuine appreciation for the first time in history – of what true freedom actually meant. It was as if people now understood the importance of supporting each other, even if it was borne of a fear of ever finding themselves back in a global dictatorship. Perhaps Vincenzo Codardo could be permitted a nod of posthumous acknowledgement for his cracking of eggs in order to make this particular omelette? Maybe. Maybe not. But his devastating error of judgement had come full circle and at least now, once again, people had the chance and the choice to decide for themselves what they thought and what they wanted out of life. Had the world healed itself? It certainly seemed as if it had started to.

What more could be done to ensure that it continued along this peaceful path?

It was this question that became the biggest motivation for Toby Hurst to enter the world of politics himself, and from the age of eighteen he became an active member of his mother's Democratic Party. Now, ten years later, he hoped one day, perhaps when his mother retired from politics, to become the member of parliament for his constituency in west London. There was still a little way to go with finishing off smoothing out the details of the transition back to the System of Nations, but these things took time and his small contribution towards it felt good. He wouldn't make a challenge until his mother decided to quit; she deserved her time as an MP, even if she'd long since stepped down as prime minister to spend more time with his little sister, who came along two years after their return to England. In his opinion, his mum had earnt the right not to be challenged for her seat until she herself chose to leave.

Yes, he thought, as he opened his computer on the desk in front of him and pressed the relevant buttons to activate the students' devices and link them to the chapter he'd opened on his own device of the still relatively new history e-book, which once more taught the truth rather than the web of lies that had sullied his own education, and watched as his class settled themselves into their seats, chatting and happy, it had all been worth it. This new generation would not be afraid to live. Their parents may still remember the traumas of the past, but young minds adapt easily, and the years of mental anguish that had been expected to follow the return to the old system had not been nearly as taxing on them as it had been imagined it would be.

'OK everyone, settle down now please and pay attention.' The class quietened down. 'Look at your screens, please. Today we're going to be looking at an issue from a couple of hundred years ago that's still very relevant and important to all our lives today, and which will remain important, probably forever.' The children looked eagerly at their screens. 'So,' said Toby. 'Chapter three: Vincenzo Codardo.'

At the back of the room, a young boy sat sullen and alone, drawing little pictures of guns in the margins of his notebook with a red pen. He enjoyed shooting. His re-married and now ageing father took him clay pigeon shooting and he'd become very good at it. He wished he were there with his dad now. It'd be much more fun and interesting and useful than this stupid lesson. Codardo, for God's sake! His father had already taught him all he needed to know on this subject, so he probably knew more about Codardo than his stupid teacher. He scowled. He hated school; it was such a waste of time. He couldn't wait for the day when he left and when he'd no longer have to sit and listen to all this rubbish. He began kicking the leg of his desk.

'Simon Ward, please stop that and pay attention. I was going to ask the class whether any of you can tell me anything about Vincenzo Codardo. Perhaps we can start with you.'

The boy raised his head from his doodling and looked directly into the eyes of his teacher. There was no fear of reprimand and no respect in his attitude as he spoke, ignoring the question.

'Is it right that your mother used to be the prime minister and that before she was prime minister, she was the one who helped get my dad arrested?'

The whole class sat staring in horrified wonder at this outburst from their usually quiet classmate. A couple of them gasped. One giggled.

'It was rather more complicated than that, Simon.'

'Why? No, it's not. It's true. My father knows everything. He says that the world's gone soft.'

'Simon...'

'OK, o*kaaay*. Vincenzo Codardo was the man who began the Free World and the World Administration,' he said huffily. 'Everyone knows that, unless they're stupid. And my father was the leader of them twenty years ago and he was the most important person in the world. Everyone knows that, too. And he was the only one who understood what laws the world should have and how the world should be run, and I believe him. Codardo's ideas were good, but my dad's ideas were better, and he made the World Administration the most powerful party in the world and the best party in the world, and everyone was frightened of him, and one day I'm going to run the WA and get my dad's party back in charge, and everyone's going to be frightened of me, just like they were frightened of him, and they'll all have to do what I say. Even you.'

He threw down his pen which bounced off the table onto the floor. Folding his arms, and with two round patches of red anger burning in his cheeks, he turned his head away to stare out of the window where a class of children could be seen playing a game of football and having fun. His dad was right, the world was stupid. No one had any control anymore.